The Game

A Grumpy Sunshine Sports Romance

Leonor Soliz

Contents

Author's Note

My books always end in a Happily Ever After. My stories are generally fluffy, with a good mix of humor and low-level conflict. Nevertheless, I believe it's important to give readers every chance to consent to reading my book. Although I write generally happy romance, if you'd like to access content warnings for these stories, check https://leonorsoliz.com/books/the-game.

Did you know you can get other free short stories by signing up for my newsletter? There's art too! Some of it spicy...

Sign up to always be in the know! visit leonorsoliz.com/newsletter

This book is for all of us big girls,
who need someone to find their
way into our heart,
and who want a partner
who can *handle* us

Chapter 1

Logan

Six years earlier

A long-haired beauty watches me from across the bar, and it's irritating as hell. She has a casual but feminine look, like she took care of her appearance but couldn't be bothered with going the extra mile. It's hard to tell, but she's probably around my age or so, maybe a year younger. She wears a tank top in her college's colors. I know, because we just defeated their football team on their turf.

Can't say I'm upset about that part. In fact, I'm here to celebrate a season where we remain undefeated. My teammates insisted. As the quarterback, I play a big part in our success. They don't care that I hate crowds, and that being approached by people wanting to ask me about my famous, football-legend of a father is my literal nightmare. Yet here I am, evading questions about Kenneth King and my own future in the game. And being given a dissecting, unwavering stare by Mystery Girl from across the room.

Her hair is a wavy, glossy-brown waterfall. A few tendrils get lost under the hem of her neckline, like they're snaking their way closer to her breasts. It's probably on purpose, but it works. It draws my eyes to her chest. I keep stealing glances at her, because she's nice to look at... and because of the prying intensity in her eyes. I frown. Someone is talking to me but I ignore them. I'm used to people staring, but this is different. Mystery Girl has a bone to pick with me and it irks me.

Despite the temptation, I refuse to march to her and ask for an explanation. I swivel on my barstool and pretend the beer in my hands is fascinating. The smell of cleaner, alcohol, and fried foods reaches my nose, and I scowl at the combination.

Chatter continues around me. A teammate makes fun of me for my grouchy attitude, and one of the girls who's been trying to chat me up asks if I'm worried about the combine.

"It's a big deal, isn't it?" She speaks into my ear. "That's when scouts decide if they want to draft you to a big team. What's your record?"

I set my eyes on my drink and don't let them waver. I've barely tasted it. Beer isn't my favorite, but I can't have anything stronger during the season and I need something to busy my hands with.

"Is your dad going to be there?" The girl leans closer to me, until her breasts are plastered on my arm. "He must be so proud."

"Excuse me." I get off my stool. "I'm going to take a piss."

I walk away. She'll probably decide I'm too rude for her efforts and I'm okay with that. It's not like I blame her for flirting with me by stroking my ego. She's probably been taught this is what guys like me want— often, she'd be correct. Many of my teammates would take her up on her offer. Once in a while, I take up such offers for myself too. All I know is that tits on a platter aren't doing it for me tonight.

The bar is a nondescript college pub and I don't take much note of it. The light has that woody, reddish tone of so many such establishments and it's *packed*.

Beyond catching those details, I do nothing more than find the restroom at the end of a hall and get busy with my zipper.

A displeased curl pulls at my lips. I hate it when people gas me up and ask about my father in the same breath. I don't play football to follow in his steps. This sport is something I excel at. I love the way my body feels when I throw the ball, and the speed at which my brain works when I'm reading the field. It may be the result of some genetic predisposition, perhaps, but the blood, sweat, and tears I've put into it are what made it happen.

It goes even further for me. This sport is my future. My college team and I are likely to win this year's championship. The combine comes after and finally, finally I'll make it to the big leagues. My stats suggest I might even be a first round pick. None of that has to do with who gave me half my DNA, or how many rings he has, or whether he really looks like his bronze bust in the Hall of Fame.

The time has finally come to get out of my father's shadow. My rookie year is my opportunity to stand on my own two feet. Proving I can be one of the greats on my own merit.

With some luck, I may even find brotherhood in my teammates for once. As the only child to a distant, quiet mother, and a hard-to-read, too-busy father, I want to build something different for myself— I just need to find the right people. But that's a problem for Future Logan. Present Me needs to focus on the championship.

I clean up and go back to the hallway, balancing the pros and cons of leaving the bar altogether, when I realize Mystery Girl is coming out of the other restroom. She doesn't see me.

"Hey," I say before I realize what I'm doing.

The music isn't too loud here, and she spins on her heels to face me. Her eyes widen when she registers me.

"Are you following me?" I ask.

I know it doesn't make sense, but I gaze at her with a challenge anyway.

She crosses her arms. "Never."

I hook my thumbs from my jean pockets and gaze down at her. She's not short, but I'm very tall.

"You've been staring," I insist.

"You've been staring right back." She rubs her lips together and watches me carefully.

I raise an eyebrow and let silence stretch between us. Maybe she'll explain herself, or escape, or something else, and I'm curious.

She takes a step closer to me. "You have a pretty face, despite that killer frown."

"Pretty?" I barely hide the jolt of surprise.

I frown. No one has called me that before.

Her head falls to the side. "Don't tell me you take offense at the word? Don't disappoint me so quickly."

People often comment on my looks. The size I inherited from my father, and the eyes I got from my model mother. It's rarely delivered in such a calculating tone.

She takes another step toward me. "Yeah, that's the intense look I was talking about. You don't look very approachable, or even friendly."

She's not the first to point out how I'm usually perceived, but she sounds like she just figured it out.

"Do you know who I am?" My question comes out terse, more out of confusion than anything.

People usually approach me because they know who I am. They follow a few different scripts— it could be something about my dad, something about my career, my future... The way she watches me isn't all that rare but, even then, it's usually because of who I am and what I can do.

She laughs. "And *that* was asshole-y. Perfect."

I shake my head. The words come out with snark and a sense of victory that say a lot about where her mind is at. My eyes never leave her, but I'm looking at her anew. Things finally click. She's pissed her team lost and would like to insult me to alleviate the sting.

"I see." I snort. "You're one of those fans."

I make to walk past her, but her next words stop me.

"I'm not a fan," she says. "I don't know who you are."

We face each other again. I'm a man who can assess a field in half a second but, at this moment, I'm baffled.

The hallway is a bit darker than the main room. Old dial-up phones hang nearby on the wall, like they were forgotten from a time when people didn't carry a computer in their pockets. A neon sign shines bright pink on her dark brown hair.

"Bullshit." I squint at her. "You're wearing your team's colors and came to this one bar, where I'm told all players and their fans come to."

She shrugs. "That's true. It's why I came here. I chose this shirt to blend in, but I don't follow football much. College or professional. Not my thing."

She's probably lying, but I don't know how to make sure. Or even if I want to.

"I don't have time for this." I make a second attempt at leaving.

It's her hand on my arm that stops me in my tracks this time.

"Wait!" She releases me.

Her arms rest at her sides now, hands fisted. Despite myself, I gaze at her again.

She lifts her chin, a resolute look in her eyes. "I'm here because I want to get laid."

My lips part in surprise.

She's breathing faster now. "I'm here because you guys leave tomorrow and I want something with no strings attached. Players are known to come here looking for one night stands, and I want one."

I gaze down her body. This close, the tank top she wears isn't particularly racy, but enough flesh fills the neckline to make my fingers flex. My sight travels lower, and her body offers lush fullness everywhere. The kind that could fill my big QB hands. The kind that feels like a challenge, daring me to prove I know how to handle myself around generous territory. A body I might want to manhandle somewhat, to feel fire in my muscles and a hint of safe defiance.

Resistance of my own fuels my words. "And I guess I'm supposed to believe you don't know who I am, but chose me for a mysterious reason, even though you don't seem to think too highly of me."

"It's not a mystery. I assume a guy who frowns as much as you do won't mind me being direct and skipping all pleasantries. That a guy who reads as grumpy from all the way across the bar, is someone who'll be happy to be all *wham-bam-thank-you-ma'am* with me— consensually."

She studies me with rebellious eyes. Her chin is up in a bold pose. But the way she's chewing on her lips tells me there's more going on underneath it all.

I take a step closer. A mix of scents reach me from her— hair products and other scents. I can't define if they're soap or moisturizer.

My heart beats a little quicker.

"Why?" I frown. "Is there something going on? Something weird?"

"Nothing weird. I'm angry at— people. The way they need so much of me, all the time, and I just—" she shakes her head. "I want to forget. Be young. Free to do whatever I want and not think about anyone else. Just me and you and some casual sex. Then we shake hands and go our own ways."

Probably an ex, then, and I'm the rebound.

I search her eyes. They're a warm, dark brown in this light. Her makeup seems minimal. With unpainted lips, I could kiss her and not taste lipstick, just her.

A one night stand, no fake pleasantries, a mutual understanding that this won't lead anywhere... a body I'd be happy to make mine for a little time... no roles for me to play, pretending this could lead somewhere, or I enjoy the person's company.

I lick my lips. I could get behind it.

"So let me get things straight." I take a step closer to her. "You want to get laid, and think I'm the right candidate because my frown makes you think I'm not the kind to get attached."

She takes a step back. "You're one of the people I wanted to approach, but then I didn't have to choose because you found me here in the hall. But whatever. I can go ask someone else."

She makes to step away, but this time I'm the one holding her back with a hand on her wrist.

She turns to me and backs up closer to the wall. I take another step towards her.

"So you don't know my name?" My cock twitches.

It's a game, one where I'm meant to chase, and I'm into it.

She shakes her head. "I won't tell you mine, either."

I crowd her space until she presses against the wall. My blood rushes south. It seems this— her— is what I want tonight.

I cage her with one hand next to her head, and the other next to her waist. "Before we agree to do this, we should test if we have the chemistry for sex."

She licks her lips. "How do you propose we do that?"

My answer is to lower my head until our mouths are a breath apart.

"Do you want to kiss me?" My voice rasps out of my throat.

Her mouth opens. A single nod tells me what I need to know. I taste her bottom lip.

It's enough to kick my body into gear. The next second, I'm devouring her.

She clutches my shirt in her hands. I plaster my body to hers and nibble on her lip. She rolls her hips against mine. We kiss mindlessly for a while, until I'm fully hard and we're close to dry humping in the hallway.

Someone whoops at us and we come apart.

"Get a room!" someone else screams.

"Fuck off," I say to the onlookers, and pull Mystery Girl by the hand.

"Don't disappoint me," she says, breathless.

We go out of the bar together.

Chapter 2

Evie

He takes me to his room. The college offices dealing with visitors put him in one of the dorms. I've never been to this building before, but it's one of the newer ones on campus.

The walls are white cinder block, lacking all decoration. It doesn't surprise me. The players won't stay here more than two days and these rooms are no more than a basic replacement for a hotel room. A large bag is open on the desk, and some clothes are strewn about the place, but not enough to call him messy.

It's all I get to see before he grabs me from the arm, turns me to him, and kisses me.

Fuck, he's a good kisser. My skin warms up fast, and my heart races with anticipation. His tongue explores my mouth and my mind quiets down.

Finally.

I've kissed a few guys before, and slept with my ex with the regularity of a semi-long distance, long-term relationship. Never was I kissed in a way that left me breathless.

It's probably the adventure factor. It's my first one night stand, and I'm all for it so far.

"You're sober?" he asks between kisses. "I can taste the alcohol." More kisses, this time down my neck. "It's hot, but I gotta ask..."

"Sober and of adult age." I run my hands down his torso, and back up to his thick, black, longish hair. "I have condoms in my jacket pocket."

I threw the thing on the floor when I came in, but he doesn't let go of me long enough to go back to it.

We're next to his traveling bag and he reaches inside, without looking. His mouth is still exploring my neck and dragging gasps out of me, but he straightens and gets a cocky gesture on his face. He shows me the strip of condoms he found.

"Never travel without them." He throws them behind me to the bed. "Just in case."

I pull up at his shirt. "Just in case someone propositions you at a bar?"

He takes over and throws the garment away. I explore the expanses of his body. His white skin has some melanin to it, from working outside so often or from DNA, I don't know yet. Something tells me it's a bit of both, and I'm going to like everything I see.

"I'm not picky about where I'm propositioned." He barely finishes the sentence when he takes my mouth again. "Are you very attached to this shirt?"

His hands land on my breasts. He gets a feeling for them, his thumbs trailing arches on me. My nipples harden with each pass he makes on them.

I moan. "No. Never wore it before."

My fingers latch to the band of his jeans and pull. I want him close. Closer. As close as can be.

"I'll tear it off you," he says. "Yeah?"

"Yes," I whisper.

He rips my shirt and it erases all remnants of thought from my mind. It's all disappeared into nothingness, now that he's thrown the rags to the floor.

This. It's exactly what I need. To not think, to not worry— about my school's latest warning letter regarding my scholarship, or my parents who just told me how much debt they are in.

He runs his hands over my torso, fondling my chest over my bra, and my breathing catches in my throat. This football player grabs at my flesh like he can't get enough, and now I don't need to think about getting a third job to help pay for everything, or how much harder it will be to keep my grades up.

His teeth close gently on my earlobe. A thrill travels down my spine and I whine. I want more.

I pull at his jeans. We stand by the bed. It's tucked by the wall and it's probably too small for the two of us, but I don't care. I'll ride him on the floor if I have to.

I unhook my bra, he helps me out of it. He finds my secret tattoo, a sun etched on the triangle of skin where my breastbone ends.

His thumb traces it. "Pretty."

"Kiss me."

He obliges and pushes me to the bed at the same time. With hands on my shoulders, he makes me sit on the bed and kneels between my legs. His fingers return to my chest, his thumb on my tattoo and fingers on my nipples. My head falls back in pleasure when he licks my neck.

"Turn around." He bites gently on my ear.

He makes room for me. I fall to my knees and do as I'm told. My thighs press against the bed and his pelvis on my ass. He rubs himself on me, his hands traveling all over my soft belly, my breasts. He grabs handfuls of my flesh, his breathing hot on my ear.

"This good?" he asks.

"More." I place my hands over his, following his movements as he discovers the hills of my flesh.

"Your body is perfect." His hands drop to unbutton my jeans. "Do you know how well you fit in my hands?"

He probably says that to everyone but I don't care. He's saying it to me now and I'm living. My heart flutters. I feel myself getting slick.

"Show me." I pull my jeans down my hips. I leave them stuck mid-thigh. "Touch me."

He gets the message and pushes his fingers under my underwear. He parts me and explores what I'm sure is wet heat.

"You're so ready for me." Index and middle fingers play with my clit, getting acquainted with it. His voice comes out rough, right next to my ear. "I want to use my strength with you. Hold you in place, shift you around. Manhandle you a little— but nothing that would leave marks— unless you ask me to. Are you game?"

My heartbeat is loud in my ears. This guy acts and talks like he has tons of experience. Maybe he does. I wouldn't be surprised if he gets propositioned every weekend.

I bite my lips. I'd do the math if I weren't so taken by his proposition, and the way the notion makes me feel— like I'm being thoroughly enjoyed. Like the fire in my body is welcome and about to get stoked some more.

"Throw me around some," I say.

I've never been maneuvered like it, and the idea this random guy wants to do it is thrilling.

"Mark me with your hands," I add. "Where people can't see."

I didn't know I could say something like that to a stranger and now that I have... My inner muscles clench in anticipation.

He slaps the round of my hip. "Like that?"

I nod. "I'll stop you if you go too far."

"I'll stop if you don't like it."

He doesn't say anything else, but hooks his hands under my arms and lifts me, turns me, and throws me on the bed.

I gasp. I didn't know I could be jostled like that.

"Fuck," he says, like he enjoyed that, too. "Did you like that?"

I nod.

He lowers close to me, his hands next to my shoulders. "Say yes like you mean it, or I won't believe you, and I swear I'll stop."

"Yes. Yes! I liked it."

He drops a hard kiss on me. "Do you want me to do it again?"

"Yes— please."

He takes off my jeans, underwear included. He straightens to get rid of his clothes, and I find the foil strip on the bed.

"A little desperate, are we?" he says, but grabs one of them from me.

I don't bother denying it. Especially when I see him naked, standing in all his glory.

Sculpted muscles that speak of a strong body. Bold ridges crowning his hips. Long lines and bulk in all the right places. He was carved out of my dreams.

"Hurry." I stand on my knees on the bed and reach for his mouth. He bends down to kiss me while putting on the rubber.

He touches my body again, before grabbing me by the hips and turning me away. I almost lose my balance and fall to the gray comforter, but he keeps me up with firm hands. The bed is instantly a mess.

Shivers run down my skin, born from the way he touches me. How he handles me.

"Fuck," I mutter.

"Hands on the wall," he growls.

I obey without hesitation. He bites my shoulder. His fingers dig into the soft flesh of my thighs and he jiggles it. The tremors of it run up and down my flesh. It's like he savors how my body responds to his commands.

My insides respond to him too. Tingles cascade through me, and pressure builds low in my belly. The sensations go supernova, when his hands come off me, only to get his tongue on my pussy.

"Holy shit." I imagine him kneeling again, my sex in front of his face. He nibbles on me, kissing me and licking me into oblivion.

The drumming of my heart. This eagerness, the need to be filled. An empty mind, and my body melting like warm wax. I could dissolve into the mattress, disappear into the ether. I would love it there.

It's exactly what I wanted out of this. More than that, because I'm discovering parts of me I never knew.

He uses his fingers on me, then sucks on the back of my thigh. I'm sure it will leave a mark, and it only intensifies the raspy sounds coming from my throat. He bites my ass, and I whine.

I don't question it next time his touch leaves me. All I do is arch my back in search of him. Soon his foot is on the mattress next to my knee, and his cock notches my entrance.

"You're going to let me fuck you so good." He slaps my ass again.

I moan.

"Is this what you want?" He pushes another inch in.

"More."

"Is this why you went to the bar tonight?" He pushes further.

Infuriatingly slow. I press back and force him deeper.

"Fuck. Greedy." He pulls away and slaps my ass again. "Don't move."

"So bossy," I complain.

I reach between us, grab his cock, and nudge back again. He makes a strangled sound.

I'm forced to let go of him the deeper he goes. He's not fighting it anymore. He seizes the soft flesh of my hips and holds on to them as he fills me.

"That's right." I moan. "Fuck me."

"Now who's bossy?" he asks, before pistoning in and out of me.

Both my hands are back on the wall. I help him along, meeting his hips with my own rocking. My nails cling to the rough texture of the cinderblock. My breasts sway with the force of our thrusts.

It feels good— too good. My orgasm builds fast. I've never come from penetration alone. I know I can, because I can get there with a dildo, but a partner? I've always helped it along with my fingers.

My heart skips a beat. I'm not sure why, but I don't want it to change.

I snake one of my hands between my legs.

"If you're going to touch yourself—" he leaves me and pushes me to my side— "I should at least be allowed to watch."

He pulls from my knees until my hips are at the edge of the bed. Within a second, he stretches me again. I practically slap myself in my rush to play with my clit once more.

I can't see his eyes, they are locked on the place where we join. I don't know what sounds I make anymore, but my chest is in overdrive. Flutters start in my core and I don't stop it or warn him— I come. He notices anyway, because his groans change, but I can't keep track.

Everything is calm for once, except for the pounding of my heart. Even as he continues to seek his release, still pumping hard, my mind is blank. No responsibilities that are too big for me. No uncertain future. Just bliss.

It's all I wanted.

A loud moan escapes me when I return to myself. I don't silence it. If I let my body do as it wants to, maybe the thoughts and worries will take a bit longer to return.

I keep them at bay by clenching around him again, this time on purpose.

He mutters a few extra swear words. I lift my torso to face him, and keep myself up with my hands on the bed.

One of his hands clings to my hips so hard he'll leave bruises. The other grabs my breast almost as hard.

I bite his lip. "Should I mark you, too?"

I don't get to. He comes and I swallow his moan with a kiss.

He stands still for a few extra moments. The same intense frown I saw back at the bar is present, his eyes closed.

Eventually, he pulls back and sits on the bed, a few inches away from me. He deals with the condom. I lean back, my hands still on the mattress.

My body feels limp. I've mostly melted, after all.

He takes a few deep breaths. He looks at me with eyes that are a rare shade of light blue. I don't think to question it. He's probably wondering if I'll stay true to my word and leave, or if I'll ask for a cuddle or try for something else after all. Guys like him are probably like that. Assuming everyone wants a piece of them.

To be fair, if he's famous enough to be surprised I don't know who he is— and I don't— maybe plenty of people want pieces of him.

It's fine. He doesn't know anyone can be like that. Plenty of people want pieces of me, too. Case in point, my ex. I don't plan to tell my one night stand that there's nothing that makes my skin crawl like keeping people around who take and take and never give back. I'm done tearing myself apart for people. I have enough of that, taking care of my parents.

I get on my feet and allow myself a stretch. I'm about to collect my clothes when he grabs my hand and calls for my eyes.

"Hey," he says. "Where are you going? Come here."

He moves back on the bed until his knees meet the edge of the mattress, and pulls my hand as if he wants me to straddle him. I resist and do not move from my spot.

His head drops to one side. "Everything okay? I thought we might... prolong the night. Do that again."

He studies me carefully. Now I realize I got it wrong, and his eyes are actually gray.

I shake my head. "I thought I might go."

"Are you in a hurry? Can I take you somewhere?"

"No, but I promised you I would leave right after."

And I don't want to stay, if it means ruining the amazing moment we had somehow.

He pulls at my hand again. "You also offered to mark me, and that hasn't happened. I don't think we're done, do you?"

I still refuse to move. I'm naked in front of him, while he sits without a stitch on. His cock is half hard on his thigh.

I frown. "Look, I'd love a repeat—"

"Good. I'm ready for a repeat."

"No. I don't do that."

It's his turn to frown. The gesture echoes the worst of his moody expressions at the bar.

"I thought we could go out for dinner," he says. "Come back for more."

I shake my head, but I'm torn. I want to indulge in a repeat, too. The way we seamlessly fit into a night to remember should probably be taken into consideration. I rarely get to indulge like this.

This may be my first one night stand, but it's already teaching me critical lessons. The chances of my future sexcapades being as perfectly matched as the past hour are low. Moving forward, I will only do this once with every guy.

But tonight I might be open to more. This footballer touched me in all the right ways, even in those I didn't know would singe my skin. Like we've been doing this for years, and he can still surprise me with a trick or two. I would be foolish to decline... as long as he follows the rules.

Fuck it. This is my night to indulge.

I lick my lip. "One more. But I don't want to learn anything about you."

He's staring at me like he wants to fight me on this, but is unsure whether he should.

I smirk and sit on his lap. His lips open in instant lust, and his hands grab the rolls of my hips— hard.

"Hmm." The sound comes from deep in his throat.

"I am one for hedonism, once in a while," I whisper. "But you have to promise you won't tell me who you are. You won't ask for my number. You won't ask who I am."

His cock hardens again between us, and I roll my hips to tease us both. We shift in place, until the head peeks between us, trapped between his flat stomach and my soft flesh. The heat of his erection, the hardness of his dick press onto my lower belly, impressive enough to demand being seen.

"Fuck," he mutters. "We'll do it your way."

"Manhandle me some more."

"Mark me."

I kiss him, but end it with a bite on his bottom lip. "Like that?"

He's still groaning when he twists and pushes me onto the bed. "Oh, we're just getting started."

It's too late to leave once we're done. The shuttles that take students back to town are done for the night, and I'm stuck on campus.

He says it's a sign and convinces me to stay. A few hours later, in the middle of the night, I wake him up and we do it again. I left a bite on his shoulder, too.

Next time he's asleep, I use my phone flashlight to find my clothes. I have to steal one of his shirts, as mine is torn too badly to wear.

He doesn't hear me, and I'm about to close the door behind me when something stops me. The light of the hall is faint at this time of the night, and my eyes land on him again.

His shape makes mountains and valleys under the sheet covering him. The shadows are stark, and a prickling in my chest wants me to go back, maybe check if his frown is still there while he sleeps.

Would it be that bad if I stayed?

Fuck. Yes. It would be bad.

Quietly, I close the door behind me and drill into my brain that I can't afford entertaining fantasies, when my reality demands so much of me.

It's early morning. My breath creates clouds as I walk through the practice fields and toward the library, next to where the small dark red buses park. I take the first shuttle into the city with the break of dawn.

I sigh. The night was exactly what I needed. I can carry the memories of what it felt like to be thoroughly enjoyed, and to enjoy someone back. The feelings and sensations of finding such a compatible hookup, it won't only leave marks on my skin— it will leave marks on this time in my life.

Now I'm a little more ready to finish the year, work extra jobs during the summer, and come back for my last college term. After, I'll find an internship. Then a job. Then I'll pay my parents' debt, before I finally focus on me.

That's when my life will be my own, and I'll start building something just for me.

Tonight is the first night of my five-year plan.

Bring it on.

Chapter 3

Logan

The first thing I do upon waking up is to reach out for her. A part of me knows she's not there, and still I search for her as if needing to confirm it.

Yeah, she's gone.

The bed is small, and yet too big without her. Her smell is embedded into the corner of the pillow, maybe the sheets, but it's subtle now.

Mystery Girl left without a word.

A frown takes hold of my brow, and doesn't leave for days.

Chapter 4

Evie

Present time

The elevator starts its journey upwards and gravity pulls at my stomach. My hands shake. I'd like to say it's caffeine withdrawal, since I ran out of pods at home and I can't afford to stop for my morning fix at the moment. But, no. My hands tremble because my boss got fired last night and I'm terrified I'm next.

I step out of the car on the fourth floor and make my way through the large distribution hall, waving at Mallory in reception, and going past her toward the executive suite. Only a few steps later, I make it past the big glass doors that welcome everyone to the organization's front office. The logo of the Seattle Strike is embossed across the double panes and it hits me again— I ended up working for a pro football team and loving it.

It's not strange that I'm hyper aware of this fact today. If I get fired, I would miss everything I've learned as a PR executive for the team. I would miss the players and admin that keep my skills sharp. I would miss working at a building with secret spots that overlook Lake Washington, and which remind me I'll get to relax one day by the water in a tiny cabin with no one around.

Above all, I'd miss the salary. I can't afford any more financial stress, not with the way I've taken responsibility for my parents' debt. They have tried to do better with time, but it hasn't been enough to fix things. With their general insolvency adding to it, I've been in trouble for a few years. Always on the first day of my five year plan, it seems. Now, if I end up without a job, things would get worse fast. Especially when my parents' house is on the line, and we have only one year to save it.

I chew on my bottom lip as I walk through halls with a shiny-but-muted treatment on the walls. It's a hint to the silver lightning that serves as a symbol for the team, and it contrasts with the deep warm tones of the wood details and the shade of blue popping all throughout the space. That one is in honor of the main uniform color, and all the water surrounding the city and satellite towns. I smile and take a deep breath. I smell clean office materials but, if I try hard enough, I can pretend I can smell the ocean all the way from here.

One day, if my parents ever stop surprising me with more debt and it's all finally, *finally* paid off, things could change. I could save for a vacation where there's sand and sun and sea. Staycations have their charm, but a girl needs to recline on a beachside chaise lounge once in a while. My old trusty couch can only do so much for me these days.

That won't happen for a few years yet. First save my childhood home, then pay the rest of the debt. Then I can have an emergency fund for myself for the first time in my life and then, just then, I may be able to save for a trip. A proper vacation— a dream. As long as I don't get fired.

I curl my hands into fists to hide the tremors, and reach the new owner's office. Ms. Carmichael bought the team a few months ago and things still feel unsettled. I thought I was safe, but everything went to shit after receiving a curt email this morning. It informed me my boss had been fired and I was being summoned to the owner's office.

I ignore the instinct to run away and hope they'll forget I exist. Instead, I enter the owner's suite and wave at Ms. Carmichael's assistant.

"Hey, Marta!" I exclaim and plaster a grin on my face. "How are you doing today?"

"I'm great, thanks for asking."

I met her a few weeks before, when Ms. Carmichael had all of the front office staff together to introduce herself and get to know us. I made a point of remembering the assistant's name, because it makes people feel good, and you never know when you need to count on someone's favor for something.

"How's the pet?" I ask. "I think you mentioned Mister... Sniffles? Was that the name? That Mister Sniffles was sick?"

She gives me a genuine smile. "Mister Sniffles is much better! You have a great memory."

"I try." I wink at her. "But I have a meeting with Ms. Carmichael, for whenever she's ready."

"Yes, she's waiting for you and Mister King." She makes a gesture with her hand, pointing behind me. "Please take a seat. She'll be ready in a second."

I freeze. I'm sure I stare at Marta dumbfounded, but there's not much I can do about it.

Based on the assistant's words, Mister King is sitting behind me. Also known as Logan King. Also known as my first one night stand, and the man against whom I measure everyone else.

And he might be in the meeting for some reason?

Fuck!

"Uhm..." I tap my chin a few times, buying myself time. "Where could I get some water, if you don't mind?"

Surely there's a kitchenette somewhere nearby, where I can go hide for a hot minute and kill time. Figure out a plan, beyond smiling and crossing my fingers behind my back.

I'm not ready to face Logan yet. As soon as it was announced a few months ago that he would replace the old quarterback, I've been imagining the moment. I expected we would cross paths on a hallway or at a team event, and I'd be casual. I'd be vague. I'd inspect his reaction carefully, and act like I don't immediately remember... if he says anything at all.

He probably won't recognize me— I wear my hair mostly straight now, there are honey highlights in my chestnut hair, and my makeup game has leveled up. My outfits are a new style, too, with dresses and skirts and vintage heels I've painstakingly curated for a mix-and-match wardrobe. It was necessary. Coming to work in a professional, entertainment-focused environment, I needed to find ways to fit in without breaking the bank.

I didn't expect to meet Logan in the owner's office, but the hope remains he won't recognize me. I can't have that kind of past hanging over my head. I go to great lengths to avoid truly bonding with anyone. I'll smile and be kind and make their life easier somehow, but I won't get close. I will look at their vacation pictures and *ooh and ahh*, but no one will know that underneath that I'm aching to be the one going on adventures.

When it's easier to give than to take, and when I don't know how to say *'enough, I'm done'*, I can't risk attachments. At work, I have job descriptions and policies. In life there's no manual, and I can't afford to dissolve into an empty shell that has nothing left to give.

And it's not like I can ask if he knows who I am. I can't fathom the embarrassment if he doesn't remember— a pro athlete playing for one of the biggest, most popular leagues in the world, pitying me for thinking he remembers the random girl he slept with years ago. So if I can walk away for a hot second and not allow him to look too closely...

Marta stands. "Oh, please take a seat! I'll bring you water in a minute."

I take a deep breath. My stomach twists into a knot. There goes that option.

The assistant leaves the office and my fate is sealed. I have to turn and face the man that defined my whole adult romantic life— or lack thereof.

I square my shoulders. He either remembers me and it's awkward that way, or he doesn't remember me and it's awkward a different way.

I turn. He wears a team hoodie and joggers in the uniform blue. He's somehow bigger than I remember, like maybe he wasn't done growing when we met... or like playing professionally did wonders to his shoulders. He's standing for some reason, and the famous frown I remember— and saw many times over on TV afterwards— is firmly in place.

Tingles feather my stomach. I erect the best shield I have, and smile. The rest comes to me without conscious choice. Whatever parts of me built my work persona take the reins.

"Hi there!" I cross the distance between us and offer him a hand. "I'm Evie Moreno, a PR executive for the team."

His hands remain in his pockets as he inspects me. It all probably happens in a single second, but time slows down and it feels like forever. His thick, black eyebrows furrow further and those eyes... gah, those eyes. In this light they look blue.

In the dorm room years ago, I thought they were gray. It wasn't until I recognized him on TV later on, and casually followed his career from far away, that I realized full debates are held in comment sections about the exact shade of them.

His right hand comes out of his pocket in slo mo. Full of hesitation, his fingers wrap around my hand. His warm palm engulfs me, and a shiver goes down my spine, like maybe my nerve endings recognize him.

"Logan King." His voice is deep, and his name curt.

"Oh, I know." I let go of his hand, hoping it doesn't seem like I'm ready to bolt. "I'd be poor at my job if I didn't have an understanding of who's on the team each season, and when someone leaked the news of your acquisition we were all paying attention."

I hold my hands casually in front of me. He stares at me like a hawk studying the landscape.

"Mmh." The sound is grumpy, this time.

He doesn't get to say more. Marta returns with a tray she leaves on her desk.

"I see Ms. Carmichael is available now," she says. "Please go right in."

"The two of us? We're both in the meeting?" I ask.

I hide my surprise well this time. I wasn't sure what I expected, considering Marta's comment earlier, but it wasn't to have a three-way meeting with the owner.

"Yes." Marta takes the tray. "If you'll open the door for me, please, Evie?"

"Of course!" I manage to say.

I tame the nerves in my belly, knock a happy pattern on the owner's door, and come in when I hear her voice giving me the green light.

I have no idea if this bodes well for me, or if I'm going to get fired in front of Logan for a Machiavellian reason, but there's only one way to find out.

"Good morning, Ms. Carmichael." I smile and approach her big, elegant desk.

The stunning Black woman smiles right back, and stands to shake my hand. "Hi Evie. Please call me Selena. Nice to see you again."

She wears a muted blue pant suit and a printed fuchsia blouse, and flat twists giving her hair an intricate pattern. She seems effortlessly chic, and even though my style is different, I appreciate her taste.

Her grin is warm, too. I allow it to reassure me somewhat, because a boss that smiles like that isn't planning to kick you out of the building. I subtly cross my fingers anyway, just in case.

"Please, take a seat, Evie." Selena directs her gaze at the silent man behind me somewhere. "Hi, Logan. Take a seat as well."

The Strike trains in a practice facility by the water on Lake Washington. Its official name is the Callum Fraser Athletic Center for the Seattle Strike, but no one calls it that. We all call it the Thunderdome, or TD for short.

Selena's new office is at the corner of the building. It overlooks the outside training field as much as the water. Marta leaves our drinks on Selena's desk and closes the door behind her on the way out. I take a deep breath when I realize this would have been my chance to ask for coffee, but we're done with pleasantries.

"Thanks for joining me this morning," Selena says. "I have to discuss something with you both, and it made sense to see you at the same time to talk about it."

I steal a glance at Logan. He hasn't said more than his name since I faced him, and he doesn't look at me. The constant frown on his face makes him hard to read, but he must be wondering why we're here. He doesn't seem to be paying much attention to me.

Relief moves through my chest. I don't think he remembers me, and now I'm free to focus on work. I'll think about his perfect face and those eyes of his another time.

Any memories that want to attack my mind will have to wait until I'm alone in bed tonight. It's how I'll reward myself for my courage in facing this meeting, when all I want to do is hide.

Selena taps her long nails on her thigh. "With the new season coming up sooner than we know, it's time to prove the Strike is ready to leave poor performances in the past. My goal is to take us to the playoffs in my first year, and the big game in my second."

Confidence infuses her voice, and it's easy to believe her... except the team has struggled to have more wins than losses in the past few years. At least, if she's talking about this, it's even less likely she wants to fire me.

"You know this, Logan." She gazes at the quarterback. "It's one of the things I told you when I convinced you to join us. I know you want to prove yourself as much as I do."

"That's why I'm here." His voice is monotone, yet there's determination in every word. "I'll do my part."

I gaze at Logan again. It's well known that his previous team dealt him a poor hand of cards. They kept him as the backup, despite being a first round pick, because the coach didn't trust him. Many rumors went around for the coach's reasoning, but none of them were confirmed.

Selena gives him a slow, considering nod. "Part of my plan is to engage the fans and get them excited for the team again. Hopeful. That's why we agreed to have the film crew following you around."

I frown. My boss was in charge of the TV special tracking the Strike's new era, with Logan as the quarterback. Rumblings traveled the halls that it wasn't going well, but I wasn't privy to the details.

"You won't regret bringing me to the Strike, Selena," Logan says.

"I'm glad to hear that," she replies, "because some things will need to change. You may have heard that Charlie was let go, but you may not know it was a direct result of his management of the TV show."

I straighten in my seat. Selena hasn't paid much attention to me, but I haven't missed a thing. If I read between the lines, the new boss wants me to use my PR powers for something Logan-related. Gears turn in my mind, bringing a hundred ideas to the tip of my tongue. To be in charge of anything related to The Strike 2.0, in particular something New Quarterback related, could secure my spot with the organization even further. And if it involved any kind of raise...

I take a deep, calming breath.

Selena looks out the window. "The production team from Sports Media Network complained to me earlier in the week. They showed me the material they have filmed since they were given access to the team at the start of training camp. They believe it's insufficient to make for a good mini-series, and they're threatening to pull the project."

"I thought the interviews were fine." Logan crosses his arms.

"And so did Charlie." Selena stared at Logan. "Unfortunately, he and I couldn't come to an agreement."

The owner of the Strike is a woman who commands the room. Her last statement sounds self-assured rather than threatening, but I understand the implication. She wants what she wants and she will make it happen.

"The network and my team, we all want the same thing." Selena gazes at me now. "Imagine this. The new quarterback with a chip on his shoulder finally has a chance to come out of his father's shadow. He never got his break with his old team, so what will he do to prove himself to the masses? He's going to show his old coach how wrong he was, by turning into the glue that finally makes this team cohesive. He's going to help take us to the playoffs. He's going to be the new King of football."

I'm a PR exec. I know a good story when I hear it, and this one could drive the whole season's media push. If Logan performs, the fans would go wild. Maybe even newscasters would stop comparing him to his dad, the old King of football.

My gaze lands on him, handsome to a fault, and with eyes that look hazel in this light. I don't know his history in great detail, but everyone knows of Logan's thirst to be a player whose stats speak louder than his last name.

If this is the story Selena wants to push... and if she sees me involved with it in some way...

I latch into every fiber of professionalism I have not to rush her. Biting the inside of my lip is a good way to keep quiet. A door seems to be opening for me, and I won't risk it closing before I can see what is on the other side.

Selena frowns and studies Logan for a second, me for another, to finally gaze out to the field again. "I want everyone to be thinking about it, Logan. You included. That means you need to give them what they want. Help me sell this story to everyone."

The man sitting next to me doesn't say anything, but the room cools a few degrees at Selena's words.

It doesn't matter. If Selena wants me to work with him on this TV show, then I very much will. I can handle difficult people, whether I have a past with them or not. One night many years ago won't be the thing that keeps me stuck in the tiny apartment I live in, or carrying the burden of my parents' wrong decisions. No matter if the mere thought of working so close to him causes tingles to my insides.

If making Logan shine is the way I prove myself, then I'll cover the new quarterback in rhinestones until I could pass him for a diamond in Selena's eyes.

"I want you to work closely with Evie." Selena stares at Logan again. "I want you two to create the perfect story for your first season with the team. What do you say?"

Chapter 5

Logan

Mystery Girl is sitting next to me. Her name is Evie Moreno. She doesn't look at me like she wants to dissect me anymore, she doesn't seem to remember me, and my limbs have gone stone cold. After years of wondering what her name was, why she left like she did, and if she thought about that night as much as I did... Now she sits next to me, impassive, unaware of the questions multiplying in my mind.

My heart beats fast, doing everything it can to pump blood into my extremities again. It barely works. Worse, I don't have the time or space to process the shock. My stomach is on the floor, because Selena wants to push the TV special further than I expected.

It's one thing to have every move I make on the field recorded, exploited for social media and the Sunday shows. Another is to have a TV crew following me off the field and making a spectacle of this year. Worse, if the interviews they want ask for more than I'm willing to give.

I already have the attention of everyone on staff, of fans in their homes, hell, even my teammates. That's something I've learned to live with. It's part of the job.

All I have to do is help take the team to the playoffs, and everything else will fall into place on its own.

The part I dread is being accosted on the streets, dealing with people who think they get to know my deepest secrets because I play their favorite sport. I want to excel at this game I love, have a team to be loyal to, and a small circle of friends to call my own. Beyond that, people get to enjoy the game with me, not question who I am. I doubt a TV crew would honor my boundaries.

I study Selena's face carefully, seeking more clues— or an exit— and keep still so as not to show my reaction.

"I'm listening." My words are about buying myself time more than anything.

I grew up with the few family meals we had disrupted by the demands of the team and the public. Every outing resulted in being swarmed by my father's fans. Plans cancelled because of an interview. Learning who he was from the write-ups in magazines, rather than a chat between father and son. This is to blame for how detached we are from each other— it robbed me of having a close knit family. My whole life has been distorted by my father's fame, and I've been trying to detach myself from it for a decade.

It's ironic, really. Football was supposed to pay me back by giving me a team to be close to. A family of sorts. All I had to do was find the right people, and prove myself my own man. Discovering how powerful I felt while playing was the gift I didn't expect, and what kept me going despite every frustration. The game became my refuge, when teams fell apart and people compared me to my father.

My career is my own. I've learned from how my dad handled things, and I've kept the media at a distance. If I don't give them extra material, no one gets to see me for more than what I can achieve on the field. It's the one thing I can do to prevent the intrusion.

I badly need time to work something out. I can't lose that distance from the media now.

Selena is serious as she speaks. "I don't want to lose this project. I want to take it farther, and that's why you're here, Evie. The show is one thing, and we definitely need to keep an eye on it to make sure it fits the story we're telling, but we can do more."

The owner turns to the woman I've thought about for years, sitting so casually next to me. Sunlight shines in the office, and it casts a glow on her I could get lost in.

Evie. I like the sound of it. Finally putting a name to the memory comes with a shake to my foundation. She's sitting next to me, and I have no reason to believe she remembers me. What the fuck am I going to do about that?

No time to make a decision about that just yet. Especially when I can sense she'll join forces with the boss before it happens.

"For sure." Evie nods and jumps in, like she's waiting for her chance. "We can set up a few things with the in-house media offices, and reach out to a few podcasts and newscasters."

"What about community events?" Selena asks. "Maybe some handpicked sponsorship deals to really sear Logan in their brain?"

"Definitely. If the fans learn to love him, we'll have brands knocking at the door."

"A couple of comments." I interrupt with the first few things I can cling to, if I hope to do some damage control. "Brand deals are for me and my agent to discuss, as long as I follow the league and team's rules. Also, I'm not a subject fit for a documentary— or fit for other media outlets either. Maybe that's why they haven't been getting the material they want."

Both women give me calculating looks. Evie's eyes, a beautiful shade of brown, reach deep into me— it's a harpoon to my memories, and suddenly I'm remembering how good it felt to kiss her. To have her in my arms.

Fuck. No. Nope, not going there. All recollections will be ruthlessly corralled into a corner of my mind, and chained there until they're not tempt— distracting anymore.

I don't bother straightening in my chair. I can't show how all of this affects me. My reaction is limited to raising a challenging eyebrow at her.

She echoes it. "Unless there's an exception I'm not aware of, my understanding is that all contracts include the standard clauses requiring participation with the media."

I return her scheming stare. With the years, details had frayed. Now I have her next to me, and my memory is sharp again. She's still beautiful. Her makeup and hair are different, but I can still see the girl I remember.

But that night she ran away when I couldn't stop her, leaving me with a million questions. And she clearly stands on Selena's side. Her beauty and our brief history are something I can compartmentalize.

I'll just go back to thinking of her randomly as I live my life, or sometimes when I'm alone in bed using my hand.

My jaw tightens. It's fine. I'll cope. I'll find a way.

"There is no exception in my contract." My concession is reluctant. "But I don't want anything affecting my concentration."

"I can help you handle it." She seems resolute.

"It's not that I can't. It's that it doesn't make me better at my job, so I avoid it."

My goals are simple. I want my performance to speak for itself. I want a close knit team, dammit, and not just one ring. I want at least three.

Within two years, I will call my teammates brothers. People won't see me simply as my father's son, and a player who had promise but never got the minutes on the field to earn anything.

The Strike's offer is the ticket to finally proving I can stand on my own. It means getting free of the weight of my last name, being known for who I am, and finding the place where I belong.

It's not the time to be sucked into the spectacle of the sport I actually enjoy.

"Helping the Network's crew do their job will help the narrative not only around you," Evie argues, "but the whole team. With the fans' support, the team will have a better morale. That means a closer team. That helps you do your work better."

I frown. I don't like where this is going. It's true that things were never right with my old team. The coach had a vendetta against my dad I didn't learn about until too late. Rather than giving me the chance I deserved, he relied on the starting quarterback instead. Plenty of alternative reasons were provided. He insisted I was too high a risk for the success of the team and fought the GM over it for years.

"Not to say anything about supporting the start to my tenure as an owner," Selena adds. "With a redemption story like this, we can kickstart the new age of the Strike."

I clench my jaw and gaze out the window. Fuck.

Charlie may have been a senior PR exec, but he never pushed me. The whole TV special deal was annoying but not too bad. What Selena wants will radically change that. Considering how short football careers can be, this run with the Strike may be my last chance. To have it televised to a greater degree than the standard game broadcast...

"I know how I come off," I say as a matter of fact. "Eighty percent of the content they'll get is me glaring at something. Or someone."

I don't mind my personality too much. Most people see my frown as intimidating and that helps— if I'm a little scary, people give me a wide berth. I may need to curb the effect if I want the brotherhood of a team, but I prefer it that way.

I'll tone down the grumpiness with my teammates. People on the street are a different matter, and one I don't want to think about.

"We can give it a spin." Evie gazes at Selena, as if she doesn't share my concerns. "We can call it focus, or passion, or..."

"Yes, that's the whole idea." Selena leans back on her leather chair. Her crossed arms make her look confident. "Evie— I brought you here because with Charlie gone, there's a spot open on the Senior Exec team. I need to think about who I really want in the PR team at large, and who's going to replace him. I know you don't have the tenure, but if you can help me with this project..."

"Absolutely!" Evie practically beams with excitement. "It will be my pleasure."

"I'm giving you this project as your top priority," Selena says. "Remember I'm making decisions on the PR staff as a whole depending on how this goes. Make sure the story I want is what we get."

"You can count on me," Evie responds.

Mystery Girl's eyes lock with mine. She studies me like I'm a challenge she's ready to tackle.

Deep in my belly, a small flame sparks to life— again. I enjoy being provoked. A person who defies me and makes me work for it will keep me in her bed for several nights. A few mornings. A handful of afternoon escapades.

Except I can't afford the distraction this season. That person can never be Evie again, not now that she smiles more than she challenges me, and not the way she left. Not now that we work together, and she's not on my side.

Selena studies me. "I'm sorry, Logan. I will have to insist on this. It's a choice I'm making in the team's interest."

I purse my lips and stare out the window. Fuuuck. It seems I will have to find a way to survive the scrutiny... and the proximity.

I will not think about that night. Simple as that. It's fine. It will be fine. I'm too damn stubborn to break for the ghost of a memory, and the reality of a beautiful woman. Everything I want is on the field.

I can play Evie's and Selena's game if it means a better season and a closer squad. I'll do anything for the team. But I will draw the lines on the playing field.

"Understood." I give Selena a single nod.

I've always known I would be in the spotlight, if not for my last name, then for my performance alone. I've fought it my whole life, but I won't let the camera be the thing to derail me, either.

My whole career, I've tackled one challenge at a time. Joining the Strike has its fair share of trials, and media would be the tribulation.

I will tackle them one at a time, too.

Chapter 6

Logan

It doesn't mean that I don't avoid Evie for a couple of days. Or several.

If I'm thinking of Mystery Girl every night, and her hair looks a bit different now, it's not a big deal. If I catch myself replaying that night again in my mind, with the way I believed she wanted me for me and wasn't there for the wrong reasons, and how she didn't ask anything of me but that moment together...

Alone in my bed at night is the only place where those memories are welcome. Everywhere else, and it will be chained in place.

A few of her emails wait in my inbox, but my eyes are on the team and training. This is the time to get to know everyone, and work on that cohesion we'll need to get to the playoffs. It's a big part of what Selena wants, too, and it's my number one target.

That's why I'm laying down on one of the treatment tables and getting a massage I don't need. A few of my teammates occupy the medical-type examination beds around me, and chatter flows easily.

Leon groans next to me. The sound is deep, almost cavernous. It fits with his big, offensive lineman size, the tattoos covering his form, and the thick beard he keeps. Even the white scar on his top lip matches his general vibe. No wonder they call him The Bear.

"You okay?" I ask.

We're both on our backs. I'm getting work on my shoulder and upper arm, but the physio working on him hovers around his hips and in my line of sight.

"I have an elbow digging deep into my groin." Contained pain etches his words. "I won't apologize for the noises I need to make."

"Go right ahead. Do what you must."

"Didn't mean anything by it, but... groin. It's the worst."

"An elbow dig hurts anywhere." Saint is getting work on his thigh, two beds away from me. "But a deep tissue back massage is bliss."

I glance at the wide receiver with quick dimples and an easy smile. Gael Santiago is well known for being the handsome athlete going through dates like he's on a mission to sleep with every eligible person in the city. He's the friendly type, and the kind to dress in fashion-forward clothes and happily pose for the cameras. Total opposite to me, but so approachable I'm looking forward to getting to know him.

"Do you have a massage therapist you trust?" I can't see Saint properly from where I am, so I stare at the ceiling instead.

"Yeah, I'll hook you up," Saint says.

I've been around everyone for a few weeks. There's a lot I don't know yet, but I'm slowly getting there. I've learned that the athletic center we're in has a long, fancy name, but everyone calls it the Thunderdome or TD for short. I know Leon and Saint are part of a closer group of friends within the larger roster, though there are no evident cliques or real contention among the team. And I'm pretty sure everyone is still deciding what they think of me.

Being myself around them while finding ways to create connections is a hard balance to manage, but I'm determined. I may be serious and even cranky at times, but I want the closeness I never got with my previous teams. I lost precious years of my career to the wrong coach and group of guys. This is my time to make up for it.

The TD training rooms have an open space layout. Leon, Saint, and I are on the rehab tables in one corner, but the big space also has a taping area, several treatment machines, stretching cages and other physio implements. On the long side toward the front, the wall is made of collapsible glass panels that open up the room to the outside field. On the left side, the space connects to the weight room, across from where the coaches and other trainers offices are, and through which we have to go to get to the bullpen, locker area, and showers. To the back, the wet room, with its three pools designed for different conditioning and recovery treatments, and five ice dunking tubs. The final side holds a few of the physiotherapists' and other professional offices, and the hallway that connects the area to the rest of the building.

It is through that hallway that Evie appears, and I groan. The sound catches my teammate's attention, and the two of them glance in her direction.

"Miss Moreno," Leon says. "What a treat seeing you here."

She settles between him and Saint. Today she wears a navy pencil skirt, tight around her wide hips, and a loose, wine-colored blouse tucked into it. Her hair falls loose and straight down her back, and her lips are painted the same color as her top.

The curve of her hip down her thick thigh is calling for my hand. It needs to be caressed. Or slapped again.

Into a metal box it goes, closed with a padlock. Instantly compartmentalized.

I may have casually looked up the relevant policies. I may have learned that relationships are allowed in the organization, as long as there are no power imbalances and everyone involved consents. A meeting with HR and it's all good. And sure, I double checked and Evie and I are considered peers according to the Strike's hierarchy structure, but romantic relationships are far from my goal. Not even a repeat is in the plans with her. This knowledge is useless, when she wants to push me to perform for the media.

"Hello, Bear." She high fives him. "The groin still bothering you?"

She doesn't look my way, but focuses on Leon closely.

"Just a temporary setback," he says. "I'll be good in a minute."

She shifts her eyes to Saint. "Is everything okay with you today?"

"It's just maintenance treatment today, Evie. Thanks for handling that one issue for me the other day, by the way."

I frown. She looks so friendly interacting with the guys, so approachable. Her energy now is so different from what I saw all those years ago.

"You didn't need to send me flowers." She grins at Saint. "I'm glad to help."

"To what do we owe the pleasure?" he asks.

Her face sets on a mock frown, and it's clear Bear knows what it means because he chuckles. I squint and track the show closely.

"I'm missing one of your teammates," she says. "He's new, and maybe he doesn't know the lay of the land yet? I've heard he's the new quarterback. I've sent him a few emails but I haven't heard from him."

"You must be talking about Logan King." Saint's dimples make an appearance. "I think I've seen him around."

Pilar, the physio treating my shoulder, presses her lips into a thin line to hold back her laugh. I frown at her but it doesn't deter her. She lifts her eyebrows, as if to say, *what did you expect?*

"Yeah, I think that's the name!" Evie exclaims. "I really need to talk to him."

Leon runs his hand down his short beard. "We can give him a message. What do you want us to tell him?"

She crosses her arms and stares directly at me. "That he should stop hiding, and meet me in Media Room 3 in half an hour."

Pilar snorts. Leon whistles. Saint chuckles.

"Anything for you, Evie." He gives her a solemn nod. "We'll tell him."

"Thank you both." She pats their shoulders simultaneously. "Let me know if you need anything."

"You're the best," Leon adds, before she arches an eyebrow at me and leaves.

My teammates and physio study my reaction. I purse my lips and hum in displeasure.

"No one plays with Evie," Saint says with a smile. "You'll thank us later."

I'm not sure if he means that as a threat because she'll be protected, or a threat because she won't tolerate games. Maybe both. Either way, I hear the warning clearly.

Chapter 7

Evie

I wait in media room number three, half-expecting Logan not to show up. Just in case, I send him an email with a map of the building, with a big red cross on the target meeting place. He sends me a three-character response— o, k, and a period— and I sit back to wait.

It's cool. I'm collected. One-on-one meetings will not be an issue, when he clearly doesn't remember me. The pang behind my breastbone will be ignored. I'm glad he doesn't think of it enough to recognize me. So, so glad. This way, I get to keep the memories for my own, uhm, *pleasure*. I can keep things with him professional.

The time has come to find a way to convince myself that fitting as well with someone as I did that night with Logan isn't magic. That the fact my hookups have only been *sufficient* in comparison doesn't mean it will never happen again.

The Strike's new quarterback comes into the room on time, teeth clenched and a frown on his brow, but with an otherwise calm demeanor.

A small round table sits in the middle of the room. It's a simple office, with a projector hanging from the ceiling and a bunch of connector cables sprouting from a plastic-rimmed hole in the middle of the circular surface. I brought my laptop as part of my plan, and it lies closed in front of me, already connected to the right cable.

Four chairs flank the table, and Logan sits in the one facing me. His hair is halfway dry, and he wears tracksuit pants and a team shirt. In this light, his eyes look gray. I don't think much about how good he looks. Nope, not at all. In fact, the only reason I'm staring at his eyes so much is because of how strange it is to notice the way they seem to change each time.

On the way to the media room, I picked up the two coffees that sit between us.

"Thanks so much for making the time, Mister King." I offer him one of the drinks. "I tried to look up online how you drink your coffee, but couldn't find anything. At all. You've been quite private to date, it seems."

"Call me Logan."

He takes the cup but stares at me. Without breaking eye contact, he brings the drink close and sniffs it.

I scoff, and the words escape me before I can edit them for professionalism. "It's not poisoned, Your Highness."

"This has sugar. I can smell it." He takes a sip. "I usually prefer my caffeine from sugar-free energy drinks."

"You don't have to drink it. I made it the way I like it, with cream and sugar. I've been known to have two cups in a row. I'll have it."

I still don't have pods at home. Getting my caffeine fix from the team offices is one of my favorite employee benefits.

Logan takes another sip and closes his eyes. "Mhh. I think I'll keep it."

"Noted," I say, and drink some of my own mix. "Can we have the meeting now?"

A man of a few words, he doesn't say anything and waits for my directions. This time, his sip is long. He finishes about a third of the cup at once.

Ugh. He's challenging me, but I'll handle it. Selena dangled my escape in front of my face, when she suggested I might get a promotion as a result of this project.

I did the math. As long as the bank accepts our offer to restructure my parents' mortgage again, a raise will solve all my problems.

"Right." I staple my hands on the table. "Did you read the emails I sent you previously?"

"I've been busy. I filmed a few intro cards and other material for the team."

"I heard. All in-house media stuff. I've been keeping an eye on things, to make sure everything has a coherent narrative. I've been using it to establish a few arrangements with the Sports Media Network crew."

"I have done their interviews. Isn't that enough? Can the network use that at all?"

I purse my lips and open my laptop. After a few clicks, the ceiling lights in the media room dim, and Logan's face appears in all its glory, projected on the white screen hanging a few feet from us.

"Mhh." The single syllable comes out grouchy.

I press play. The recording shows Logan in a close up, lights shining on him from all angles so we can see every little detail.

I bite the inside of my lip. Even if he doesn't like the camera, the camera definitely likes him. Just like his fans do. In my usual social media morning check, I caught a bunch of them arguing about his eye color in the comments of a fan-made video. Maybe that will help with his TV charisma somewhat, but that won't help me. I know what my job is, and it isn't to provide an answer to the long-held questions about his eyes.

"Can you tell us about getting used to playing with the team?" the producer asks from behind the cameras.

"It's good. I'm getting to know everyone." His face looks stern and his tone sounds deadpan.

"Can you repeat the question in your words?" the producer adds. "Something like, 'Playing with the team is...', then fill in with your thoughts."

"Playing with the team is good. I'm getting to know everyone."

A long silence fills the video. Interview Logan runs his fingers through his longish hair and looks up to the crew. With the lighting in the studio, his eyes take a hint of green.

"Fans are coming to watch the team train." The producer's voice barely contains her frustration. "People are excited for the new quarterback and your first season. What's your message for the fans?"

"I hope they enjoy the season," he says on the screen.

Someone from the TV crew we can't see clears their throat.

The producer sighs. "Repeat the question as part of your answer, please."

"I hope the fans enjoy the season." Logan's tone continues to be monotonous.

I pause the video and stare at the quarterback.

He crosses his arms. "Fine. I get it."

"Selena said they're pissed, Logan. The way they talked to me when I called them, they will need some coaxing. Since I couldn't reach you, I've started the conversation on my own. Tried to sell them on the narrative again."

"The redemption story."

"Yep. With a hint of *the chosen one* for spice." I've been no-nonsense up to this point, but I add a small smile to the space between us.

The man in front of me is way too serious, and I fully expect my smile to be the only one making an appearance. It doesn't intimidate me. I'll amuse myself in any way I can and, through the years, I've learned I get much more done with sugar than with salt.

He snorts. "I'm the team's savior now?"

"Rather, you're going to be the glue."

"Thanks to my charming personality?"

"That seems like a stretch." I arch my eyebrows. "But we can say you brought everyone together with your dogged determination and passion for football. No pressure."

"As long as I get to focus on that. Playing a good game, being a good teammate."

"Exactly. They will probably ask for mini-interviews from you and others on the team. Do you think we can get your father involved, too?"

This meeting is the third time I get to see Logan up close, if we don't consider the past. Every time, no matter what, there has been a frown on his brow. It has ranged from a simple, mild notch above his nose, to the deep furrow and intense look he's best known for.

Right now, the frown is so fierce there's something sinister to it. Perhaps even evil— perhaps not. Perhaps that's all in my head, but it's definitely *killer*. With those grayish eyes of his, it makes him look like a shark swimming figure eights, ready to catch its prey.

A shiver runs down my spine.

"My father will not be a topic," he says in a tone that leaves no room for question. "I will not talk about him. He cannot be invited."

"But— Logan—"

"Non-negotiable, Miss Moreno."

"Please, call me Evie."

"Evie, my father is out of bounds."

We stare at each other in a standoff.

For a second, I'm back in the bar where we met. The way he openly inspects me as if to predict what I'll do next. Those eyes of a color no one can define, steady and scrutinizing. It rattles me, and I break. I cast my eyes down to my coffee.

Getting into football was circumstantial, when I got an internship with the Strike at the end of my last year of college. I consumed everything I could about the game, to the surprise of no one who understands the despair of an only child daughter of immigrant parents. Overpreparation is part of the strategy.

I had not forgotten my one night stand, but I hadn't thought about it in the context of my career either. When I snuck into the screening room where the team reviewed tape and saw Logan's face, handsome and large and frowning as usual, glaring at the Strike from his team's bench... I had to remind myself to breathe.

Since then, I've done my research. I've noticed that neither Logan nor his father talk about each other much. His old man is a commentator for the Pirates, the team with whom he got two rings and where he broke several records. He would only say a few things when the Pirates played Logan's previous team but still, everyone compares them. Kenneth King is a legend, and from a PR perspective, a big angle in our new quarterback's story.

"I may have to push, Logan."

Regardless of everything else, I can't risk the promotion. Or the potential for getting fired after all, if I fail Selena. She didn't hesitate to kick Charlie out. I better keep that in mind. This is my chance to turn my life around.

"I have made my decision," he says.

I purse my lips. The King Senior could be an asset, but having Logan on my side for this season is even more important. On the other hand, getting our new quarterback's father on board for bonus material could be the cherry on top to please Selena with my work.

I may have to get creative with this one, but I don't have to solve it today.

"Fine," I concede. "But you have to do your part."

"Which is?"

"We need to do something about the interviews." I take a deep breath. "You've been great with letting them film you without being antagonistic but, as an interview subject? That's a different story."

He purses his lips and stares down to his lap. "I'm saying everything I have to say."

"Then you might have to dig deeper for a few extra words. Honestly, Logan. You must have had PR support before."

"Yes, and see how that went?" There's no humor to his quip.

I chuckle anyway. "Okay. Let's try again. What do you hate about this? Maybe I can fix it."

"I thought your job was to handle this project with the filming crew. Set up a few extra opportunities. Not monitoring me."

"Of course it's with you, too. You know this. I'm the bridge between the players and everyone else. I help you guys get what you need, and make the fans love you at the same time."

The frown grows deeper. "I hate this stuff. With a passion. Asking me to suddenly be personable makes my teeth ache. All the media has ever done for me is make my life harder and ruin good things."

"You've been playing ball for years. You have to know how important the relationship to fans is."

"Can't they keep it to the comment section? I'll shake a few hands and sign a few shirts if that helps."

"Go right ahead and do that, too. But you'll have to do the media stuff as well. We need the world to love you."

His restless energy escapes through a shaking leg, and he runs his fingers through his luscious hair again. "When they see me play— when we start winning, they'll call me eccentric and move on."

He crosses his arms, his eyes hard on me. Thoughts cloud his eyes. He may be remembering his history with his previous team, or he might be imagining the upcoming season and feeling the pressure of it all.

"If we can sell this redemption story to the masses," I add, "you'll shine. For yourself and the rest of the team. So let's control the narrative, okay?"

"Control the narrative."

He doesn't ask it as a question, but I respond to it anyway.

"Think of the media as the place where you tell people what you want them to think about you. Sure, a bunch of them will disagree, but a whole lot more are going to take you at your word— especially with how serious you are."

He squints at me and I take it as a win. It's the opening to get him doing what we need him to do.

I smile to add confidence to my pitch. "Media is the megaphone through which you steer people's opinion. If you learn to speak their language, you can steer things your way. What do you want them to think about you?"

He rubs his lips together and doesn't respond, but I know I have his attention.

"Let me help you," I insist. I keep my grin, because smiling at people is what I do. It puts them at ease.

He thinks about it for a moment. "I still hate it."

"That's okay. Hate it but do it anyway. And manage it."

When he studies me this time, there's less resistance in his... blue-ish eyes.

"So you'll help me," he says. "How?"

"I'll come up with a plan. Trust me."

"Why? For a promotion? You're going above and beyond your role. Most PR folk have let me get in trouble before."

I hesitate for a second. I'm usually the one offering help and getting things done for people. I'm the one bringing cupcakes to the office and collecting signatures for someone's 'Happy Retirement' card. I don't open up to others in the process. Especially someone I've had sex with and now work with. Talk about fuzzy boundaries.

But if it may bring down a few of his walls, and he lets me make this project a success, I'll share a tiny piece.

I shrug like it's not a big deal. "Yes. I want my old boss's position."

He doesn't get to know why I need that raise so badly.

Logan stares to the ground and doesn't say anything else.

"This time things will be different with the media," I say. "I promise. All you need to do is play nice and talk to reporters. Go to the community and charity events we set up for you. I'll be there every step of the way, to make sure they don't do anything shady or cross any lines. I'll make this work for you and the organization. You win, I win."

"Fine." He stands up, arms still crossed over his wide torso. "But whatever you come up with to help me, I refuse to engage in role playing."

I laugh, to distract from the way my cheeks burn. The night we had years ago hides in plain sight, if I hear the words *role playing* and think of him asking me to bend over because I've been a bad girl.

I shake my head to dislodge the thought.

"I'll find a way." I stand and offer him a handshake. "Good luck to us."

He stares at it, then at me. It takes him a moment, but he finally takes my hand.

His large palm and long, thick fingers engulf mine again. Warmth seeps into my skin, but I push all of it out of my consciousness.

"I never count on luck." His voice is rough, and his words are clipped.

The way he looks at me— it sends a wave of awareness down my back.

I believe him, too. It's a thrill cascading down my spine.

"Good." I release his hand. "Because I don't give up."

The work has just begun.

Chapter 8

Logan

The team and I are in the locker room after a long training day. People chat, rest, and hit the showers before changing into fresh clothes. My stall is between Dom, a tight end, and Rafa, a defensive tackle. Rafa is a quiet guy, silently untying his cleats, which makes him a great neighbor for me. Dom, on the other hand...

"I think I'm breaking out of my routes too slowly," he says. "I keep missing the timing."

Dominic Wright is the team's starting tight end, and another serial dater. His hair is black and buzzed short, and his beard is short and dense. It suits him. He's as tall as I am, with similar complexion and build but, unlike me, he has tattoos down his arms and up his shoulders.

"We'll get there." I hang my hoodie in my stall and take off my shirt. I stuff it in my bag.

Encouragement doesn't come naturally to me. Theoretically, I've always known it's important. I've wanted it myself. But even if I believe that the right people will like me how I am, I know I have to do my part.

I clear my throat. "We need to practice more. Wanna get together earlier next week and get ahead?"

"Might have to reschedule a couple of dates but priorities are priorities." He grins. "I'll let you know."

The smile is cocky rather than a sign of friendship. The guys are cordial to me, but I know better than to take that gesture as a sign of closeness. It's too soon for that. Maybe that's why he's non-committal, but I don't bring it up.

I stare at him. "You have dates at seven in the morning or...?"

"I'll let you guess," he laughs, before we're interrupted by a mild commotion.

Saint comes into the locker room carrying a big panel of some sort. A ruckus follows him.

"Finally," Dom says. "Come on, King. You're going to want to see this."

Rafa joins us and we approach everyone by the wall that separates the locker room from the showers. It's been an empty space up to this point, but Saint hangs the panel from a hook, and I raise my eyebrows at what I see.

Glitter and shiny ribbons surround a whiteboard. Bold patterns in wildly cut paper letters title the monstrosity. It reads, *The Seattle Strike Best of the Best Betting Board Team* ~~destroyer~~ *Builder*: The B-Hypercubed!

"Who made that?" I ask under my breath.

"No one knows," Dom replies. "Saint has never revealed it."

The board is in place now, with some initial bets written in whiteboard marker. One of them places the bets for the highest score on the bullpen pinball machine, and one for the Pac-Man machine. There are a couple others, and also plenty of space to add new ones.

Bear places a crown on a hook above the board, and mocks a trumpet sound effect.

Saint faces us with a big grin, and gestures to the board and the crown like he's the ringmaster of the circus we're in.

He bows. "Good folk of the Strike's locker room, homed in the revered Callum Fraser Athletic Center for the Seattle Strike, our beloved Thunderdome."

A couple people cheer and clap. I wear only my training shorts, and cross my arms over my naked torso.

"The season has officially begun, thanks to the annual, honored, illustrious, Hypercubed Team Builder!"

Now everyone claps and cheers and I can't help it— I snort laugh.

"Place your bets, everyone," Bear roars. "You know you want the crown! But only one of us can claim it for the off-season."

Damián, a kicker, takes the marker attached to the board by a string. He writes his name under *the highest pinball score of the season*.

"Whoever gets the most points takes the crown," Dom explains. "Side quests happen— extra bets not on the board that may or may not involve bragging rights and or embarrassing dares."

"I see." I rub my chin. "Would it be fun or asshole-y if I came in to destroy everyone in pinball?"

Several sets of eyes land on me and take my measure. Some of them are playful, most are suspicious. If everyone jokes around, I know better than to take it as a ready welcome. The team is a pack with a fresh wolf in their midst, and the new pecking order hasn't been determined yet.

"Oooh." Dom grins and raises his voice. "The new quarterback is ready to throw down! Damián, you have a contender."

"What?" Damián turns to face me. "Did you see the record on the machine yet, King? It hasn't been rebooted for the season yet."

I shrug. "I'm not scared."

I take the marker from him and write my name on the board.

"Oooh," comes out of several onlookers.

"You're on, King," Damián adds.

I give him a confident smirk and shake his hand. Being accepted into the group requires that I be myself and join in their traditions in equal measure.

We move to the side and let others add their name to the board. I aim for my stall, when Evie's voice reaches me from the hall.

"Please cover all goods! I don't want to see any dicks in the wild unless it's mutually consensual!"

I raise both eyebrows and turn toward her. She enters the locker room with her hands at an upward angle on her nose. It's a well-placed screen to keep her vision above our necks.

No one seems to react, except for a couple of the guys coming out of the showers. They wrap their hips in a towel and go on as usual.

Not a rare occurrence, then.

Evie stops near the entrance. "Is everyone decent?"

"Come in, Evie." Rafa, the quiet guy, motions her forward with his hand. "You're always welcome."

"Thank you, Rafa." She drops her hands. "You know how it is."

He nods but doesn't say anything else. She returns his nod, before gazing across the room and settling her eyes on me.

She puts on what I'm starting to think is a professional smile and strides to me. There's something about it that seems... restricted. No one else seems to notice or, at least, no one mentions it. I frown and keep my impressions to myself.

"I don't know how it is." I'm still shirtless and my arms are still crossed. "If you don't want to see dicks in the wild, why come to the locker room? This isn't the place to care about modesty."

Her eyes scan my shoulders, my arms, and go as low as my navel. Her face is neutral but, at the last second, she adds a downward curl to her lips.

She doesn't look impressed. "I don't announce myself to protect my virtue. I don't care about your guys' dicks."

Saint walks by and adds his two cents. "We all have a small crush on Miss Moreno, but I'm afraid she's immune to us."

"Mmh," I utter.

She wasn't immune to me once.

Except the way she left, maybe she truly meant to use me to get laid and nothing else. She could still be immune, if she rationally picked me for the task more than half a decade ago.

Evie raises an insistent index finger. "Immune."

"Wonderful news, I'm sure." I raise an eyebrow and let my words drip with sarcasm.

The fact she doesn't remember me scratches down the walls of my mind. Long nails on a blackboard kind of thing.

I haven't decided what to do about it yet.

She sighs. "You're a little bit of an ass, did you know?"

"I've been told."

"But we shook hands and now I'm going to help you."

"Can't wait."

She rolls her eyes and it's salve for my prickled ego. It helps to know that while she's not someone to shrink in the face of my grumpiness, she's still bothered by it. That she may not be spooked, but she's irritated.

I'll take it. It means I can affect her today, even if she forgot about me.

Fuck. I hate that she forgot about the one night I think about the most.

If I could jog her memory, I could make her remember. I could drop hints here and there. A word that echoes those hours we shared. It can be a game, one where I poke and test how far I'll go, before I remind her we had sex once. All for the moment I get to look into her eyes, and demand answers to all my questions.

"Anyway." She jerks her head in the general direction of the hall. "Follow me to my locker room office, a.k.a. the service room around the corner."

"Are you serious?"

She doesn't respond and starts walking that way instead. "We could also go on a journey all the way to my actual office but, unless you want that, this is a simple place where we can talk in private."

She's wearing a dress that hugs her hips. My eyes fall to her behind. It sways as she walks, and it's indulgent enough that little tremors echo her steps.

Just like it did when her hands were on the wall that night.

Dammit, I need to keep myself in control.

"Fine." I follow her and stop complaining.

A man can look. Once in a while. Recreationally. As part of this game with loose rules I'm embarking on. But letting myself get hard with the memories has trouble written all over. Especially while surrounded by witnesses, and while so early in this one-sided match.

We enter the service room. It's bigger than I thought it would be. A cleaning cart much like the ones they use at hotels waits at the back of the room. Behind it, what I think are industrial size washing and drying machines. The side walls are shelved and full of cleaning supplies and folded towels.

The space is filled with the smell of laundry detergent and cleaning products. Even so, I can smell traces of wet towels waiting to be washed, and the faint odor of a mop in need of replacement.

Evie turns to me and crosses her arms. "This is where I come with your team-mates when I need a quick word with them."

"You could have sent me an email."

"Sure, and then you would have ignored it."

"Only if I didn't like what you had to say."

She grins. "Exactly."

I close my eyes and groan. "Can I still avoid you for a couple of days?"

"Can you be a little less irritating?"

I smirk to hide the smile that wants to curl my lips. "Can't make any promises."

"And this is why I don't want to date you."

I should be happy to hear her say that, but confusion overpowers it.

"Thanks for letting me know." Sarcasm is my go-to. "But that's coming out of nowhere. Explain."

"We're not going to date, even if it looks like it," she adds.

It quiets everything inside.

Fuck, it reminds me of that night when she left while I slept. We had agreed on one night, and yet I wanted to get her number in case I made my way back to town. We could have had more nights like it, no strings attached. Instead, she gave me a few hours and disappeared into the night.

The same feeling I had the next morning drips down my back.

"Excuse me?" I ask.

"It's how I will help. We're going to go on pretend first dates— in private. We'll let it be awkward and stilted and push through it."

"Is this a joke?"

"I would never joke about work! It's a great plan. We're going to desensitize you to small talk."

I blink a few times. I'm frowning so hard the muscles on my brow threaten to cramp.

I scoff. "You mean, you're going to torment me with small talk."

"We're going to let you loosen up and answer random ass questions." She smiles and gives me finger guns.

Finger. Guns. I'm tempted to grab some of the bleach I'm sure is here in the room somewhere, to erase the image from my brain. It's way too cute, and it threatens the severe persona I need to keep. Her proposal is too chilling to have fun with any of it.

"I changed my mind," I say. "Role playing sounds good all of a sudden."

"You're lying. No one likes role playing."

"But how is this any better?"

"We're going to meet in my office. Just coffee or you bring your energy drinks or whatever. I ask questions. You answer. Easy!"

She's smiling like this is a wonderful plan. It doesn't do much to soothe the knot in my stomach.

I'm still wearing my training shorts, but I feel naked.

To think she didn't even want to know my name, once upon a time...

"Listen." She takes a step forward, hands between us in a gesture that one might see on someone approaching a wild animal. "Your interviewing skills need work. Your answers should consist of more than five growled words. You need to pretend to be interested and engage like you're trying to impress whoever is listening. Doesn't that sound like a first date?"

"It does. It's sickening."

And precisely the reason I don't date. I hate the performance of it all.

"Evie, you're not helping your case."

"Okay, so how about this. We talked about getting close to the team. How's that going?"

"Well enough."

"Right. The thing is, I know these guys. They're a close bunch. After Matt— the previous quarterback— left, everyone was shaken. They understand why he was released, and why they brought you in, but they're going to need more than time together on the field to truly feel connected with you."

I frown. I'm sure she's thinking of cohesion and team spirit, and how that can lead to winning, but her words tickle my interest for a different reason. I want to find a family with them, and I'll take any clues that might help me get there.

"How would these fake first dates help?" I raise an eyebrow.

"Did you see the betting board? That's only one way they bond. They have group chats and get togethers and like to spend casual time with each other. How are you going to build rapport if all you do is frown?"

I'd offered Dom more time to practice, but my gut told me Evie was right about this. It might not have been the right call. Besides, challenging Damián on pinball might show I want to be part of the team, but it won't necessarily ingratiate me with a lot of them. And unless they understand my humor is dry where theirs is lively...

She reads my thoughts as doubts.

"Logan, we shook hands. Let me help you the best way I know how."

I purse my lips and study her. Hope glimmers in her eyes. A soft smile curves her mouth. She's showing me who she is with everyone on the team.

"I prefer it when you bite back, Evie."

A gasp escapes her. The shake of her head is subtle, but I'm looking closely. She composes herself quickly, and her warm smile turns into a smirk.

"Then see you on Monday after you're done with training. My office. Bring your own food and drinks."

She turns to exit the service room, and goes as far as to flip her straight hair over her shoulder.

"Mmh, quite the date, I see," I grumble.

I tell myself I'm not looking forward to it. I highlight the part of my brain that knows I hate dating. That I find the spectacle of it dreadful and useless.

But I know I'm lying.

Chapter 9

Evie

Back when my parents first told me the extent of their debt, I went into a bit of a crisis. The weight of caring so much for them and wanting to help overwhelmed me, and I ended up locking myself in my room for a few days.

Two people noticed and checked in on me. We shared a few classes together, and they knew I wasn't the kind to skip my responsibilities like that. So when I ditched every other friend, I held on to Ren and Pri.

Maybe it helped that I knew they'd return to their small town after they finished their degrees. I've been hesitant to get close to people for years, and it's easier to keep people at a distance when they live far away. My conversations with Ren and Pri mostly happen in the group chat we have together, and all our plans to visit tend to fail for one reason or another. The fact we're only tied by our phones means they are friends that live in my pocket.

They are my only friends, and I smile when I see texts from them on my screen.

> Ren: Hey, city girl. How are things?

Evie: same old, same old

Ren: surrounded by big, sexy guys you swear you're not into?

Evie: that's correct

Pri: Not even Saint? Or Logan King?

Evie: Not even

Ren: still don't buy it!

Pri: me neither tbh

Evie: how are my two darling, darling friends?

Ren: missing you! The town's summer festival is about to happen in a few weeks. Are you sure you can't make it????

Pri: we've been inviting you since we met in college. You've never come

Evie: I'm sorry, friends. I can't make it. I was given a huge project at work that I need to excel at. It could get me a promotion! So it's a big deal. But please don't stop inviting me, in case I can make it one of these years? Pretty please <3<3<3

Ren: we'll invite you every year

Logan finds me in my office for our first not-a-date. The skies are a patchwork of white and blue, and the forecast predicts a balmy temperature for the next few hours. The team won the preseason game the day before and spirits are high. Trapping ourselves in my office for our first not-a-date feels depressing, so I guide him out of there.

I stride toward the back of the executive suite, rather than the elevator. "This way."

I go past the reception area toward the copy room, past the kitchen, and into the storage area. At the back, I find the door leading to the elevator electrical room and to the stairs.

"I know I haven't been at my best with the interviews," Logan mumbles behind me, "but murder might be too extreme a reaction."

"I don't plan to murder you..." I leave the sentence hanging, so he can hear the *yet* I don't say out loud.

He sighs. It's a heavy and peeved sound. It's the only way I know he follows me. For a big man, his steps are quiet.

I open the service door and step onto the roof terrace.

It's not a pretty place, but it's got a great view. A section at the back is hidden from the field and the outdoor parking lot alike. Tucked in the corner, two large paint buckets wait to be used as stools, to sit and stare at the water or the island across it. I may have done it a few times in the past when I needed time alone, but I'm willing to give up my escape place if it may help bring down Logan's guards. The openness of the space invites honesty.

I sit on one of the upside down buckets, taking care that my pleated skirt rests appropriately over my legs. Logan takes a beat to make up his mind, but eventually sits on the other one next to me.

"All right," he says. "Shoot."

I smile up to him. "Congratulations on the win yesterday."

He acknowledges me with a single nod. His hair is still half-wet from his shower, and today he's wearing training shorts and a shirt. His defined thighs tempt my eyes as do his arms, but I stop myself from ogling. I frown at the cup he carries instead. It's a big, reusable glass cup with a straw and a colorful silicon sleeve that I've seen before.

"That looks like one of Saint's smoothies," I say.

"He hooked me up with his chef. Her team delivers these fresh after training."

He doesn't add more and the thread seems to wear off. The second after has that feeling of *quick, find something to say* that happens in awkward conversations.

I chew on the inside of my lip.

He tastes the concoction with a gesture full of suspicion. I snort. At least he seems wary of all new foods, and not only the coffee I brought him that day.

I sigh and reach for a container of food I left by my feet earlier, and open the plastic lid. "Saint swears by those smoothies. I'm sure it's fine."

"I've been told it has all the nutrients I need to recover."

It sounds like he's giving away a fact, rather than keeping conversation. I need to find a way to get him to chat with ease.

"Will you eat something else later?" I ask. "I can't imagine being so physically active as you guys and then eating a liquid diet for dinner."

He sips from the cup again. "I'll have proper food later. I'll be hungry again in two hours with this drink. At least it's tasty."

He steals a glance at my food.

"What's in your drink?" I spear roasted peppers and chicken from my pasta meal.

"A bunch of things apparently." He appears to think it over, like he's looking for something to say as well. "Oatmeal, apple, ginger, and avocado are the main ones."

I raise my eyebrows and take another bite of my dinner. "I wouldn't have thought to add avocado."

I don't rush him and take in the landscape view. There's enough sunlight to bring the water alive in a deep blue. The trees on the other shore move in the wind in shades of deep green.

One day I'd get to sit somewhere and gaze out at nature, with a cup of a delicious warm beverage in my hands. I would have no work to get done, no problems to solve. No fires to put out for teammates or my parents or anyone. It would be me and a few days to do nothing. Ah, glorious *nothing*.

But that isn't today. On this fine training day, I'm taking care of my biggest challenge of the upcoming season. Logan King and his media reticence could get in the way of the team's and my goals alike, and we can't have that.

"How's your food?" he asks in a begrudging tone.

I chew and glance at him. "I appreciate that you're putting effort into the small talk."

He rolls his eyes. "I feel ridiculous."

"Aw, it'll get better. We'll figure it out. You're doing good."

"It's been five minutes. I know how I come across. Don't be so generous with praise."

"Would you like it better if I used degradation?"

The words are out of my mouth before I realize what I'm saying. I don't know what it is about Logan, that my tongue gets loose and I say things I would never say to other people at work.

Maybe it's because he's been inside me, and he's the only partner I've ever had who almost made me come without my help.

Nope! Can't think about that.

He studies me with one of his famous frowns. "I'm not one for praise or degradation, thanks."

I stuff my mouth not to ask what he's into. From memory, I'd say he's more into being bossy.

Shouldn't think about that either.

A small group of people row past the Thunderdome on kayaks. Their bright-colored vessels catch the eye, a big contrast with the dark bluish gray of the water.

I grab a coffee I left by my feet earlier as well, and I sip from it.

"I'll try to be neutral, then," I say. "We're keeping it casual."

"I thought that this would be more like media training."

"But you don't want role playing or proper coaching... this is what I can do. I'm trying, Logan. It's for both of us."

"I'm trying, too, believe it or not." He drinks more of his smoothie. "I've never cared for small talk."

"But how do you get to know people, then?"

"Small talk doesn't help me know people."

"No? I'll prove you wrong."

He arches an eyebrow at me.

"Ask me about my food again," I say.

"How's your food?"

A breeze plays with my hair, and a lock flies over my face. I smile, imagining Logan and I are on a picnic and being friendly for once.

Not that we can be friends. Even though personal relationships are generally allowed in the Strike's organization, I'd rather keep things professional. Clearer, stronger lines that way. Especially with Logan. There's too much past to imagine that between us.

I clear the hair from my face. "My food is tasty, but it got cold fast. I wish I had a microwave closer."

"Right." He stares at me like he has no idea what I'm doing.

"Do you want to try the pasta?"

He squints at me with skepticism.

"Please." I roll my eyes this time. "Your Highness, will you require a food tester? It's still not poisoned."

His nostrils flare as he studies me, but eventually agrees. "Fine. Give me some."

I give him a bite. He tastes it thoroughly, eyes across the water. "It's good. Did you make it?"

"Yep. And thanks. Did you think you wouldn't like it? Everyone loves pasta."

"I like pasta." He avoids the question and drinks more of his smoothie.

"Nicely done! We small-talked."

He smirks. "I know, thanks for pointing it out."

"Now you know I like my food still warm, that I love pasta, and that I'm very generous of spirit because I offered you some."

He shakes his head, and some of his hair falls over his eyes. It's long enough to curl over his temples, and past his ears.

"Evidently." He snorts.

"What else did you learn?"

"That I still hate small talk."

"Anything else?"

"That you're snarky under the smiles you offer everyone, but I don't know if other people know that. And that you will likely call me 'Your Highness', even if it's a cheap nickname for me."

My lips open in a mix of surprise and vexation.

He smirks. "Do you want to hear more of what I think?"

"I'm not sure, actually."

"Tell me when you're ready."

A hint of humor appears in his tone, but I ignore it.

"You'll have to wait for a while, King."

"I've noticed you help everyone, but share very little about yourself."

"Uhm, excuse you. We're here to help *you* open up."

"I can open up if I want to. I just don't want to."

It's like he enjoys aggravating me.

I stare across the water to one of my favorite houses. It has contemporary lines, with whitewashed and natural wood walls, and huge windows all over.

"I don't know," I say. "All I see is that you're direct and don't mind speaking what you think, but that's not the same as opening up."

"Maybe I have my reasons not to open up."

"If you tell me why, you'd be opening up and proving me wrong."

"Tempting. Proving you wrong, that is."

"Come on, Your Highness." I stress the nickname with high eyebrows. He snorts. "What's the worst that could happen? I'm not asking you to reveal your deepest secrets. There's an art to giving answers that are truthful, that you mean, that reveal a bit but never too much."

He mulls over my words. His gray eyes are locked on me while he gets lost in his thoughts for a minute. Nerves bubble up in my belly, like my guts know I don't really want to know what's going through his mind.

A small part of me wants to know, but I quiet it easily.

He doesn't stop inspecting me. "When did you learn to measure your words like that?"

The question comes as if he's known me for ages, but he doesn't recognize the new me. Unease settles in my stomach, because it's the kind of thing he might ask if he remembered we have a past.

I find comfort in the fact he doesn't know we've had sex. Even if he did, it doesn't mean he knows the depths of who I am. He couldn't have discovered my secrets, after only a few hours together and an amazing fuck. Without knowing me, he can't see I've created this mask where I take the best of me, and highlight it for others to see.

I dig into my food again. "I'm someone who had to be responsible from a very young age. I'm also someone who looks for silver linings. When I got an internship with the Strike in my last term of college... it came out of nowhere. I'm still not sure why they picked me, but they did. I quickly learned that taking charge like I always have, and finding a positive spin to things, were going to make me good at my job."

"And the smiles? They smooth the process?"

His frown is one of his focused ones. He's paying attention, so I give him another honest answer.

I nod. "It makes people feel more comfortable."

"You smile at me." He sips from his smoothie again, thoughtfulness all over his gesture. "But you're sarcastic, too. I haven't seen you do that with other people."

"I know. I'm not sure why I'm sarcastic with you."

"I wasn't complaining, Evie. I told you I prefer it when you bite back."

"I can't promise I'll do that, either."

"Don't apologize."

"That wasn't an apology. I would rather be myself, and find our way with you being you, and me being me."

"That I can stand behind."

A micro smile appears at the corner of his lips, so small I might have missed it if I blinked at the wrong time.

"Did it hurt?" I ask.

He raises a questioning eyebrow. He stretches his long legs and crosses them at the ankles. The buckets we're using for chairs aren't very comfortable, but he doesn't complain.

"You had a tiny smile there for a second," I explain.

"I smile sometimes. This wasn't a smile."

"Ha! Lies and deceit. I have never seen a proper smile from you. Not live, not on the screen. A mini-curl at the corner of your lips barely counts— but it counts."

"That's libel. Careful, Miss Moreno."

"In any event. Congratulations, King. We're conversing."

He shakes his head and finishes his drink. "I can't banter like this with Melanie the TV producer and her crew."

"No, but you can banter like this with the rest of the team. They'll get more comfortable as you show them a bit of you, and you learn more about them. That will help loosen you up, too."

He gives me a long, suffering sigh. "I still hate the awkwardness of it all. So infantilizing, trying to teach me how to talk to people."

"Next time, we're talking about you in depth."

"Fuck."

Chapter 10

Logan

I'm in the bullpen with the guys after a gruelling training session. Despite the exhaustion, the energy is great. We've won both of the pre-season games we've played, and practice shows we're being consistent all over. No one says anything so as not to jinx it, but I don't think I'm the only one who feels the hope building in the Thunderdome's halls.

I sit in one of the couches, drinking from my smoothie. Dom and Bear are in spots nearby, chatting about Coach Clark's new strategies. Their conversation is easy to follow, but I only half-listen. Damián is playing at the pinball machine, with Saint playing Pac-Man next to him. I'm in no rush to set my record to win the bet with Damián. The way points add up on the counter, I'll shock them all with my score soon enough.

The hangout at the bullpen was spontaneous. I have a not-a-date with Evie tonight, but I thought she'd appreciate the effort I'm putting in getting closer to everyone. Not that I'm doing it because she told me to. I'm doing it because I'll do anything for the team and the bond I want with them.

As someone who comes across as grouchy, and with a family that didn't teach me how to get close to people, I've spent a lot of time alone. I'd rather that than being with the wrong people, but I crave an inner circle.

It's only natural that I'm willing to continue with her version of media training for me. It's going to help the team and my own goals to work with her. It has nothing to do with any fun I may have had with her of late. I'm here because it's a chance to test if I'm getting any better at small talk.

I check my phone. It's almost time for our meeting, but I haven't heard from her yet. I sent her an email to let her know where I'd be, just in case, and my number in case she needed to reach out more easily. No notifications light up my phone. I frown.

"I have a question for you," Dom said in my direction. "Does your forehead ever hurt?"

"My forehead?" I ask.

"With all that frowning. Don't those muscles ever cramp?"

Bear snorts at my side, at the same time as Saint celebrates something related to his game. None of us respond to it.

I cast my eyes at Damián again, quiet and focused on his own pinball practice.

"I've been frowning since birth." I sip from my smoothie. "These muscles don't know anything else."

"Since birth?" Saint calls from his machine. "I have to see pictures of it."

"Can you imagine a baby with thick eyebrows frowning the way King does?"

"I was an adorable baby." My tone is deadpan, but the guys are starting to recognize my humor. They laugh.

The bullpen is painted the same combination of blue and shiny white as the rest of the building, with a sitting area, and a snack and drink section by one of the walls. On the table, a muffin carrier Saint brought from home, to share his baked goods with the team. It's half-depleted. Everyone seems to love the sweets he makes and, after trying one, I understand why.

Big windows overlook the field and the parking lot, too. A bulletin board hangs next to the arcade machines and, on the wall above the biggest sofa, a few Strike jerseys from decades past hang in shadow boxes. The bullpen isn't particularly cozy, but it's a decent place, and better than the locker room for casual time as a group like this.

I check my phone again. Still nothing.

"Aaarrgh!" Damián grabs his head in a frustrated gesture.

The counter shows he just lost.

Yeah, I'm going to win that bet.

"Oh well." Damián turns to the group with a placid smile. "It's time for me to go home anyway. I want to make it there before my girlfriend, and I need to pick up my dog on the way."

Still nothing on my phone.

"I'm coming with you." I stand. "I need to find Evie."

"Take a muffin for her," Saint says. "She likes them."

I start to follow Damián out of the bullpen, but stop halfway.

I speak in a teasing tone. "I've heard the stories, Saint. I'm not doing your flirting for you."

It's still deadpan, compared to other people's joking voice, but it seems he gets it. Saint abandons his game to study me, a curious smirk in place.

Apparently, Saint dates a lot, never for long. Everyone knows the current fling is over when he bakes her something before he breaks up with them.

Damián waves at all of us and leaves, but I stay and return Saint's gaze.

The wide receiver crosses his arms. "Muffins are for friends. As are cookies, pastries, and baked bars. Cakes and pies are for break ups. Evie knows that."

He inspects me like what I said is suspicious, but I ignore it. He doesn't seem happy to leave it at that.

"Now," he says, "if you have any issues with me flirting with Evie, or would like to do some flirting of your own..."

"All good," I growl. "I'll take you at your word."

To stress the point, I take a detour on my way out of the room. I grab a muffin in a napkin, and wave goodbye to everyone with the smoothie still in my hand.

Evie's office door is ajar, but I knock anyway. Nothing happens at first. When I listen carefully into the room, I hear her quiet voice. From the sounds of it, she's alone.

I push the door open and peek inside. It's not a big office. The desk area is across from me, framed by a big painting behind the chair. It's flanked by the window looking out to the parking lot, and a small sofa on the other wall. Evie sits on it, leaning forward with an elbow on her knee, and her head heavy on a hand.

She's speaking on the phone, but lifts her face when she hears me.

She looks sad. Exhausted.

I freeze. It strikes me as a rare view of something I'm not supposed to see.

"Listen," she says to the device. "Te llamo después, ¿bueno? Okay. Yes. Okay. Chao."

I hesitate for a second, before sitting next to her on the couch.

She hangs up and gazes at the phone. "Sorry, Logan. Didn't realize time went so fast."

"I was wondering why you didn't find me on time to start the interrogation." I purse my lips. "Everything okay?"

"My parents..." she doesn't finish the sentence. She sighs and shakes her head. "Never mind."

I study her. She closes up swiftly. In the second it takes her to firm up and rearrange her beautiful face, I see the mirage of the girl I met years ago. Even back then, she gave me the bare minimum of information, only as much as I needed to make up my mind about being her rebound— or whatever I was to her.

This is who she has become. Someone who closes up. And all I want to do is learn more. Solve the puzzle of everything she hides. I want to understand her and make up my mind about her again.

All the questions she told me not to ask that night— her name, who she is, or to see her again. I get to ask them now.

I give her a smirk and hope it will loosen her tongue. "I thought today's not-a-date was about opening up to more personal stuff."

"For *you* to open up. Is that one of Saint's muffins?"

I give it to her. "If you open up, it will probably teach me a lesson."

"That's a cheap trick, King." She takes a big bite of the muffin and moans. "Besides, this is fixing my whole life."

I snort. She doesn't react, except to take another bite.

I missed my chance to learn more, but I'll get other opportunities. These not-a-dates can serve more than one function. Not friendship, all things considered, but they can help satiate my curiosity after years of asking questions in my head that I thought would never be answered.

She swallows. "I should look into getting Saint on one of those celebrity bake off shows."

"Should I go get him? He was still here when I left the bullpen, if you want to talk to him instead."

I want her to say no.

She gives me a sideways glance. "Jealous, Your Highness?"

Not that I would ever admit it.

"Please. I'm just hoping to escape this meeting."

"Aw, don't hurt my feelings." She chuckles and reaches for a coffee mug from the side table. "I know you like me."

I narrow my eyes at her. "What makes you say that?"

"We converse. You almost smiled the other day."

"Because of work. Because we have a deal."

"Works all the same."

"I would have expected you to have higher standards."

"Oh, I do." She smiles. "How's the smoothie today?"

I take a sip. "Good."

"How are things with the team?"

"Good."

"Logan." She gives me a look that makes her thoughts clear. She's asking what a producer or a journalist might ask, and I should play nicer. Say more.

I lean back on the sofa. The office is dark. It's still daylight outside, but the windows point East and no lamps are on in the room.

The team. I'm doing this to get closer to them. Gaining extra points with the owner doesn't hurt, either, since I have no choice.

I sigh. "We're getting to know each other. Our strong and weak points. The quirks. It's working."

"Are you ready for the last preseason game tomorrow?"

"As ready as I can be, but there's a lot of work left to be done. This is only a warm-up for the real challenge."

"The first game of the season will be against the Pirates. What do you think about that?"

She drinks from her cup, eyes clear and sharp on me. The Pirates are my dad's team, and he'll be a commentator that night.

I frown.

"If not me," she says, "someone else is going to ask you."

"Didn't you write in the outlines that they shouldn't ask about my father?"

"I did, but it doesn't mean they won't. Especially tangentially like I just did."

I know she's right. It's one of the reasons I hate the media so much.

I finish my smoothie to gain some time.

Evie leans slightly closer to me. "Are you sure you don't want to talk about your dad? It would cause a buzz and get the fans looking at you."

"I'm sure," I growl.

"Why?"

"What's going on with *your* parents, Evie?"

She crosses her legs and runs her fingers through her hair. "This isn't about me."

"If you can keep things private, so can I."

"But your dad is a public figure—"

"I am my own person. If you say I need to give football fans something to chew on, let it be about me."

She watches me closely, looking for any weak points in the wall I built around that subject. She won't find any, but I give her a stern look regardless.

She takes a deep breath. "Fine. So what do you think about playing the Pirates for your first game with the Strike?"

"The guys and I have prepared for the season. We've studied the Pirates' plays. We're ready to show the hard work we've put in."

"There you go. What are your goals for the season?"

"Always the big game."

"Ambitious, much?"

"What's the point of playing if it's not to win every time?"

A tiny smile appears on her lips.

She straightens the skirt of her dress, her hand sliding down her thigh a few times. "I know everyone at TD would be satisfied with getting to the playoffs, but that's a better answer."

"Playoffs are the bare minimum, not what I want."

"Tell me what you want."

I lean forward. It's easier to speak my mind now, and it'll help with the next interviews if I imagine it's just a conversation like the one I'm having with Evie. I'm of half a mind to share my every ambition with her, and reveal the goal of rings and brotherhood.

Except she looks at me with a spark in her eyes, and it shifts my attention to a different type of wanting.

She's beautiful. No wonder the whole team has a small crush on her, according to Saint. It's even more understandable that my body responds like this, when I remember what it's like to have her in my bed.

It was... unforgettable. It became the template by which I measured every other passing encounter. How free I felt, and how sure.

No one compared to how we fit that night.

From what I gathered with all of those comments about her immunity to the team, no one else on the team has the privilege I've had. Only I possess the knowledge of Evie when she's in the mood for sex. So who cares if Saint sends her a muffin and she moans to it? She has come with my cock inside her.

I lean closer. Maybe I should ask if she remembers that night. Or drop a few hints that I do, and see how she responds. Perhaps it will shake a few memories into place.

But I take a deep breath, collecting my thoughts, and it hits me that she smells different. It burns in my lungs with the need to get closer, take in her smell again. Lick her— taste her.

My frown deepens. "You changed your perfume."

"I... didn't. I just..."

I take a deep breath again through my nose, and don't bother to hide I'm seeking her scent.

"Lavender," I say. "It's faint, but it's there. I'm pretty sure it was a different fragrance before."

I usually try to ignore the million smells around me, but some deep part of my brain knows this isn't what she's been wearing since our paths crossed again... or whatever she used years ago.

I'm close enough to see a faint blush appear on her light brown skin. Her pupils dilate. She stares at me with a hint of lust and plenty of panic at being caught.

"It's my soap." Her voice is tight. She gulps. "I ran out of perfume a few days ago."

It's a strange thing to say.

I gaze down at her body. She wears a sage pleated dress, and somehow there are no wrinkles on it despite the long day. Her hair is clean and lustrous, shorter than when I first met her and well-styled. She doesn't strike me as someone who forgets this kind of thing.

"I didn't realize the scent was so strong." She seems sheepish.

I could reach for her. Surround her neck with my hand, and caress the spot where her pulse is the strongest. Come in close, put my nose on her skin, and breathe her in.

I don't.

"It's not." I purse my lips. "I have an unusually heightened sense of smell."

She licks her lips. Her eyes drop to my mouth, before she squirms in place and looks away.

Mmh. Interesting.

Her eyebrows wrinkle as she chooses what to say next. "Sense of taste, too? Is that why you twitch when trying new things?"

I welcome the change in subject. I'm not sure why, but I would have regretted revealing what I remember so soon. We're not close enough to change the rules of how we see each other professionally. For the rules would change, if she knew how often I've been thinking about that night.

I lift a shoulder. "I doubt that's something I can share with the fans."

"You could, if you want to give them a few random facts to add depth to your persona."

"Somehow I don't think interviewers will be asking if I have hyperosmia."

She straightens in her seat, a surge of excitement replacing everything else. "We could come up with a way to share it— an article somewhere or even social media. A 'get to know the new quarterback' segment somewhere. A Q and A..."

"Slow down, Evie."

"Never!" She chuckles. "You gave me good player answers to my professional questions. Maybe you just needed a poke there and we should shift to the general persona."

"General persona...?"

"Social media." She gives me a determined nod. "When was the last time you posted on one of your profiles?"

"I don't have *profiles*."

"Just the one then? Not ideal, but I'll work with you. Which one do you prefer?"

"I prefer none."

She gasps. "Logan! Don't tell me you don't have *any* profiles?"

"What's your wildest guess?"

"Give me your phone." She opens her palm in front of me. "We'll sign you up right away."

"We will do no such thing."

"I'll manage it for you."

My chuckle is dark. "You won't."

"I will. Selena gave me a job—"

"And we're going beyond the requirements—"

She takes away her hand and crosses her arms. "We're not! What did you call it? The bare minimum? We need to give the fans a story—"

"I'm sold on giving proper interviews moving forward, but social media is too far."

"Make your assistant run it for you."

"I don't have an assistant."

She closes her eyes in an exasperated gesture. It almost pulls a smile from me, but I'm too busy dueling her on this matter to let her see that I enjoy it.

She's the one to give me a stern look this time. "Then I have to run it for you. Logan. Social media is a big part of the team's engagement with the fans. Just say yes and I'll figure it out."

"That proposal is too open. Too suspicious. What will you do?"

"I'll figure it out."

"That's what you said when you came up with these dates."

"Not-a-dates."

"Sure. What I'm hearing is that I should be worried."

"Hey, the not-a-dates were a great idea."

"We'll see about that. I have an interview with the crew tomorrow after the game."

"You'll do great. Look how fluently we conversed today!"

"You could be scary, Miss Moreno."

"Is that a yes?"

All I do is nod.

I don't see her the next day, but I get a text from her that brightens my morning.

> Evie: I forgot to say it last night~~ Good game, Logan. I would have wished you good luck, but I know you don't believe in that.

I might not like the reason we're currently working so close together, but I think I'm enjoying the time I have with her nevertheless.

Chapter 11

Evie

A couple of days after convincing Logan to let me run a social media account for him and receiving his agent's approval, I create him an account while sitting in my parents' living room. I've stolen my lunch hour to come check on them. Worry still plagues my mind after our last call.

"Un café, hija?"

I nod. "Gracias."

My parents work in the restaurant business. It's a merciless industry. Most of their debt comes from attempts at having a place of their own, and growing too fast with too many liabilities. Now they run a small sandwich shop that opens until late in the night. It's almost time for them to go to work, so I get to the point as soon as we're all sitting with our drinks.

"So?" I ask. "Are you still thinking about expanding?"

They share a look.

"Yes," my dad says. "It won't be like before."

I bite my bottom lip. "Are you sure?"

Nerves swirl in my stomach. My whole life, I did what needed to be done. When my parents got too nervous calling insurance? I called for them, who cared that I was eight. When it was time to renew visas, and they couldn't make sense of the checklists, multiple documents, and submission requirements? I did it at the tender age of twelve. Did they sign things with the bank they shouldn't have? I went there and did damage control, no matter if I was sixteen.

They tried to do better as I grew up, but the initial mistakes were big, and smaller ones followed despite their efforts. I did my best to help with that, too. For a long time, I've known we have boundary issues. The conversation we're having is my latest attempt to find a balance with them.

"We're doing things right this time," Dad adds.

"It *has* to be done right, Papá." I swallow through a tight throat. "The sandwich shop is your retirement plan. We already have enough with trying to save the house, and the bank hasn't given me an answer about the renegotiation."

I promised to help with their home, if they focused on building a good business this time that they could sell later on. That way, they'd have money to live off of as they grew older, and I would have a light at the end of the tunnel— a time when I'd be free to live my life and just be their daughter. The idea that could be at risk is freezing the blood in my veins.

"Tranquila," Mom says. "This will help."

I'm tempted to ask for a business plan, like they're kids and I can check their homework before they're graded for it.

I sip from my coffee, press my lips tight, and stare at my lap instead.

"Hija." My dad's voice is soft.

I lift my eyes to him.

He gazes back with understanding. "Adding a food truck will be the right way to grow our equity and keep fixing our credit score. Poquito a poco."

"But who's going to lend you the money? I really can't pinch any more cash out of my paycheck, and my credit score is in the dumps too. No bank will let us borrow any more. We need to get the bank to give us a bit of extra time. We have to pay off the principal and then focus on the penalty we negotiated last time. It's the only chance we have—"

"Tranquila," my mom says again.

At least, their shop is safe for now, and the bank can't touch it if they take the house. I would rather they never do, so we get to keep both.

Even though they keep reassuring me, it doesn't have the effect all of us hope for. Anxiety still plays with my nerves like they're the rope and I have to continue skipping. One wrong step, and I'll be out.

All I can do is monitor the situation, do my best to stop my parents from creating more dangerous debt, and focus on my promotion.

I'll make the fans obsessed with Logan. I'll impress Selena. That raise will be mine.

It's with those thoughts that I enter the Thunderdome and walk straight onto the sidelines of the training field. My bag still hangs from my shoulder, but I take out my phone and start filming the equivalent of b-rolls for my new project—making Logan into a social media sensation.

The fans will *love* him. I'll make sure of it.

"Miss Moreno!" Saint runs to me. "What a pleasure seeing you here."

"Hey, Saint." I point the camera to him. "How do you feel about the new QB?"

"King?" He gives me a dimpled, glorious smile. "Oh, we're going to do amazing this season with him. The team spirit is high."

"You won all the preseason games."

"It's a new era for the Strike."

"Hear the thunder?"

He lifts both arms and roars. "Hear the thunder!"

I laugh and pan away from Saint, recording the rest of the field. I find Logan and zoom in on him. He's frowning at nothing, staring at something on the field or the horizon. His hair is long enough that he tied it up in a half-bun.

It changes the angles of his face. With thick, heavy eyebrows and his straight, long nose... with his tanned skin after being outside for the pre-season, and big, shapely body... his legs and arms, thick and defined... Gah, he is a gorgeous man.

Tingles appear in my belly, and I clench my teeth to contain them. I'm not supposed to react, and even less to wonder if we would have fun again if we were to have sex. My one time with him has to stay a sexy memory. Not an interruption to my work.

Sure, we would probably have fun, but we will never have sex again. I'm a one and done kind of person since— him, I suppose. That night, I decided I would only do one-night-stands, and I've kept that promise to myself. He doesn't get to change the rules, especially not after all these years.

Heat has raised up my body, and I have to resist fanning myself with a hand. I keep filming him as he goes off on a sprint. The plan is to use music for this section, so conversation doesn't interfere.

"Thanks for that, Saint." I glance at him with a smile. "Congrats on an amazing preseason. Ready to beat the Pirates this Sunday?"

"Evie, don't talk sports to me. When are you going to talk to me as a friend? Ask me if I'm still dating Tabitha, and not because you're offering to do disaster management."

I snort. "You've seen her twice. I'm going to guess she got a breakup pie already?"

"Saw her thrice, but yes. She got a breakup pie last night."

His grin is impish, and I shake my head.

"You're such a playboy, Gael Santiago."

I track Logan again. It's cloudy today, which lights up the players clearly on my screen. No sharp shadows to obscure their pretty faces and strong bodies, and professional training alike. Fans will be delighted. With Saint's close up, this video is going to be amazing.

The new quarterback makes a throw that Dom catches seamlessly. The play is smooth, and Dom celebrates with a dance.

A smile tilts my mouth. It will be great content and I can't help it— it makes me happy to see the team optimistic like this. It's much better if I focus on this instead.

I stop recording and face Saint. "We're professionals at our place of work, though. If there are no broken-hearted girlfriends having a difficult time letting go and you don't need my help with that, I may have a different type of proposal for you. With so many pies and muffins under your belt, what do you think about participating in a baking show during the off-season?"

"I'm not giving up, Evie." His dimples pop. "You'll be my friend one day, you'll see. For now, don't sign me up to the baking show. And remember I don't have *girlfriends*. You know I don't give that title away."

"I know, I know."

We smile at each other, and I give him a good-natured punch on the arm.

Many people think his smile is flirty, but I know it's the effect of those dimples and he doesn't mean it that way when he grins at me.

"I better return to practice," he says. "Do you want me to call anyone for you, or did you get what you needed?"

I gaze out to the field, to find Logan studying us from the fifty yard line. With a wave of my hand, I gesture for him to approach me.

"I'm good. Thanks, Saint."

Logan jogs to me. I get my phone up again, and record until he stands in front of me.

He crosses his arms. "What are you up to?"

His eyes are a bluish gray today, and they scrutinize me through my phone. He looks incredible with his hair tied up like that, his eyebrows heavy with a severe frown. The shirt he wears and the way he holds his arms around himself, it makes his arms look big and toned.

I bite my lip and order my body to keep quiet. "What do you want everyone to know, Logan?"

All tingles are swiftly suffocated. Partially suffocated, if I'm honest. Fine, they are there but I ignore them.

Melanie, the producer from the Sports network, sent me an email this morning. She thanked me for the work I put in. She said Logan has been giving short-but-sufficient answers to the crew, and things are looking up in that realm.

His lips twitch, and I know he's thinking of a professional answer. "This is going to be an amazing season. Keep an eye out, because lightning will strike."

The words drip with confidence. He stares at the camera with the self-assurance of a veteran player. One who has had years to learn how to engage with the fans. I'm certain— they will go wild.

I stop the recording and put my phone away. "Thanks. That was great."

"Do I want to know what you're going to do with it?"

"Probably not."

He sighs. "I'm going to guess it has to do with my agent's email this morning. I heard you called him yesterday."

"What I'm hearing is that you actually pay attention to your emails and, when you've ignored mine, it's been on purpose."

"I've never denied it, Miss Moreno."

"Anyway. I'll be posting the video to your brand new social media profile later. I'll let you know how it goes."

"No need, thank you."

I chew the inside of my lip. A mini-report for Selena might be a good idea, too, just in case. If the social media push goes as I hope, I want her to know how far I'm taking this. Anything for that promotion, and the extra cash that comes with it.

Logan peers at me. "Did something happen?"

I'm not sure if he's seeing something on my face, but I clear my worries in case I'm showing them despite myself.

"I'm good." I wave the question away. "Since we've established you read your emails, you must have seen the one I sent you about the library event. I need to know— are you going to ignore that one?"

His mouth takes a downward slant. "No. I'll attend."

"Good! It's going to be great."

"I will also attend a barbeque at Damián's house."

That makes me genuinely happy, and I grin. "That's amazing! Not everyone gets the invitation, you know? The fact he's included you means you're finding a spot within the team. There you go, building that team cohesion!"

"I'm not a child in need of a participation trophy, Evie."

His grumpy statement doesn't affect me.

I laugh. "Sorry not sorry, Your Highness. This is good news. You should take a treat for his dog Barkley. It will earn you a thousand points."

He raises an eyebrow. "How do you know so much?"

"I make a point of knowing as much as I can about everything."

He takes a step forward and brings his face closer to mine, like he's paying careful attention to my pupils dilating. It gives him the aura of a human lie detector.

"What?" I ask.

"I get it now."

"What?" The word sounds breathless this time.

"You are Miss Fix It, aren't you?"

My mouth goes slack.

Logan straightens but his eyes never leave me. He continues to inspect me, this time with a proud look on his face.

"I should have seen it sooner," he says. "Always checking in with people. Everyone's always thanking you for something. You're always thinking of the next thing that needs mending."

"It's my job."

"So you don't do it for people outside of TD?"

I purse my lips. I tell myself it's because I don't like that Logan put this together. He's supposed to take my help and use it to be successful. He's not meant to try to look behind the veil to ask why I do it.

The truth is, I'm uncomfortable. I don't like it when people look too closely.

Letting people in means I'll care. If I care, there will be more people needing things from me. It's too much. And if they care and then yank it away...

My heart loses its rhythm for a moment.

All I want is peace. Just peace, please.

"Nope." I raise my eyebrows in an expression I know will read haughty. "Less than a handful of people get that privilege. Otherwise, I'm getting paid for my skills."

The way he dissects my answer tells me he thinks he received a new puzzle piece, and is trying to fit it with the rest.

It's unnerving.

"Stop looking at me like that," I say.

"Won't stop me from thinking about it."

"King!" One of the coaches calls. "Come back! Training isn't done."

Logan smirks. "Saved by the bell, Evie."

He takes a step back, a corner of his lips curled up in a micro smile. His eyes shine with as much humor as I've ever seen on his face.

I ignore how it lightens him up and stop him. "One last thing. There's one last angle I need you to tackle."

"Shoot." He takes another step back, but continues to face me.

"Are you dating anyone?"

"King!" The coach calls again.

"I'm sorry, Malik!" I wave at him. "I'll give him back in half a minute."

"I think we're done for today." Logan makes to go away, but I stop him again, this time with a hand on his arm.

"I thought you'd be happy about this one!" I say.

"I am not happy about this one." The wrinkle between his eyebrows is deep as he stares down at me.

"If you have a life here in the city— if people see you out and about, people will love you more."

"That's a step too far."

"The new quarterback has thrown himself into life here," I say as if I'm quoting a newspaper article. "He's here to stay!"

"He's here to win the trophy, not to party."

"He can do both, can't he?"

"He doesn't want to do both."

"Ask Saint to take you out. Or Dom. There's a club the team likes to go to. Make it into a bonding event."

"Send me an email next time."

I smile. "I'll include tickets to an event. You can take someone who catches your fancy."

Any jealousy I might feel at the thought gets pushed out of sight. If a part of me wishes to be the one going places with him, I trip it and let it lie sprawled on the floor.

This is work. I'm a professional with a plan. Logan and I will follow it until we get what we agreed on.

"Evie."

I wink at him. "Talk to you soon!"

I'm the one walking away this time.

"Evie!"

All I do is give him a wide grin and a wave, pleased with my distraction technique, enough that I don't mind letting him have the last word.

Chapter 12

Logan

We're flying back from an away game. In the whirlwind of the first month of my first season with the Strike, I don't see Evie much for the rest of September. We've won every game, and the interviews, community events, and related obligations have multiplied. It only adds to the hours watching tape and learning defenses.

The pressure has gone up. Fans are going wild.

But Evie relies heavily on communication via email for a while. She does not back away and helps coordinate everything with efficiency, but we do not share space. It's not far-fetched to think she may be avoiding me. I may have spooked her with my comments on the field that day. It's only fair that she rattled me with her suggestion that I go out and be seen.

I should date, she said.

Yeah. No.

Dating requires a performance. A honeymoon where you show the best of you and hope it's enough to make things work. I've never wanted to follow the rules of romance, if it means having to conform.

Worst of all, dating means having to put effort into figuring out why someone is with me. Even in the rare cases when things feel good at the start, it fizzles out when they tire of my personality. My energy is better allocated into a spectacular season, rather than decoding the nonsense of romantic love, or managing someone's expectations.

The plane lands back in Seattle. Everyone gets restless around me, itching to start their journey home even as we still taxi to our gate. I remain calm in my seat, and take a minute to check my texts when I connect to the cell network. Two messages appear on my screen.

> Dad: Good game today. You're doing well.

I take a deep breath and stare at the text. My relationship with my father is strange. I want to get away from under his shadow. We're not close. It's been years since I've had a proper conversation with the guy. Yet he's not a bad person, and he'll have a few encouraging words for me once in a while.

It isn't enough to feel like it's a fatherly pat on the shoulder, or to grant more than a simple message back. To this day, I still don't know if he's happy I followed in his steps, or if he dreads that I might beat his legacy.

> Logan: Thanks. I hope you're good. Say hi to Mom.

I swipe away from the chain and check the next one. This one brings warmth into my chest— humor, probably. It comes close to smoothing my frown for once, too.

> Evie: Great game today. Social media is in love with you. Though that one is probably more to do with my influence than your own

I haven't checked the profiles she's managing for me, but I know she keeps a steady stream of content going. She uses several sources, including her own recordings. According to my agent, she's doing a great job and a few of her videos have gone viral. I'm told that's great news.

Logan: I wash my hands from all of that. Happy to leave it all to you.

Evie: Excellent. I plan to make a few thirst traps and I'm pleased you have pre-approved.

Logan: I revoke said approval

Evie: Too late. I already posted those. They are doing really well, so I'll post more

Logan: How are you getting this material, exactly? I haven't seen you in the locker room recently

Evie: I don't need to go to that extreme. Carefully edited training videos and slow mo do wonders for the fans' gaze

Logan: So you're saying I'm effortlessly sexy

She doesn't text back right away. I smirk. It's easy to imagine her weighing her words, hesitating between banter and flirting.

Not that we're flirting.

Or at least I am not. I don't think she is either.

Evie: I'm saying the fans are starving for content about the new QB, and will take any scraps and think they're gifts

I snort. Clearly she's not flirting. I should have trusted the way she approached me at the bar years ago. At the time there was no flirting to be seen, just a proposition. Straight to the point.

Though she has changed since then, and maybe I don't know how she would act if she were attracted to me again.

Fuck. To have her come close to me. Have her give me one of her real smiles and sultry eyes that gaze at me with desire. That she would tell me what she wants from me, in a husky voice that—

I clench my jaw. That is not on the menu. I cannot be thinking about that.

The chains I keep around such thoughts clatter as I tighten them. They're coming too loose of late. I might need extra padlocks soon.

Evie: In fact, I may work with your agent to get you a swimsuit ad so I can crash the photo session and get some content that way. Maybe with the help of stylists, make up artists, and the right lighting, we'll get something worth thirsting over

This time I snort-chuckle.

Logan: now it sounds like you want to thirst over me, and that's not very professional, Miss Moreno.

The three dots appear and disappear. I bite the inside of my lip and watch her start and delete a few more messages, until Saint leans on my airplane chair and gazes curiously at me.

He raises an eyebrow. "I was going to invite you to a blind date tomorrow, but maybe you already have plans?"

"What?"

"You look like you're sexting."

He probably didn't see who I was texting with. If he had, he would have known Evie and I were only playing our game, the one where we poke and see how far we'll go. The subject matter was purely coincidental.

I lock my phone and put it in my pocket. Saint makes room for me and I stand in the aisle.

I grab my carry on and give him an unconcerned look. "How would you know what I look like when I'm sexting?"

"I don't know, man. You looked very focused and, dare I say it, eager over what was going on with your phone. We've all been there, haven't we? Sexy photos coming through and all. Especially after a win like today's. You're doing great, QB."

I give him one of my ghost smiles.

I return his raised eyebrow. "Now I know not to interrupt when you're on your phone."

We stand in the aisle, waiting for the door to open. Several of the other players wait too, impatient to get home after game day.

He ignores the comment. "If you weren't busy with someone just now, then maybe that's a yes to the blind date? I heard through the grapevine you may be looking to go out and about."

"Who said that?"

"Evie. I said I'd take you out." He gives me a dimpled grin. "Tell me if you have any guidelines— genders you're attracted to, personality traits— and I'll set us up. Double date."

I frown. My nostrils flare. I'm trying to be less grumpy with the guys on the team, but this set up brings my grouchiness right back to the surface.

"Woah," Saint says. "I haven't seen you glare like that from up close. I'm taking that as a no on the double date?"

"It's a no on the double date."

People start shuffling out of the plane and I follow them. Saint walks behind me.

I have never been in a relationship. Dating is out of the picture while I'm playing. My hand is enough for me until the offseason.

"Still no to a date," I add for Saint's benefit. "But brunch on Tuesday sounds good. You and the guys."

"Where?"

"No idea."

Saint laughs. "Okay, I'll plan something."

I thank him and we take the team bus to TD, where I get in my car and drive to the house I got fully furnished and decorated. It's a modern looking place, with a big yard and trees all around. Big windows allow for lots of light. It's furnished with cream and light wood furniture, and off-white walls. Even the big paintings are in gold and honey tones. It's a pretty place that I didn't have to put effort into, and it works for now.

My phone stays in my pocket while I unpack and get ready for bed. I know a text from Evie waits for me, but I don't want to reply until I know exactly what to say. How far to push the conversation, this time.

After a long shower, I get in my bed in my underwear and sit with my back against the headboard. She may not respond right away, but if she does, I'm going to be ready.

> Evie: the only reason I'm thinking about this stuff at all is because of my top priority job as assigned by the owner herself. Don't forget I'm immune

Bullshit. She's not as immune as she likes to say. I've made her moan from kissing her in the hall of a bar. I convinced her to stay for more sex when she could have left right there and then. Those hours had more than chemistry— it was alchemy.

When the day comes I remind her what we had, we'll see how convincingly she can insist she's immune. But that is not today.

I shake my head and address the urgent matter at hand.

> Logan: you asked Saint to set me up with a date? Really?

I check up on my emails while I wait for a response. For a moment I consider spying on the account Evie manages for me on social media, and see what she means by thirst traps. My finger hovers on the links my agent sent me, when I get a text back.

Evie: Saint is a friendly guy and he's in the social scene, which is precisely where I'd like you to be. He hooked you up with a massage therapist and with his chef, why not with a date?

Logan: how about because I don't want to date?

Evie: What? Why not?

Logan: this is definitely going beyond your scope as PR exec

Evie: we all know PR involves your private life when seen by the public, and that my job is to make the public love you

Logan: I thought they already love me

Evie: and we're still building your social credit with them. Come on, Your Highness. We need more

Logan: I'm doing everything you've asked me to do, but dating is where I draw the line

To my surprise, my phone rings in my hand. I answer her video call with a frown.

"Why?" she asks. "Tell me your issue with it and I'll try to fix it."

She's frowning, too. Otherwise, all I see is her hair up on a messy bun, and the light blue of a wall behind her.

She's not wearing make up and now the call strikes me as an intimate moment. The fact I'm in my underwear only adds to it.

It draws me in. My cock twitches, like asking me if we're getting some action soon. The rattle of chains comes louder from the basement of my mind.

I frown harder. "You can't fix my disinterest in other people."

"Oh, Logan. I know you don't hate people as much as you like to pretend. I've seen you with the guys, you know? You like them."

I purse my lips. "And yet I don't plan to date any of them."

She rolls her eyes. "Fine. Don't date if it's going to aggravate you so much to wine and dine with someone, but please be seen?"

"Fuck, Evie. This is the show around the game I didn't want to get involved with."

"I thought we were on the same page about this? We're trying to make sure you get what you want out of this, rather than let other people dictate the conversation about you. Tell me again what the big deal is, so we can fix it."

I rub my brow. Evie and I may have been on the same page at the start, but this particular strategy brings me too close to feeling like a puppet in the entertainment machine. Coming out of my father's shadow involves doing things differently at all levels, including the way he handled the media.

My stare is hard on the screen. "If you're throwing me to the center of a coliseum for the fun of the plebs, at least let me choose the beast I'll fight."

"Okay, a bit dramatic, Your Highness. This part may be a show, but it's going to help you become the new star of football. And if you go out with the guys, it will get you closer to them! Consider it an investment for when this wonderful winning streak inevitably ends. Your haters are going to get loud then, so let's prepare, all right?"

I grind my teeth. She's right. It's why my father spent so much time doing media things while I was growing up. If I want to fully own my corner of the league, I need to do it, too. At least for a while.

"Fine," I concede. "I'll go out, but I'll set it up myself. Don't put Saint up to it next time."

"Deal."

"We should have another one of our not-a-dates, too. I've been told I'm going to have to do a post game conference soon."

"Uhm..." She adjusts her position and she comes out of focus. "Sure, yeah. Next week?"

The field of vision moved around enough that I see she's on a sofa, wearing a tank top and with a blanket on her lap.

A random memory hits me. Does she still have the shirt she took from me?

Shit. I want her to have kept it. I want her to remember I tore her top away when we had sex. I want her to have thought of me every time she wore it, and that it took on her smell and has turned soft with wear and the passage of time.

"Since I have to be *seen*," I say, "we should go out and eat together somewhere."

My cock twitches *again*.

I clench my jaw, irritated with myself. What the fuck is up with me? I must be tired.

"What? No." She frowns. "In my office."

It's a good thing I'm only being practical and arguing for fun. The only reason chains clink away in the dark and padlocks strain to keep things secure, is because once upon a time I thought of seeing her occasionally for some casual fun. Which isn't dating, either.

"I have limited time to do things, Evie. Two birds with one stone and all of that."

"I don't go out."

"You have to eat."

"I do. I eat at home."

"Are you inviting me over for dinner?" I suppress a smile.

It's so easy to tease her. The quick quips really work for me. It's one of my favorite games.

"I am not!" she complains, though she has to press her lips together to hide a grin of her own.

"Then go out with me. Professionally. I'm not inviting you on a date."

"Good! We agreed on not-a-dates, and I never date."

"You don't date, but want me to date?"

"I'm not a public figure."

"So this shouldn't be a problem for you. We can go out for dinner somewhere. Nothing romantic going on. Two colleagues going out with no pleasantries and a mutual understanding that this will lead nowhere."

My chest works faster. This is the closest I've come to prodding at her, to check if she remembers our past. I'm repeating words we exchanged that night. It's not a checkmate, but I'm getting close to her king.

The risk makes it fun, but I should be careful.

She sucks in her bottom lip. "Not now. I need to do something first. Let's meet somewhere at TD next week, okay?"

I frown. I didn't expect the caginess. She's spooked, all right, but I may not know all the reasons why.

"Okay, Miss Moreno. We're doing it your way."

Relief softens her face.

"For now," I add.

I can't help myself.

She looks at the ceiling like she's summoning patience from the deepest corners of her being. I pull back from grinning again.

"Thanks for all that benevolence, Your Highness. Now go rest."

"Good night, Evie."

She gives me a small smile and hangs up without a fanfare.

I turn off my light and take a deep breath, and do not use my hand. We need the reminder. The discipline.

As sleep takes over, images of Evie weave into my mind, dreams and reality mixing. Her going to bed in a room with light blue walls. Us cuddling close so we fit together in a twin bed, exactly like the one in the dorm room where we had sex. Kissing her in the hallway of a bar. Us having dinner and going on a banter match until deep into the night.

My last conscious thought is that maybe she's also thinking of me as she falls asleep. If talking to her late at night has kept her in my mind, I might also be on hers.

I'm not sure if I want her up tonight thinking of me.

That's a lie. I do.

Chapter 13

Evie

It's been a week since Logan and I talked on the phone. The team lost their first game the day before. Not by much, but they lost it, and the vibe feels different in the Thunderdome today.

That's why I'm at the main doors to the building, waiting for Saint's private chef, Amelia. After coordinating with my superiors and with Ames, we decided to bring a treat to cheer everyone up at the end of the day.

Ames and a staff member from her kitchen park a van at a service spot in the parking lot. I've met Ames a few times. She's known Saint since they were in college, and she and I have crossed paths every once in a while.

She gets out of the van and I approach her. Ames has wavy hair down to her shoulders, and dresses in jeans and a black linen shirt that suits her really well.

"Hey, Ames! Thanks so much for accommodating my sudden request."

I greet her and her staff person, named Jo, who wears a graphic eyeliner in a way that highlights her epicanthal folds.

We go to the back of the vehicle, where Jo and Ames load a cart with a hundred cupcakes.

"I'm glad to help!" Ames says. "This is the best start to a season they've had in years. Must be extra hard to lose when you've been winning so much."

She grins at me while she works, while Jo's long ponytail swings from side to side as she gets through the task.

I nod in agreement with Ames. "Yeah, but it's to be expected. I just want them to cheer up, you know?"

"And a treat is a great way to do it."

I guide them through the building toward the locker room. I explain that I need to announce our arrival and, once everyone assures me all private parts are covered, I bring Amelia and Jo in.

"Surprise!" I say. "I cleared a little something with management to put a smile on your faces."

"Ames?" Saint exclaims and jogs our way.

I catch a new look on his face when he looks at his friend, and I store the tidbit of information away. Interesting.

He reaches us before everyone else, but soon cupcakes with happy faces are being passed around the room.

Saint kisses Amelia on the cheek. "Ames, I didn't know you were coming."

She shrugs. "I thought it would be a nice surprise. We don't see each other as much these days."

"No, we don't." A small wrinkle appears between his eyebrows.

I already plan to ask him about it as soon as I get a chance but for now I let him be. Damián and Bear are grinning my way in thanks, and I go through the room patting shoulders and sharing words of encouragement. I chat with several people, before I notice Logan isn't among them.

I take a full turn of the locker room and still don't find him.

"Hey, Bear." I gaze up at him. "Have you seen Logan?"

"Him and Dom were still in the weight room. I think Dom was going to get in a pool. He took a beating yesterday."

I nod in thanks and steal a couple of cupcakes. One of them goes to Dom's locker, wrapped in a napkin. I'll text him if I don't see him, so he doesn't miss out.

The other cupcake, I take with me.

The clinking of metal reaches me before I enter the weights room. With most everyone gone, the sound echoes throughout, unencumbered.

Only one of the machines is occupied, and it's easy to recognize Logan's form in it. He sits on a bench while pulling down from a bar. From my limited knowledge it looks like he's exercising his shoulders. I approach him from the back. I can't see his face, and I don't know if he's listening to music or not, or how concentrated he is—

"If you're hoping to record a thirst trap, Miss Moreno," he says, "I'd appreciate a say in the final take."

He doesn't stop working out. Our reflections catch my eye. He saw me appear on the large glass doors that open to the field, closed now for the evening.

I don't respond right away. A machine just like the one he uses stands next to him, empty, and I sit on the bench. He steals a glance at me, but mostly focuses on his routine.

He wears his usual shorts and shirt combo to train. He got a haircut, but didn't chop a lot. The straight strands curl softly to his temples and down the curve under his ear. Mild sweat shines on his forehead and down the thick cords of his neck. The frown he's famous for gives him a look like an assassin training for a hit.

My body immediately responds to it. It's something ancient, the kind of thing that has kept humanity alive, because it led to procreation.

It's a base instinct. I don't have to act on it.

I clear my throat.

"I could film a thirst trap." I make my voice sound technical, despite the havoc rising inside of me. "They always do well."

They add spice to the shots of his skills on the field, and it makes a certain fan demographic really happy to have that kind of content. As for me, it doesn't hurt to film it... or edit it... or watch it a few times to make sure it looks professional.

He stops the rhythmic movements of his arms and takes a break. Both hands land on his thick thighs, and his gray eyes fix on me.

"But that's not why you came to the weight room?" He arches an eyebrow.

"Nope. I came to bring you this." I offer him the cupcake.

He takes it and, when he sniffs it this time, I don't take offense.

I read that people with a highly sensitive sense of smell and taste can struggle with flavors and bitterness in foods more often. Some of them will be really picky eaters or at least cautious with food.

"I organized a treat for the team," I explain. "Just to lift everyone's spirits a bit."

"Miss Fix It strikes again." He takes a bite, frowns, then eats the rest of it fast.

"You're welcome."

He snorts. "Is this something you did before I came to the team, too?"

"No, I've never done it before." I lower my voice so it sounds like I'm confiding with him. "If I did it in past seasons, with their track record before you joined the team... well, I would have had to do it too often and that's not how treats work, am I right?"

He stares at me, and the ghost of a proper smile slants his mouth. A spark of humor shimmers in his blue eyes.

They should really work harder at settling on a single color.

"Are you trying to lift my spirits?" he asks.

"Why does it sound like an accusation?"

"I don't need to be placated. I need to work it off and I'll be fine by Wednesday."

"Work it off. Eat the cupcake. Grin and bear it. You don't have to choose."

"I thought you'd want me pushing harder for the win. It's all about the team and making Selena happy. I thought we're here for the same thing."

"You're doing well, Logan. Selena is happy. The fans are happy. Ticket sales are at an all-time high. Did I tell you that I got an email from Melanie? The network is very happy with your answers these days."

He grabs a towel hanging from one of the metal bars on the machine, and he dries his forehead and neck. "Are we having an impromptu not-a-date?"

"No, we're still on for Friday. I only wanted to check on you."

"Sounds like you care."

"I care. Professionally."

I have to be careful about not caring much more than that.

He gazes at me for a while. It's less scrutiny, and more understanding this time. I've seen hints of this look on him before. As recently as when I called him on the phone, and I was in my pajamas, and he may or may not have been naked.

I don't know why I called him that night, but I think it brought us closer.

I'm approaching dangerous territory. If I learn to care about Logan as a person, I might go too far. He might assume I'm here for anything he needs. I might end up wanting to do what he needs, because caring means wanting him to be happy. Suddenly, there are more people to take care of. I have too much on my shoulders to add another commitment like that.

He takes a deep breath and stands. I don't immediately imitate him, and cast my face up at him.

He purses his lips. "I'm going to guess we still need more with the fans? I think you called it social credit?"

"Of course. Always."

He nods. In the next movement, he takes off his shirt, opens his water bottle, and splashes his hair, face and neck.

I thank whatever guardian spirits may still be on my side that his eyes are closed and he can't see the way my mouth hangs open at the sight.

Good lord, the man is gorgeous. Better than I remember from years ago, and that's saying something. He's sculpted like a Greek statue of old, depicting the best Olympian of the nation. It is a double-edged sword that I remember his cock is much better than those carved into marble thousands of years ago.

I close my mouth with a snap when he dries his hands with the towel. Only one of us has an excuse to be wet, and that person is not me.

"So about that creative license for sexy content," he says.

I blink a few times and stand. It takes all the strength I possess not to follow some of the drops trailing down his skin. Eyes, fingers, even tongue would enjoy the privilege.

Stop it, Evelyn Moreno.

At least this has nothing to do with feelings. Arousal I can deal with. It's all about denying myself until I am home alone and can take the matter into my own hands.

He stares at me. I don't know if he's aware of the strain he's causing me, but I hope he isn't.

"I hate the cameras," he says.

"I've heard," I croak.

"But I know I'm helping everyone if I call a truce and play nice."

"It would certainly help me."

He tilts his head down, eyes on mine. "So how about I work out for another five minutes, and I let you record it as you will?"

"That would work well." I take a deep breath. Professionalism is the right move. "If you want to splash some more water on yourself that would be amazing, but you know I don't like to push you too hard."

Oops. At least my tone sounds technical and I can pass it off as expert PR advice.

He scoffs, but humor is back to him. The water bottle is nearby and he drenches his hair, allowing the liquid to drip onto his shoulders.

I scramble to get the phone from my pocket and start recording.

"How close can I get?" I ask.

He stares into the phone. "As close as you want."

I bite my lip and film a close up of his clavicles and shoulders. This is going to go viral, I'm sure.

He runs his fingers through his hair and sighs. He dries his hands on the towel once more, then takes chalk and slaps his hands together to spread the white powder across his palms. It creates a cloud.

In slo mo with a good song, this section will be a fan favorite.

Just as is, it will engrave itself into my memories for the rest of eternity. I can barely breathe, because if I do, he might see how much this affects me.

For the next five minutes, while he uses the same machine, I film him from different angles. I record his face, then the working muscles of his shoulders and back. The grooves, hills, and cords of his anatomy, with drops still pooling and sliding down his skin...

I wouldn't be surprised if it makes its way into my dreams tonight.

He stops soon after and gets on his feet. I stand in front of him, my phone between us.

"Logan, what would you like everyone to know?"

"I want you to know me." He stares deep into the camera again. "I want you to remember me."

I gasp.

I freeze.

He smirks, takes the phone from my hand, and stops the recording. "I'm of half a mind to film the look on your face right now."

I shake my head. "I'm not made for the spotlight."

"You'd steal it, Evie."

"Stop." I chuckle, because I need to pretend he's joking.

If he isn't, then I might believe he was talking to me when he said he wants me to know him, and that he wants me to remember him.

I'm not available for that, but the public will love every second of it.

I have to make it about the public.

"That was great," I say before he can add anything else. "Thanks for being such a good sport these days."

He's not as serious as he usually is, though he continues to track my movements as if he's studying me.

He lifts a still-uncovered shoulder. "Good practice for the ad you want me to do."

"It's not like I directed you much or asked for a hundred takes."

"But admit you objectified me."

I laugh and gaze up at him. "If it's going to put a smile on your face."

He runs two fingers down my cheek. "We both know I don't really smile."

"You're still around?" Dom shows up from the pool area. His hair is wet, and a towel hangs from his shoulders, but he's dressed in the usual shorts and shirt combo.

He gives us a curious look, one eyebrow raised high.

"I'm done for now," Logan says. "On my way to the showers."

I have to shake my head to put my thoughts back together.

"I'll walk with you to the locker room." I fall into step with them. "I need to make sure you get your cupcake, Dom, and I need to see Amelia is all good to go."

It hasn't been that long since I came in search of the quarterback, but a third of the people have left when we make it there. Bear reassures me that Saint took care of Amelia and, after chatting with a couple of the other players for a few minutes, I go to my office, reply to a couple of emails, and finally leave work.

It's not until I get home and go to take off my makeup, that I see the chalk lines his fingers left on my face. Everyone saw me, but no one said a thing.

It keeps me up at night. If I didn't know better, I would question if Logan was flirting with me.

It's territory that is too dangerous to entertain for long.

Chapter 14

Evie

Logan doesn't flirt during our not-a-date that Friday. We meet in my office. I eat a snack with coffee, he sips from his smoothie. I ask about work, he answers to the point but sufficiently.

Forty minutes into our conversation, I've relaxed enough to get into it.

"One last question." I finish my coffee and stare at him. "People have been commenting on your performance, and wondering if the team has recovered enough from the slump of past years to make it into the playoffs. Some people think there's no way, some others say it's the perfect underdog story. What do you have to say to the detractors?"

"That we'll prove them wrong. We've worked hard and we'll continue to go out there and show everyone what the Strike is capable of."

"Great answer, again."

"You were right. Practice has helped."

"Wait. Did I hear...? Did you say I was right?"

He rolls his eyes. "Don't let it get into your head."

"Why wouldn't I? You're Mister Confidence on the field. I'll take your words and let it build my confidence in my field. Media training comes to save the day."

"What I've learned in our many dates is that media training is all about taking turns saying a whole lot of nothing, saying the same thing in twenty different ways, then saying something new once in a while when the questions are actually good."

I laugh. "I'll give you this. You're right about that."

"Thank you."

"Now we need to focus on keeping the momentum. You're doing so well. The photos of you with the guys for brunch the other day were so cute—"

"Cute?" He scratches his eyebrow.

He's leaning back on my couch. There's enough light in my office from the window that I see the confusion in his hazel eyes.

I should look up what the changing colors are about.

I sip from my coffee. "And Dom and Saint have said great things about working with you and feeling like you all are getting to the point you can read each other's minds—"

"The guys and I are going out on Monday night again. Want to come?"

That shuts me up.

"I'm glad you're going out with them," I finally say, "but I try not to... implant myself in players' lives outside of the professional realm."

"Why?" He frowns and peers at me. "Everyone adores you."

"It blurs the lines."

"Going out with my teammates is making us friends. Would you call that blurring the lines?"

"That's important if you need to read each other's minds. I don't need to read your minds."

"Sounds like an excuse."

It is, but I don't want to tell him the real reason. I can't pay my way when going out with them, and I won't ask them to pay for me.

They may be rich, but they owe me nothing. Even if we become friends and it somehow comes to light they don't mind, that means letting them do that for me. Depending on them for it. I would owe them.

I can't add that to my plate.

I cross my legs, my arms, and lean back on the couch as well. "I have to be careful, okay? I can't keep up with you guys."

"Keep up? Stamina wise?" He gives me a dubious look. "I don't buy it."

"I just need to have a very good reason to go, and I don't have one at the moment."

"Is that what you need to do before you come and keep me company while I'm *seen*? Have a good excuse?"

"I have my reasons."

"Which are...?"

"Why do you want to know?"

"I like to understand people. Doing media training while out and about is a very hands-on approach. It will help us both. It's what I'm proposing. Why are you avoiding it?"

I purse my lips and struggle to keep it in. He's so direct it makes me want to match him. His quick wit reads as steadfastness to my brain.

When I first saw him across the bar years ago, it was the frown and serious demeanor that gave me that feeling. Today that's here, too, and it's weakening my resistance.

In our fast-paced conversation, it's harder to push down a quick truth.

"Evie..."

The deep notches in his brow mark lines of concern. His thick, black eyebrows are heavy, just like his eyes when he peers deep into my face.

"What are you not saying?" he asks.

I believe his concern. I shouldn't do anything with it, but I've been holding my situation in for too long. None of this conversation was expected, and the surprise finds the cracks in the walls.

The truth drips out of me.

"Going out is not in my budget." I cast my eyes down. "That's all."

He doesn't say anything, and I don't look up at him.

"Now you see it's not a big deal." I lift a shoulder in a half shrug. "Just an issue of responsibility and living within my means."

"I can pay for you."

"No way I'm letting you do that."

"Evie. If you have a tight budget, or if you are struggling financially, a night out is something simple I can help—"

"It may be simple for you, but it isn't for me, okay? Please, let it be."

He studies me for a long time at my *please*. I hold myself in place, even when I want to shrink away. His scrutiny, careful as it is, makes me feel like I'm in a petri dish under a microscope.

He purses his lips. "The more I learn about you, the more questions I have."

"Don't ask more right now. I don't like to open up."

"I gathered."

"It's going to give me a vulnerability hangover, you know?"

He stands up and finishes his smoothie. With one of his small smiles tilting his lips, he offers me a hand. I frown, confused, but I take it.

I stand, and he keeps my hand in his.

"No one here knows this is why you keep to yourself, do they?" he asks.

"That's another question, Logan."

He lets go of my hand. My palm tingles from the touch, and I interlock my fingers in front of me to curb the sensation.

"You can save the answer for next time we chat," he says. "But I think I know what you will say."

"I can neither confirm nor deny."

His lips stretch in a closed-mouthed, barely-there smile. It's mesmerizing. It's like a gift I received for showing him a tender piece of me.

He takes a step back, on the way out of my office. "I would say I've graduated from media training, wouldn't you?"

"Nah. But we're in the maintenance phase. Reinforcing the gains. As long as you don't get yourself in trouble."

"Keep an eye on me all you like, Miss Moreno." He smirks. "I'm learning to enjoy it."

He disappears into the hall. With him gone, I release some of the tension that kept me ram-rod straight on my feet.

I lean my hip on the side of my desk and cross my arms. Nervous butterflies skip over my diaphragm. Not only because I shared something I've kept close to my chest for a long time, but also because it was easier than I thought it would be.

It's evidence that Logan and I are getting closer. That even if I've been trying to find a line where I don't care too much about him, I think he has started to care about me.

The fact that it's easy to believe blurs the lines for me, too.

I'm worried... but not as worried as I should be.

Chapter 15

Logan

The club Saint invited me to is dark and loud. We're in the VIP section with another twenty people, half of them friends of Dom and Saint's. Damián is here too with his girlfriend, Natalia, as well as Bear who brought his best friend Penélope.

While Damián and Bear are happy to chat with their guests and other friendly people, Dom is occupied talking into a redhead's ear. Saint, on the other hand, takes turns chatting with two brunettes competing for his attention. Based on a few comments I've overheard, I think he's taking both of them home tonight. Good for all of them, if they're all happy with that.

Me, I try to interact with Damián and Bear's group. I'm not here to chat anyone up, nor am I interested in being seduced either. Not even a direct proposition would work on me tonight... unless Evie was the one making it. I admit to that only because she was successful once. Since she's not here tonight and it's probably a bad idea anyway, I don't have to fret about what it means.

Despite all the work I've been putting into being friendlier with the guys, I'm not feeling chatty. I keep quiet, listening to the conversation and nodding or chuckling at the right time. It's a fun group, at least, since they don't talk about football. I learn about them as people, with stories such as how Pen was the first to give Leon his Bear nickname, or how Damián and Nat would be confused as a couple even before they were together, and still never clued in about their feelings.

"For years people assumed we would get together," Nat says. "But it took me a long time to figure out my real feelings. Now I feel we lost years to it!"

Damián puts an arm behind Nat, over the backrest. "We didn't lose any time, Nat. We were still living our lives together, in a way. Just missing out on a big thing or two."

The VIP zone has several lounging areas, set up as interconnected sitting sections with velvet sofas, plush divans, and upholstered seats. Deep purples and blues on every surface keep the ambiance elegant, while teal, neon lights hidden in the recesses of furniture and alcoves give us just enough light to see each other. Side tables make room for food and drinks, conveniently placed within reach of the patrons.

"I know what you mean about people expecting you to be a couple," Pen says. "People think Leon and I will get together one day."

"Will you?" I raise an eyebrow.

Bear snorts. "Nah. There's nothing like that going on between us."

"And you, Logan?" Nat asks. "Any friends you're never getting together with?"

I smirk and pretend to be thinking of the answer. Evie's face flashes through my mind, but we're not friends, so it doesn't count.

"To borrow Bear's expression, nah," I say.

I wouldn't call whatever Evie and I have as friendship, per se.

We have a past. I remember the sounds she made when I was deep in her. I know she has a secret tattoo. I'm as attracted to her today as I was that night we met at a college bar. The look on her face while filming me at the gym the other day tells me she's attracted, too.

Immune, my ass.

But that doesn't mean we'll get together. Even if we end up having sex again, it will never be more than a hookup to release the tension building between us. Feeling good together and enjoying each other's bodies for a short while is not the same as a relationship. Neither of us is into dating, last I heard.

All it means is that I care. Especially when she lets me take a peek at what's at the other side of the veil. I'm privy to things no one else knows, and it makes me want to learn more. Help in any small way she'll allow. I may have kept myself away from romance, but I have thought about friendship and found families a lot. It's clear a part of me wants her in my inner circle.

Damián opens his mouth to add more, but we're interrupted by club staff. Two people dressed in black stand by the group, one of them looks feminine with long blonde hair in a high ponytail, while the other looks masculine with a pixie cut.

"I apologize for the interruption," the pixie cut person says. "We wanted to let you know that a group of reporters and fans are gathering outside. It's our policy to let you know when that happens."

"As usual," the blonde staff member adds, "we will do our best to aid you in leaving when you're ready to do so. Simply let us know and we will help coordinate your exit."

Saint has both arms over his companions' shoulders. The three of them seem to be in their own little bubble next to us, and yet he's the one to respond to the club staff.

"Thank you, Ryan, Alex." He smiles at them. "As usual, great service."

The two of them nod to us and leave. Everyone goes back to chatting with each other, like this is par for the course.

The stress raising my hackles isn't as strong as it used to be, but it's there. People out in the world don't have interview guidelines, and it's too close to what I watched my dad go through. I've spent years avoiding situations like this and keeping them to a minimum. Now I've cornered myself into having to figure out how to handle the potential interaction with reporters and fans. Everyone else seems ready for it, and like they have no concerns about how to handle it.

I have concerns, and no idea how to handle it.

I've been sipping scotch all night, and I finish the rest of it in one gulp. The people around me are those I hope I will find brotherhood with, but I'm not there yet. Tonight isn't the night to confide in them and reveal how unprepared I am to deal with the public.

Tonight, I reach out to the one person who might help, and with whom I have no problem opening up to these days.

Logan: Evening. You up?

I have time to ask for another glass of whisky before I get a response.

Evie: Hello to you too. I'm doing well, thanks. How are you?

Logan: I said 'evening'. It should count

Evie: Sigh

Logan: Good evening, Miss Moreno. May I request your attention for a moment

Evie: Yes, Your Highness, you may. I thought you were out with the guys?

Logan: there are reporters and fans waiting for us outside. What the fuck am I supposed to do?

Evie: Are you asking me for PR advice?

Logan: You can never say I did not do my part.

I clench my jaw. The screen goes black as I decide my next steps, irritation pulling my brow low.

People have always expected me to be a serial dater, when that's far from the truth. I've never dated seriously but, and when I tell that to anyone, no one seems to believe it.

I'm not likely to change my mind. Dating short term is a performance I will always hate. In the long term it's about letting them see who I really am and risking *them* changing *their* mind.

No, thanks. I'll find companionship and friendship with my team— eventually. As they get to know me. I'll find confidence and autonomy in a few trophies and awards. I'll be happy with that.

Without a second thought, I take the device with me and hide in one of the VIP private restrooms. It smells like bleach and chemical air fresheners, and I scrunch up my nose.

She answers my call on the second ring.

"Evie. You're bringing dating up again? I said no."

Her hair is loose today and has some curl to it. It's the closest it's been to how it looked when I met her, and I file the image away for later contemplation.

She gives me an innocent look. "You don't have to date anyone if you don't want to. I said you have to leave the place with someone. Especially if folk get loud— if you look like you're protecting her from the noise and the intrusion, you'll look heroic. Points tally in your favor, et cetera."

I groan. "See what that's doing to my frown?"

I angle the camera so she sees the deep lines in my brow.

She snorts, undeterred. "People are excited for the Strike this season. Everyone wants more of you all because they have hope. That's why they're there, remember that."

"It still means I have to find someone to leave the club with."

"I'm sure it won't be hard."

"It wouldn't be hard. I don't want to, which is different."

"There must be someone there you find alluring? Even if it's only to leave the club together and take her to her place. Nightcap with her optional."

I ignore the suggestion. Evie looks pretty, in that unstudied way she had when we met, or on our first video call.

That's much more alluring to me at the moment. Especially since it means I wouldn't have to convince someone I'll take them home but I'm not interested in a nightcap.

My brow relaxes. "I have a better idea. You should be the one."

"The one... what?"

I let my lips slant into a micro smile. "Come to the club. Have a drink with me— my treat. We'll leave together."

Her eyes narrow. "No."

"You can scold me in person."

"I'm in my PJs."

She doesn't show me, though now I'm curious.

I don't ask. "Come in your PJs."

"You're ridiculous."

"It's the perfect plan."

"It's not."

"Why not? Tell me when you arrive."

"Logan—"

"I can send a car for you. We have a drink together, you chat with everyone or teach me a lesson on something. Whatever makes you happiest. Then we go out, I protect you with my large, manly size, and get those extra points you say we need. It's a win-win."

Reasons and excuses cloud her eyes. I retaliate before they click into place.

"Remember that swim ad? I said no, but I'll say yes if you come. We're helping each other out in the long term. That's all that's happening here."

She purses her lips. Indecision mars her brow— it's the closest she's ever been to saying yes, and I intend to find a way to persuade her.

"Text me your address," I add. "I'll text back as soon as I have the ETA. See you soon."

She gives me a pained expression, like I'm inconveniencing her but can't quite say no at the moment.

"Thank you, Evie."

I mean it.

She gives me a single, annoyed nod, and I hang up before she can change her mind.

Chapter 16

Evie

A staff member guides me from the club doors up the stairs, and into the VIP section. Nerves tighten my stomach, but I can't pay attention to that when Logan comes to greet me.

The staff person opens the velvet rope for me, but my eyes are on the quarterback. I have never seen him dressed like this, at least not in person. He wears bespoke trousers in what seems like a mossy green color and a matte, black shirt that fits him like a glove. The cut of his clothes highlights the triangle of his shape, with wide shoulders and narrow hips, and they make him look taller than ever.

The last part is the only thing I had prepared for, choosing my one pair of stilettos for the night. Still, when he stands next to me, I have to look up at him. I'm a tall woman, but he's *tall*.

"Thanks for coming," he says.

We banter enough that I'm surprised at his politeness, and I retaliate.

"This is my one cocktail dress, Logan. A little black something that works for everything. I never get to wear it. Didn't get to dry clean it before the evening, either, so if it's musty it's your fault."

If his hyperosmia makes him suffer, that's on him.

Humor sparks in his eyes. He takes me by the arm and leads me to the side. The staff member closes the rope behind themselves, and we're alone several steps away from the group. We can still hear the music loud and clear, but it's not so loud that we couldn't keep a quiet conversation if we wanted to.

Disrupting all protocols and without any warning, Logan dips his head to the general vicinity of my neck— and takes a long, deep breath in. The inhale is strong enough to change the air pressure balance of the space around us and, just like the skies give birth to wind, his inspiration creates a breeze that blows through the tiny hairs of my skin.

"What—" I start, but a shiver interrupts my words.

It runs all the way from my nape to my feet. My toes curl in my heels.

What the fuck kind of witchcraft is this?

"You smell great," he whispers.

It's dangerous wizardry, is what it is.

I push him back and hiss a warning only for him to hear. "Don't do that here!"

"Why? You were worried. I put your mind at ease. You're welcome."

"What a start to the evening, Your Highness." I tsk and shake my head.

I have to fist my hands to hide the way my fingers tremble. There's nothing I can do about the drumming in my chest.

He snorts, before he leads me to the group, where I say hi to everyone.

"Can't believe you finally came out to meet us." Saint smiles at me, only one of his dimples visible. The other is being kissed by one of his two companions.

Dom gazes at me as well, his arm around a beautiful redhead next to him. "Thank you so much for helping me win one of my bets, Miss Moreno."

"What bet?" I ask.

"That this would be the year we convince you to join us at the club," Dom replies.

A flutter skips over my stomach. The guys have asked me to join them before, and I've resisted each time. Spending time with them outside of TD complicates things, if they might end up needing more from me. All I've known is that to care for people means jumping to their rescue and, until I figure out how to stop myself, I can't afford the risk.

I sit on the green velvet of the couch, closer to Damián's group than to the two players getting busy in the shadows of the VIP section.

I smirk. "Does it count if I'm here for work? I'm thinking I may expense it."

"You're not expensing it," Logan says.

I keep my eyes on Dom. Logan's statement does nothing to help me create some much-needed distance between the guys and me.

"It counts." Dom grins. "And now I'm in first place on the B-Hypercubed board. Your first drink is on me."

"Everyone's drinks are on me tonight," Logan insists.

He sits next to me, and we join Damián, Nat, Leon, and Pen. Saint and Dom go back to their dates, and I leave them to it without a second thought.

Damián leans over. "Funny that Logan was the one to convince you."

I shrug. "Like I said, this is work."

Logan arches an eyebrow my way. "Admit that you like me better than the rest."

His tone is dry. One could easily take it seriously or as a joke. People around laugh, so it's clear how they're taking it, but Logan and I like to prod and poke.

I answer as if I believed him. "I don't! You're just my biggest challenge."

"It's not all suffering." The corner of his lips turn south. "You have fun in this game we play."

"What game?"

I tell myself I'm teasing. Then I tell myself that it's a genuine question. Until he leans close to me and my thoughts stop altogether.

We lock eyes, and I hold my breath in waiting.

It's like he wants me to see him clearly. I happen to know, he tries to see me clearly, too.

"You know the game," he says. "The same one where you pretend not to enjoy the way we banter."

"I don't know what you're talking about," I reply.

He leans back and gazes at the group. They all study us with varying degrees of smirks and attention.

Logan purses his lips. "Next, I'll get you to come to see us at the stadium."

"She's never come to see us play that we know of," Damián says. "We've tried."

I shake my head, unconcerned. "Doesn't mean I haven't been."

"It doesn't count if no one knows," Logan insists.

"Is this a bet, King?" Leon asks. "That's what I call team spirit."

"It can't be a bet," I argue.

"It doesn't have to be on the Hypersquared," Logan says. "I'm just calling it a challenge."

I frown at him. "You are way too confident, Logan."

"It's part of the game we have." He smirks, but a playful gleam shines in his eyes.

It gives me butterflies.

I can't accept them, so I stare at the rest of the group.

"Do you know what game he's talking about?" I ask.

"I don't know, but I'm having fun watching." Nat smiles, her lavender hair taking on an intense shade of purple in the club lights.

"If you're not aware of a game, Evie," Bear challenges, "then how is this work?"

I can't be the one revealing the deal Logan and I have. I turn to him with a raised eyebrow, daring him to come clean.

He frowns. "You may have noticed that I can come across as..."

"Serious?" Pen says.

"Severe?" Damián adds.

Nat smiles. "Grumpy?"

"Reserved," Logan says before other people can interject further.

His eyebrows pull down lower in response to the comments. It's one of the frowns I used to think were killer, and now only seem like sharp focus to me. The other people in the group don't seem put off by it. They smirk or hold back a smile, and find humor in it the same way I do.

Logan purses his lips. "Miss Moreno is helping me be more... forthcoming with people."

"I still don't see how this is about work?" Pen asks.

"Let's say I got in trouble with the boss," Logan explains. "Evie and I have meetings about it. She makes videos for social media, and comes to me at the club when I ask very nicely."

"I've seen the videos," Pen says with a knowing smile. "They're very popular."

"Have you read the comments?" Nat asks Pen. "People are wondering who is behind the videos. Now we know."

I have seen the comments. A group of fans have romanticized the videos. Assumed that whoever runs the account is in love with the quarterback. At this point I've decided to ignore the comments, and I would rather other players don't go looking.

I don't know if Logan has gone looking yet, or what he'll do about it.

"In any case," I interrupt before anyone gets any ideas, "we should go, Logan."

"You haven't had a drink." His frown turns unhappy.

I didn't have a drink on purpose. He said he would pay for me, then offered to pay for the group, and I'm not sure how I feel about any of that.

Suspicious. That's how I feel.

I came because if I told Logan that PR had a say in his personal life, and I'm in charge of his PR, I should own up to it and show up. I didn't come here to let him be the first person in a decade to buy drinks for me, or treat me to anything else.

My speech is prepared to redirect the topic again.

"And before you get any ideas," I say to the group, "I'm leaving with Logan because of work, too. To help his PR with the hoards waiting outside. But I wasn't ready to come out tonight, and I have to work extra early tomorrow."

It's the perfect excuse because it's true. Tuesdays are the team's day off, and they could party for who knows how long.

Logan stands when I do. We ask the staff to coordinate with his driver. When we're told the car is ready, we say goodbye and step out of the VIP section. The stairs have a landing midway, and we stop there.

"What's the plan?" Logan asks.

The music is louder here. I go up to the top of my feet to talk to his ear. I'm forced to place a hand on his chest to keep my balance.

"We go straight out," I say. "We walk close enough to look friendly, but I'll open the car's door to disappear as fast as possible. You can either nod at people out there or ignore them completely, with me there they won't expect you to stop. That's it."

"Mhh." It's an unhappy sound.

"Ready?"

He nods and we go to the first floor, where a few fans wave at him. He waves back, but puts a hand on my lower back and we go out.

Flashes explode. A few people scream, others ask questions.

"Are you hoping for the Super Bowl, Logan?"

"Who is she?"

"What does your father have to say about this season?"

Logan puts an arm around my shoulder and pulls me closer. I gaze at the floor, not to be stunned with the flashes. We're only a few steps away from the black SUV.

People continue to try to get his attention.

"Can we take a picture?"

"What happens if you don't make it to the playoffs?"

Logan opens the door for me and I climb in, without much time to question how he didn't follow my instructions too closely.

He sits next to me, the door shut again behind him. The driver starts the journey soon after.

"That went well enough," I say.

"Mmh. I still hate it. How soon until I can stop?"

"Three seasons. Tops. Then you can pull back a lot."

He stares out to the streets flying by. Most of his face is hidden from me, but I'm learning the lines of his profile well. His mood is somber again, and his frown deep.

"You're doing great, Logan. You'll see. It's going to be worth it. You're getting something out of it even now, aren't you? By getting better at media, you're also getting better at talking about yourself and opening up. I can see the guys like you."

All he does is nod once. I don't take offense. He's deep in thought, and I'm happy to let him process whatever he's working through.

We make it to my place a short time later. There is a deli at the bottom of my building. The neon sign on the glass shines in blues, reds, and violets to let everyone know they're still open.

The driver gets out and comes to my door.

"All right." I hold my bag tight and get ready to get out of the car. "Good night, Logan."

I push against the seat with my free hand. I'm halfway out when he stops me. His large palm is warm on top of mine, between us.

His serious eyes take a gorgeous shade of purple as he gazes at me. Fucking *royal purple* eyes.

"Thanks, Evie."

The words come out solemn, my name weighty. Unlike when he greeted me at the club, this time I believe him.

It wreaks havoc inside. My stomach is doing cartwheels for some reason, and my heart rate shoots through the roof.

He's not supposed to be earnest. He should be following the rules, and be grumpy and sarcastic so I know where the lines are. So we both remember this is work *only*. A friendliness between us at the most, like I have with the rest of the team.

This doesn't feel like general friendliness.

I'm breathless.

But the driver is waiting for me, and I can't sit and figure it out when Logan is studying me with keen eyes. The hairs in my skin perk up, because I know that if I tried to put the puzzle together now, he would read my mind.

I gulp. I nod. I pretend all is good, and get out of the car.

He doesn't stop me this time.

It's not until later when I lay awake in my bed, that I realize that if I wanted him to follow the rules, it's because a part of me understands this is a game, after all.

Chapter 17

Logan

The fans waiting outside the club a week ago were a nuisance, but the memory doesn't stop me from going out for dinner tonight.

It's the Monday evening after our second loss of the season. Saint and the guys are doing their own thing, but I don't want to be alone with my thoughts. Not many people I could call, when the group I'm getting close to is otherwise entertained, and I don't think Evie would say yes.

I end up finding my way into a restaurant Dom mentioned once. It's the kind of place where you need to make a reservation months in advance, but they make an exception for me. Despite the loss, I may have collected enough social credit with the city to grant me access.

I tell them I'm waiting for someone and they give me a table for two. There's no plan in my mind yet, but I'll come up with something. At worst, a few people might question if I was stood up, and that's fine by me. All I do for now is order an Old Fashioned and get on my phone.

My agent's team sent me another update email regarding social media. The body of the message isn't very long. It only says, "This is going well, but we should keep an eye on things just in case'. A few links to videos are included at the end. Knowing how they communicate, they like what Evie is doing with the profile, but want to monitor it regardless.

It's as good a distraction as any, and I finally give in to the curiosity and check Evie's work.

The first video is of one of my plays the day before. I recognize it within a couple of seconds. On the screen, I throw the ball to Saint. All of my guys are covered by the Hawks' defense, but Saint is the one that has the best chance to catch the ball and run with it.

It doesn't show on the recording, but he gets tackled. The music Evie chose goes into a crescendo. The camera is still pointed at me, showing to the world the way my frown intensifies and the very clear *FUCK!* I let out. The music sustains a high note, to cover the sound of my swearing and highlight it at the same time.

I snort. The video has thousands of likes and, upon investigation, the edit has hundreds of thousands of views. Most videos do.

A server delivers my drink and brings warm bread, butter, and a dish of what looks like olive oil and balsamic vinegar. Another dish with olives and a few pieces of cheese comes along, too.

"We'll wait for your guest," they say. "Please let us know if you need anything else."

I thank them and go back to the phone. There is a video with over a million views that I want to check out.

It's the one she filmed the last time we lost a game, a few weeks ago. Evie had been trying to lift my spirits, and I ended up letting her film content, just to put a smile on her face. She looked hungry instead, and it put a smile on *my* face. Metaphorically.

The editing in this video is more careful than the first one. It's not just music on this one, which has a sexy beat to it. Some of the shots are in slow motion, too. Until it quiets down, so viewers can hear our voices.

She asks what I want fans to know. When I answer, she gasps.

I remember the moment. She asked me for a sound bite and I gave her an answer that meant more. My reply came out fueled by the heat that built in my muscles, born from my workout and from being watched by Evie alike. I enjoyed her eyes on me, and the words came out uninspected.

I want you to know me, I said. *I want you to remember me.*

I want her to break and ask me about me. Let us get close. I want her to tell me she never forgot about me and the night we had.

Fuck. Evidence grows to suggest I want her close.

I tap on the comments to skim through them, but thoughts run in the background. They mix with people's opinions of the video, the team, and me.

He's so hot

At the club, I tried to tease her by taking a deep whiff of her scent. I managed to pass it off as no big deal, but I played myself. It spurred a deep awareness of her. Like her pheromones had the exact right chemistry to wake up something ancient in my brain.

They reminded me of the magic of us together, naked. Alchemy, all right.

I continue skimming, only one in three comments making it to my awareness.

What a loser. The Strike are the worst

That one barely registers.

That first night years ago, Evie didn't let me ask anything to get to know her. We didn't get a chance to see how far we could push what we had together. Just a few nights ago, she didn't let me pay for her drink at the club.

Logan King is bringing back this team!

She put her hand on my chest at the club and my heart skipped a beat.

Whoever runs this account knows exactly what we want

My hand on her back. My arm around her shoulders. It felt natural.

He'll never be as good as his father

Being close to her feels good. I want more.

But seriously. Who's running this account? She's clearly into him

That comment snatches my attention. I frown and open the comment thread.

They must be sleeping together because that gasp was full of sexual tension

Both comments have thousands of likes. Someone else adds, *'did you see the video of him with someone in the club? I bet that's her'.*

I bite the inside of my lip. It takes a few tries, but I find the video under the hashtag with my name. It's of Evie and I on the stair landing at the club, talking close. The comments on that video are more of the same.

Is that his girlfriend?

The video of them getting out of the club?? SWOON

BUT WHO IS SHE (we'll find her)

When I see the first vitriolic comment about Evie— about us, I swipe away from it all and lock my phone.

Shit. I'm pissed. Too much show, too much scrutiny about my private life. Now Evie is getting caught in the tornado, and I don't know how she feels about it.

She probably knows this is happening, but she hasn't mentioned it.

I rub my forehead, hard. Many things feel off about all of this and I don't know where to begin.

Fuck it. I need to start somewhere.

> Logan: Do you read the comments your videos get on social media? We need to talk.

She doesn't respond right away, but I'm not surprised. I kill time by checking the comments on a few more of the videos she has posted to my profile, and a few more of the ones on the hashtag. It's more of the same. I don't care so much about the ones celebrating or criticizing me. Everyone's a coach online. But the ones poking at our personal life cut. The ones saying mean things about her burn.

They can say whatever they want about me, but I can't stand the way some of them are talking about her.

Evie: I do. Talking might be a good idea. Do you want to meet me in my office tomorrow after training?

Logan: I'm in a restaurant. Alone. Come join me. We can talk now

Evie: You're alone in a restaurant?

Logan: I didn't want to be at home alone after the loss. Don't question it

Evie: … so you're alone at a restaurant instead?

Logan: I thought I asked you not to question it?

Evie: Fine, fine.

Logan: come join me, please

Evie: what exactly are you worried about with the comments?

Logan: Some people are being rude to you because they think we're dating. We should talk.

This time it takes her a minute to respond. The server asks if I would prefer to have a special service exclusively crafted for me, which is a fancy way to ask me if I'm going to dine alone after all.

"Ask me again in a few minutes. I'll know then," I say, before checking her new text.

> Evie: If I join you those comments could get worse.

> Logan: I'd call you if I could talk freely here, but I haven't had dinner yet. Join me. Please. I'll make sure we get privacy.

> Logan: Or invite me over to your place, I know your address from sending the car to pick you up.

I double text her on purpose. It's pushy, but overasking is a negotiation technique. If you start with twice what you want, you may get the middle number which is more than you wanted to start with.

Unless the counterpart decides to give you even more than half, which is a win-win, and I know Evie would let me know in a heartbeat if she really wanted me to stop.

> Evie: It can wait

> Logan: I don't want to wait. And I don't want to eat alone. Please.

> Evie: So you're going to convince me by asking me to take pity? By being polite for once? again?

> Logan: we both know I'm shameless. I won't sleep well tonight without the conversation

I go as far as to take a selfie of me frowning and coming as close to pouting as my face will allow. I send it to her.

> Evie: YOU ARE UNBELIEVABLE

Logan: Thank you. Can I send a car now?

Evie: Fine! You win. Just make sure we have privacy, and the food better be good. I'm still at work and I'm starving. It's the only reason I'm saying yes

Logan: I don't believe that for a second. See you soon.

Chapter 18

Logan

I arrange for the restaurant to set me up in a private spot. Turns out they have a small section in the back they reserve for special occasions, and it's perfect for Evie and me. If privacy might make Evie feel better about having dinner with me, then privacy she'll have.

She shows up at the restaurant twenty minutes later. She asked to be picked up from work— maybe that's why she wears clothes I've seen before. Her pencil skirt is blue-green and tight, and it shows off the round curves of her hips and thick thighs. The top is a cream blouse in a material with a subtle sheen, that drapes around her breasts. She looks just as good as she did in her black dress at the club.

"Hi, Evie," I say, because she tends to complain when I don't greet her properly. "What would you like to drink tonight?"

Our server joins us seamlessly, standing at our side and introducing himself. Evie gets white wine, and we're told the first course will arrive shortly.

She sighs. "Okay. I'm ready for our chat."

"Are you?"

"Of course. You said you wouldn't sleep well tonight if we didn't talk."

"Thank you for caring about the quality of my sleep."

"I happen to know sleep is very important."

"Your sense of responsibility over my wellbeing is endearing."

Humor builds on her face, but she doesn't crack. My drink tastes better now, too, for some reason.

"It is my responsibility as front office staff," she says.

"I like to think I've charmed you with my personality."

"That's exactly the kind of thing that could make people believe we are in fact together."

The restaurant has a soft, golden light to warm up the old Hollywood decor in gold, black, and white. It shines on her, making her skin and eyes glow.

I take it as confirmation she enjoys our word sparring, too.

She looks beautiful.

I take another sip from my Old Fashioned. "You and I know we're only having fun. I don't care so much about what they believe, but the things they're saying about you."

"I don't care about what they're saying about me in the comments. It's all engagement, and their curiosity has people talking about you. It was my goal to start with."

"But?"

"If you're going to keep trying to get me to join you out in the wild, and it keeps pushing fans to believe we're dating, I need to know you will tell everyone else the truth."

"What do you want me to tell people?"

The first course arrives. It's a seafood trio in different color combinations—green, yellow, and purple. Evie waits until the servers leave and we've had our first bite to answer.

She chases the food with her wine. "You should tell everyone that we work together."

Evie's hair is in a loose bun at her nape. It lets me see the curve of her neck, and how her throat bobbles as she eats another bite.

I gulp and fill my mouth with the rest of my plate. The taste brings me back to the ocean, and an evening watching the sun set. Like Evie and I are at the beach and having dinner together after a long day of doing nothing.

That may be why the idea of only being linked by our occupation and responsibilities doesn't feel like enough. It's not the right description.

I test a different label. "Do you think we're friends?"

She works through her last bite as she thinks. A wrinkle appears between her shapely eyebrows and she gazes down at her plate.

"I don't know," she finally replies. "Maybe. But it would be the right thing to tell people— that we're colleagues. That we're friendly now after months working together. Fans want to know about me, and it will help your engagement in socials if we explain it this way."

"I can tell people that."

We work together. We might become friends. That's plenty, and true enough.

"This is how we control the narrative," she adds. "Especially when some of them decide we're lying."

"Would that bother you?"

Servers take away our empty plates, and we both kill time making a dent in our drinks.

She lifts a single shoulder. "As long as people at work believe us, I'm fine with it."

"Fine with it."

All I can do is echo her words. I'm supposed to poke and have fun, but that sounds like, to her, us together is something to be dismissed.

Us together isn't to be dismissed. It's realistic, it's proven physically, but it's not something either of us is planning for. Very different issues.

She nods. "If I go out with you and we both know why, and we tell everyone the truth, then no one will doubt I took my priority project seriously."

I frown. The main course arrives. It gives me time to push away my irritation, that she's thinking about her promotion while I'm thinking of dating and the reasons why I won't do anything about it.

I'm quickly forgetting. Getting to know her these few months is to blame, but I can't let it change my mind about relationships.

I shake my head and hope the motion will kick my brain into action. "I do like you more than I liked your old boss."

She gives me a close-mouthed smile, tasting the food I haven't bothered to look at.

"Even though I've pushed you more than he ever did?" she asks.

"I like it when you do."

I purse my lips. It feels strange to admit this, but I want her to react and match me, and I don't care to lie.

"We agreed to it," I add. "You can push, and I'll be fair. Same the other way around."

"That's the game we'll play. We'll spend time together and then explain we're not involved."

"You should come to a game, to drive the point further. I'll get you a spot in the suite."

"As a friend."

"Of course. When you wear my jersey, we'll remind everyone it's all platonic."

"I'm not wearing your jersey, Logan."

She for sure isn't wearing anyone else's.

"We'll see," I concede. For now.

I finally try my food, to find buttery fish, pasta, and a delicious garlic and herb sauce. We eat in silence for a while, and finish our meal with me teasing her for the videos she's produced.

She accepts dessert, and I like that she's open to spending the extra time with me tonight. At the club, I didn't get to enjoy her company as much.

Her relaxation disappears when we get ready to leave. She goes quiet, and doesn't respond to my conversation with the same ease anymore, or when we get up to leave.

"Shouldn't we wait for the bill?" She eventually asks.

I shake my head. "It's taken care of."

A weight falls on her shoulders. I try to meet her eyes, but she looks away, so I guide her out with a hand behind her back.

I break the tension as soon as we're in the back of the car, on the way to her place.

"What happened? You went quiet," I say.

"You're always quiet, unless it's with me."

"Let's not ponder on that, when it only distracts from my question."

"You're not going to let me change the subject, will you?" She stares forward, her eyes lost on the dark glass divider in front of us.

"I will if you tell me to stop." I lick my bottom lip. "But you've opened up to me before, so my chances are good."

I've spent enough time with her that I'm learning to read her. I want her thoughts enough that I'm glad for it. But even if I'm willing to push, I don't want her to be uncomfortable.

I let her make up her mind, and wait to see what it will be— assertiveness or another piece of the puzzle.

She sighs. "I didn't get a chance to look up the restaurant before I joined you. I didn't realize it's the type of place where they take your credit card information when they take the reservation."

My brows pull down, but I don't say anything yet. She may offer more if I keep quiet.

She stares at her lap. "I was going to ask for the receipt so I could expense my part."

I scoff before I can stop it. "I wouldn't have let you do that."

She stares at me, a hard line tilting her lips. "I would have insisted. It's... I wouldn't... I can't accept you paying for me. It's too close to dating."

"Didn't we just agree that fans will think we're dating and we're good with that?"

"It's not about what random people think. It's about you and I. I don't date."

I hate that she keeps finding ways to point out she doesn't see that for us.

We could if we wanted to and it wouldn't go against our plans. Evie and I fit, but many reasons exist to push away the notion for myself. On one hand, the process of trying to turn dates into a relationship has always seemed demoralizing to me. It requires trust that I've never been able to give freely, and a willingness to be vulnerable that I've never been able to offer. On the other hand, my focus can't be on making something like that work, when a bad day could ruin the whole season for me and my team.

Evie has her reasons, too. That's fine. All I want is to know what those are. But I've never liked pretense. There is attraction between us. We have fun together. We have a past— an incredible night together. Plenty of people start with less. If it weren't for our reasons not to, trying something would make sense. I want her to see it too.

"I'm not saying we should." I grind my teeth. "I don't date either, but accepting that and feigning disinterest are not the same."

Her eyes narrow. "There's no point in talking about *interest*, if nothing will ever happen."

"And what's the point in telling me you don't want me to pay, when that won't stop me?"

"You're so persistent, King." She crosses her arms. "So fucking stubborn!"

"I'm logical. I have the money, I invited you, I don't care if it feels like dating. We know we're not dating."

"I care. I don't like to depend on people for anything."

"And letting me pay is depending? Or is it dating me that you have a problem with?"

She shakes her head and turns away to look through the window. "What is it about how you talk to me, that gets me admitting things I never tell anyone?"

"I'm told I'm persistent. Fucking stubborn."

She scoffs. Her shoulders turn inwards, like she's feeling exposed.

I'll get a vulnerability hangover, she told me once.

Our arguing pumped energy into my blood, heating me up. I go cold now, adrenaline evaporating all at once.

My stomach drops. I don't like that I pushed so much she's feeling threatened.

I chew on the inside of my lip for a second, two. There's a lever somewhere inside of me. It helps me contain my private world. A control panel sits next to it, measuring in painstaking detail how much I let anyone know of who I am. They take what I learn from people, and allow small pieces out if they show me constancy.

It finally clicks— Evie is like that, too, but she has a harder time with it.

My chest softens. Leveling the field is only fair.

"I first went to therapy in college." My voice comes serene. Open, for once. "It was mandatory, but it helped. My therapist back then, she told me I'm like a hunting dog. I get a scent and I pursue until I get my prize."

"Funny, for someone with hyperosmia."

She still doesn't look at me.

I snort. "I guess, but that's not why I'm telling you the story."

I don't add anything, hoping the silence will grab her and get her to gaze at me again. It does, and she turns to me with suspicion in her eyes.

"I always want the truth," I say. "As much of it as I can. It helps me find my place with people, when I live in a world that forgot I'm more than my father's son, the moment I first stepped onto a football field."

Her eyes clear. Her face softens.

The space between us opens. It's lighter, now that I shared.

A ghost of a smile curls my lips. "I'm sorry that I push so hard that I forget to take a step back sometimes. You match me so well when we talk that I make the mistake of assuming all you want is the truth, too."

"I suppose it's something like that for me as well. It's that when we get into it, your direct questions translate as honesty to me. That honesty makes me want to meet you there and give it right back. But my truth is that if it makes me feel you're dependable, it doesn't mean I can rely on you."

"You said earlier that we may be friends one day. Maybe then you'll find you can rely on me, Evie."

"I still don't want to let you pay."

I smirk. "What is it that you said to me that day? Hate it, but do it anyway."

Chapter 19

Evie

It's the middle of November. Eleven weeks into the season, the Strike has won seven games out of the nine we've played. The mood at TD is incredible, smiles everywhere— including Selena, on the rare occasion that we cross paths these days. Once she declared she liked what Logan and I were doing, she moved to more urgent matters. The freedom is reassuring.

Between that and the conversation Logan and I had in the car many days ago, I let him get me into the next home game. Some of the guys pay for a box together, and Logan texts to tell me Nat will be waiting for me.

I meet her there and she gives me a hug. It's strange as I didn't expect it, but I smile through it. The guys and I are friendly enough, but I rarely spend social time with them or their people. Somehow, whatever time I've spent with them has been enough for Nat to welcome me with open arms— literally.

The thought blows wind to the butterflies in my stomach, and they dance around as she and I go to the seats by the window. Pen is there, and we say hi as well.

"I didn't know you'd be here!" I say, before asking a server for a fruity drink.

"Yeah." She pushes her lips to the side. "Leon broke up with his girlfriend and he wanted company today."

She wears Bear's jersey, just like Nat wears Damián's.

I wear my navy, oversized shirt dress with a light blue, shiny belt at the waist. It's the team's colors, but I don't wear a jersey.

"I didn't know he was dating anyone." Nat sits at my other side.

"He likes to keep those things private." Pen sips from her drink. "So I probably shouldn't say more."

"Are you dating anyone, Evie?" Nat's eyes shine with mischief.

"Me?" I snort. "No. I don't date."

"You're here for Logan, aren't you?" Pen asks.

"Because of work," I say. "As a friend."

I roll the words on my tongue, testing them for fit. In the car we said we might come out of all of this with friendship, but I don't think we're friends. Just like I'm not friends with Nat or Pen either.

There are degrees of friendship, and all of these people are in that weird space that it's more than acquaintances but not someone I would tell my secrets to.

Do I want more with any of them? Maybe. But it's the only word I can use to describe what I have with all of them, and I have to be okay using it.

The server brings my drink. It's raspberry and mint, and sweet on my tongue.

"Right, you explained at the club," Nat says.

I'm not sure she believes me and I don't blame her. With the online chatter about us and the time we spend together, it's easy to assume there's more. At least it can't affect me at work. As long as we're clear that we're not together, no one at the organization will demand the HR meeting from us. There's no power imbalance between us, and that will protect us.

We turn to the field as the pregame show begins. Highlights from past games play on the massive main screen of the stadium, and the cheerleaders find their place on the turf. They line up outside the tunnel through which the players will come in, past the smoke machines. Music and fireworks welcome them into the field, one by one. Fans cheer.

Everyone applauds in the suite, and Nat and Pen are especially loud when their players come out. I keep my excitement even, but I track Logan when it's his turn. He runs into the field through smoke screens and cheerleaders shaking pom-poms, head down as he charges forward.

He doesn't dance like Saint or Dom. There is no fake superhero pose like Damián, or a bear walk out of the tunnel that turns into a power run like Leon. All Logan does is wave at the crowd when he goes to stand with the rest of the team.

I smirk. He really hates the show around the game, and it strikes me that I don't know why. I don't even know whether he likes football, or if he plays it only because he's good.

We stand by the windows and watch the start of the game. The Strike is on offense, and Logan stands in his position. The first play goes fast, and they gain several yards. When the next play turns into a touchdown, with Saint shaking his ass to music only he can hear, the box explodes to cheers.

Players run to celebrate with the wide receiver, but my eyes go to the quarterback again. He does a single power pose, the kind a body builder might do with both arms at the front.

"They look so good when they're happy," I say.

"Personally, I love the uniforms," Nat says.

Damián comes into the field to try for the point after touchdown.

"They are all fine, aren't they?" Pen asks.

Logan runs to the bench, the tight pants and shirt showing off his form.

Damián's attempt is good, and the three of us sit and take sips from our drinks.

Pen sighs. "I have to admit, I love the aesthetic of football."

"Not the sport?" Nat winks. "Just how it looks?"

Pen smiles. "I don't care who makes it into the playoffs or whatever. But I like to watch the game."

We laugh.

"Yeah, I get it," I say. "I was never into it, but I've come to appreciate the aesthetic, too."

"Are we just using euphemisms here? Are we saying we just like to watch them play?"

"I mean the whole aesthetic," I say, though my eyes are trained on Logan. "The plays, the bursts of excitement, the screams of the fans."

"Same, but I also like to watch them play." Pen shrugs.

Nat sighs. "And to think I used to tell myself thinking Damián is hot didn't mean anything."

"What do you mean?" I ask.

"We've been friends for years. I always knew he's sexy, but I liked to pretend it was only an objective statement."

The Strike intercepts the ball and we jump up to the window again. Logan runs onto the field now, shoulder checking players in celebration. They tap each other's helmets for good measure.

It makes me smile. They look like a close team. It's good because it adds to the story we're building for all the fans, but it also seems real. I don't know for sure but, whatever my subconscious has picked up when I'm with Logan, it tells me this is good for everyone, and what he wants, too.

I'm happy that it could be making him happy.

Fuck. That seems like I care about him, and maybe I'm closer to being his friend than I thought.

We sit again as the team continues their play. Nat asks for a second drink, but I leave mine on the window ledge.

I bite the inside of my lip. I've been careful for years about who I make friends with. I'm still not sure if I'd be able to say 'enough, I can't give anymore', or whether I would drown in a whirlpool of wanting to make things better for everyone. Even now, with two people next to me I'm getting to know better, I know I have to pay attention. And with Logan, we're in quicksand, playing as if this thing between us could lead to friendship.

From my current angle I can see the screen much better than the turf. Logan's famous frown shines bright on the cinema-sized display.

It's been years since I first saw him in a bar, brows furrowed at everyone. At the time my body responded with greed for him. A hum low in my belly. Today...

Today I still do.

I grab my drink and gulp half of it down.

It hasn't been that long since Nat's statement, and I jump right into the conversation as if it's not a big deal.

"Now that you're with Damián, did you change your mind?"

"What's that?" Nat asks, a confused look on her face.

"You used to think you could find your friend attractive and still be friends. Did you change your mind now that you're together?"

"Oh. Well." She receives her drink and sips from it. "I can't speak for everyone else, but I know I was wrong. Very wrong."

"I think it's possible," Pen interjects. "Bear is a catch. He's handsome and gives the best hugs, but I don't want to date him. It wouldn't work."

"How do you know?"

"Oh. We tried. A long time ago."

Nat grins. "That's a story I want to hear!"

Pen shakes her head. "There's nothing to it, really."

They chat with each other, but I don't pay attention. Pen's words force me to think about that time years ago when Logan and I tested the chemistry between us. That time with him is what I compare every one-night-stand to. Even if Logan doesn't remember, his words in the car recently suggest he may be attracted to me this time around, too.

If I'm already nervous about all these friendships, especially the possibility of being Logan's friend at the end of this... the attraction only makes it worse.

The Strike's defense collapses in the second half, and we lose the game.

Everyone in the suite is somber. Damián is one of the first players to come to the suite. Nat immediately hugs him tight and holds on. They embrace for several minutes, like they're alone in the box. It feels like I'm intruding in something private, and I step to the side and stand by the wall.

Leon comes in and goes straight for Penélope. She makes a joke I can't hear, he looks pained but about to laugh, and pulls her close for a hug as well.

I shift from foot to foot and wait for Logan. Saint comes in with Dom. The latter goes to meet with a redhead that I'm pretty sure is the same person he was with at the club that night, but Saint turns to me.

"Hey," I say. "How are you doing?"

Of all of the guys in the friend group, Saint is the one I'm closest to. We don't really spend time together outside of team situations, but we talk about things that are not game-related. Sometimes. Maybe that's why he ignores his guest and comes to me instead.

He lifts a shoulder. "It always sucks. Every single time."

A beautiful blonde hovers nearby. She's not one of the two people Saint went home with after the club, but I've never judged anyone for their dating habits.

"Go," I whisper to him. "They're waiting for you."

He sighs but doesn't walk away yet. He steps closer to me.

"I'm frustrated." His voice is low, only for me. "I'm preparing myself for the hell that reviewing tape with the coaches is going to be tomorrow. Maybe a bit sad, too, if I'm honest."

"Saint— I—"

He shakes his head to stop me. "It's fine, but Logan hasn't said a word since the end of the third quarter. He always looks grumpy, but I'm starting to think half the time he's just thinking hard about things. Today I think he's just plain upset."

"I see. And maybe you think that, since I'm here..."

"You're his guest. Even if you're not wearing his jersey, it means something, you know?"

I purse my lips to the side. "Your guest isn't wearing a jersey."

"Don't worry about me." His dimples make an appearance. "I'll be well taken care of."

I make a disgusted face and he laughs.

A large shadow blocks the light coming through the suite's door, and we both turn to find Logan standing there.

Saint waves at both of us and goes to his guest, freeing a clear path between Logan and me.

At first, he does nothing but stand there, serious eyes on me. Even if Saint hadn't told me of his low mood, I would have seen it right away. His shoulders are low, heavy with his disappointment. His hair is still wet, and as he gets closer with slow steps, I get to see that fresh look on his skin, the kind that comes from a recent shower.

I take a deep breath, and my lungs fill with the smell of his shampoo. He takes an extra step and stands close. For a moment I wonder if he's going to ask me for a hug, just like Damián with Nat, or Leon with Pen.

He doesn't. "I thought you might be gone already."

"It didn't cross my mind."

"Thank you."

"I'm sorry. I don't have a cupcake today."

"But you're trying to lift my spirits?"

I step closer. "Don't tell anyone I said this."

He raises an eyebrow.

"I may not be an expert at football strategy, but something tells me that it's not the quarterback's fault if the defense doesn't play well."

He doesn't smile, but there's something about how he presses his lips together that tells me he could.

I grin.

"You don't have to feed my ego," he says. "I'm supposed to be the glue. As the offense, we didn't sustain long enough drives to let the defense rest properly."

"Okay, then let me try a different angle. I have an idea. Tell everyone you won a bet and that's why I'm here. If you win the Hypercubed, then the king can get his crown in the off season."

His face relaxes further, but he doesn't smile. "Can't. I would have had to make that bet earlier in the week, or it looks too suspicious."

"Collusion!" I exclaim.

A couple of people stare our way, but his eyes on me don't waiver.

I put a hand on his chest and go to the ball of my feet.

I speak to his ear. "Bet you'll get me to wear your jersey next time I come to watch a game. I will let you convince me, Your Highness."

I'm halfway through my proposal when he puts a hand on my waist. His fingertips dig into me, like he's clinging to my body. His breathing plays with the tiny hairs of my neck.

I want to push you around, he said that first night.

I had a few bruises on my hips, and a hickey on the back of my thigh the next day.

A shiver runs down my spine.

He speaks to my ear, too. "What's this? A proposition, Miss Moreno? How many of those have you got?"

I pull back. I need to look into his eyes. He gazes at me with humor, but there's nothing else that suggests his memory came back, and he remembers I propositioned him that night in the bar.

He's just teasing me for the betting collusion idea. I read between the lines because I was already thinking of that night.

I'm always thinking about that night, it seems.

"I'm trying to make you smile," I say.

"You don't have to." He runs two fingers down my face again, though there's no chalk to leave marks this time. "Remember I don't really do that."

"I'll break you, Logan."

"I'd like to see you try."

"Uhm, sorry to interrupt." Pen shows next to us. "We're leaving, and I don't know if either of you cares, but I thought you might want to know."

Logan stays right where he was, but I feel shy about the game he and I were playing. I take a step back, and his hand falls.

"Yes, Pen?" I ask.

"Apparently the broadcast of the game showed Evie, Nat, and I here at the box. Comments online are popping up, calling us the Wives And Girlfriends. I've gotten more texts than Nat about it, since she's actually with Damián—"

"We're just friends," Logan and I say at the same time.

"And I'm friends with Bear, yet here we are."

I check my phone quickly.

Ren: how did it take me so long to put this together? You're running Logan King's account. You're the one from that club video with him. And now you're in the friends and family box?

Pri: are you part of the WAGs?!

Ren: ARE YOU DATING LOGAN KING????

I press my lips together and shoot off a quick response.

Evie: It's all work!!!!!!!!!!!!!!!

I put away my phone.

"You could have used a few more exclamation points, Evie."

"Logan! Don't read my texts over my shoulder!"

But he chuckles, and it fixes the whole night.

Chapter 20

Logan

It's early December, on a cloudy and cold Wednesday morning. We're training hard, preparing for the chaos of the traveling and special games happening this month. We can't lose any more games, if we want to secure a spot in the playoffs.

It will be an important month. I can feel it in my bones.

Rain starts falling in the early afternoon. My shirt sticks to my skin, but I don't mind. Some of the guys wear their hoodies, but I welcome the cold. I've been running hot of late. To the point that the last time I spent significant time with Evie, I almost let it slip that I remember the time we shared a few years ago.

I'm ready for her to remember.

I purse my lips and throw the ball. Dom catches it beautifully. I celebrate by shoulder checking the players nearby. I even come close to smiling, but I will only do that if we make it to the playoffs.

And if Evie keeps being adorable, trying to steal a grin from me. I'm not sure how long I'll be able to stop it. Just like I might let it slip that we had a one-night-stand.

Fuck. I think about her all the time. I want her to know I remember, and see in how many ways I can refresh her mind. The only problem is that it means I lost the game, the one where I push until she breaks and lets it slip herself.

Except telling her might be how I win the game. How I control how it happens. I'm not sure I can keep going with life without acknowledging she offered to mark me, too.

I'm thinking about it too much.

Maybe that has something to do with how Evie materializes at the edge of the practice field.

I catch her standing there and shifting from side to side, hugging herself in the rain.

I frown. With a quick hand sign, I let my coach know I need a break, and I jog to her. The closer I come, the clearer the picture becomes. Her hair is in the same bun at the nape of her neck she wears sometimes, but a few wet tendrils are glued to her temples. Tiny drops catch in her hair. Her make up hasn't run, but her chest— Fuck, she's wearing that pretty white blouse with a subtle sheen to it. Only it's almost see-through at the time.

"Where's your jacket?" I ask.

"Hello, I'm cold but fine, thank you. And you?"

"Hi, Evie. Yes, Evie. You're wonderful, but you're wearing a dark bra under this blouse, aren't you?"

"What?!" She looks down at herself and gasps. "Shit!"

I grab her by the arm. Her skin is slick with water. We stop by my bag, where I rummage for my hoodie.

"Take this," I say. "Did you forget what the water does to white tops?"

"I wasn't thinking about it when I came outside!" She slides her arms through the sleeves. "If I didn't think to bring my jacket even though it's winter, what makes you think I thought of my blouse?"

The movement jostles her breasts like she's shaking them to my face, and I bite back a groan.

I grab the zipper and pull it up her body. I need to clear the image out of my mind, and all it brings back. Like me tearing her shirt off, to find that dark bra and getting rid of it to fill my hands with her and finding ink—

Fuck. I say the first thing that comes to mind.

"Zip up and wear this until you're back in your office. Seriously, Evie? You're going to catch a cold. The shirt is stuck to your skin and I can see everything."

With a little imagination, I can see her nipples going hard and dark and visible through her clothes. I could bend down and suck—

"Damn it." I grind my teeth, aware that I'm cursing to myself more than to her.

I bite the words I want to say back, because it's the game we play and I—

And I...

I'm done playing it.

I want the rules to change.

Fuck it.

I'm changing the rules. I'm taking control again.

I stare into her eyes. "Next thing, and everyone will know you have a tattoo."

She stills.

Neither of us moves. Rain falls on us, but I wait for her response.

"Logan..."

My heart beats faster than it did during practice.

"What tattoo?" she asks in a small voice.

I release the zipper and straighten up. The hoodie is long on her, but her full hips stretch the blue material. I lick my bottom lip and stare into her eyes.

"Don't you know?" My voice is deep, only for her. "I remember everything."

Her mouth opens. Her eyes widen. She doesn't say a thing.

If she's running through my words and trying to find hidden meanings in them, I don't like it.

I lift a single finger to the appropriate general area. It hovers at the spot of soft skin, a few inches below the center of her chest, where ink marks her.

"A small sun," I say. "Pretty, if memory serves me right."

She gasps and, next thing I know, she's unzipping the hoodie like she's ready to take it off and maybe burn it in a pyre.

"What are you doing?" I stop her before she can fully release the metal pieces. "You need it."

"It's your hoodie! With your name on the back, isn't it?"

"That's what you care about right now?"

She's the one to hold me from the arm this time. She takes me further away from everyone.

"When did you remember?" Her voice is shrill and she's shivering, but that could be the remnants of standing in the cold rain for a while.

"Six years ago," I say. "A bar. You watch me from afar and then proposition me—"

"Oh my God." She hugs herself again and stares at the grass at our feet. "When did you remember?!"

"Really, Evie? Since the start. I never forgot about you."

Her eyes snap back to me. "And you didn't tell me?"

"I didn't know if you remembered. You never said anything and, believe me, I've paid attention. I've poked. I've waited. But I'm done pretending. Now I learn you've remembered this whole time. Damn, Evie."

"I figured out who you were when I came to work for the Strike— I've seen your face a thousand times since. Then you came to the team. I remember! Of course I remember."

"You could have reached out."

I grind my teeth. I hate that she didn't.

She shakes her head. "We shouldn't talk about this here. Or ever. There are a million things we need to talk about, and none of them are about our one-night-stand years ago."

"We should talk about it. You never planned to tell me, did you?"

A weight settles on my chest to imagine, but it's like she doesn't hear me.

Her eyes are wide open with worry. "I had a call with your agent, and I heard from Selena, and they want me at the gala—"

She's rambling. She's anxious.

I push my feelings away and put my hands on her shoulders.

Why does this bother her so much?

"It's fine." I try to catch her eyes but she evades me. "We're fine. We'll tackle things one at a time."

"No." Her head snaps back up, her chin high. "I'll tackle them. You'll get my emails, and you'll answer them."

"It's been good between us. Nothing has to change just because we both remember we've had sex."

"Keep quiet! No one can know. Especially when there's so much talk already about us being together— I shouldn't be wearing your name on my back."

She tries to undo the zipper again, and I stop her once more.

"It's not my jersey," I argue, her hands in mine so she can't take off the blue piece of clothing. "And you need it."

Her hands are cold.

"No need to panic, Evie."

"Easy for you to say!" She pulls away, but she doesn't try to take off the hoodie so I let her. "Fuck this. I'll send you everything in an email. Don't ignore it."

She still doesn't take off the hoodie when she turns away, so I let her go.

I stand on grass, rain falling over me, and I watch her walk away. I'm nailed in place, breathing deep and questioning what comes next. Why I am trembling like she did, to see my name on her back.

Only three words form in my mind.

This isn't over.

My day doesn't improve once I make it to the locker room. I drop onto the chair by my cubby, and it creaks with the force of it. The space smells of sweat and cleaning products, and the first scent of steam and soap coming from the showers.

I close my eyes and groan. For once, my frown has been so tight that it's threatening to cramp. Perhaps it's time to ask a physio for the right way to massage those muscles. I'm going to need it, if I'm going to keep thinking about Evie this much.

Fuck, she drives me wild. I keep wanting to do things to her, with her. For her. I keep wanting to learn all the things she doesn't tell anyone else. I want to run my fingertips over her tattoo. Everywhere, really. Every time I say her name, a feeling comes with it— frustration, irritation. Playfulness. Doubts. Desire. Curiosity. Meanwhile, she panics at the mere thought of acknowledging we've been together.

I grind my teeth and rub my face. I'm losing my cool around her, and I can't afford that.

"Hey there, King." Saint sits on the chair next to me, his friendly smile subdued for once.

The rest of the guys stand around us. Bear, Dom, Damián, even Rafa sits on his chair in the cubby next to mine, and watches the conversation about to unfurl.

If the quiet, hard to pin down Rafa is involved, this is a serious conversation.

My eyes narrow. "What's going on?"

"Just a chat." One of Saint's dimples makes an appearance. "We noticed Evie wearing your hoodie."

"Is she going to be wearing your jersey at a game next?" Dom asks.

I straighten on my chair and cross my arms. "She was cold in the rain. I don't know about the rest."

Damián cocks his head. "Did you know people online are convinced you two are dating?"

"I am aware." I frown. "We're not. We're... coworkers. Friends."

The last word makes it through my teeth.

"She stormed off the field today," Saint argues. "It looked a bit more serious than that."

"Are you surprised that I said something to make her angry?" I ask. "You wouldn't be staging an intervention if you thought I'm an angel."

It stings, but I get it. They have always made it clear, they adore Evie.

"That's not the full picture," Bear says. His big, tattooed arms are crossed, and they look even bigger. Like a shield.

I raise an eyebrow and wait for them to explain more.

"It's not that we don't get it," Saint adds. "We all understand the appeal of a full figured woman."

All five of them nod.

Saint purses his lips. "But it's Evie... and it's you."

"It has that classic Beauty and the Beast thing going," Damián says.

I take it I'm the Beast.

"We are not dating." My nostrils flare.

Saying that shouldn't bother me as much as it does.

Rafa watches me with understanding eyes. "But you wish you were?"

I purse my lips and say nothing. Even if I know exactly what they're going to think that means.

"It's not that we have a say in that." Saint shrugs. "It's that we care about the two of you."

My frown deepens. I expected them to be protective over Evie, and tell me to stay away. I would hate every second of it, but I would accept the meddling. It meant she had people in her corner, and I appreciate it. Having them include me was unexpected.

"We don't want her hurt," Saint says. "And we like you. We'd like to see you..."

"Happy?" Damián says. "Is there a happy frown we might see one day?"

I snort, and my brow relaxes somewhat.

"You say you're not dating. She says the same." Rafa's deep voice manages to be quiet. "Just be careful, for both of your sakes."

"You've gotten her to do things we couldn't," Dom adds. "She gets you talking and as close to smiling as we've ever seen."

"It looks good on both of you." Damián smiles.

When I say her name these days, I come close to having butterflies in my stomach. Dammit.

"Even if dating isn't in the picture..." Bear lets the words hang until I stare at him. "Be careful as a friend."

I barely have time to nod when a feminine voice comes to us from the hall.

"Uhm... is Saint in there somewhere?"

The wide receiver scrambles off the chair. "Ames?"

"Can I come in?" she asks from around the corner.

"Cover yourselves, lads!" Saint calls and he jogs away to her.

Damián slaps my shoulders a few times and the group disbands. At other times in my life, I would have been pissed by being warned like this. For once, the conversation settles warm on my chest. They said they care about me, too.

All the work I've put into creating bonds with the guys is slowly coming to fruition.

Their concern for Evie helps, too. I would want to protect her if she started dating someone as serious as me. Beauty and the Beast, indeed.

"Here you go, QB." Ames shows up next to me and offers me one of her smoothies.

She's not usually the one delivering our drinks after training, but today she's here carrying a cooler behind her.

"Thank you," I say. "What's the mix today?"

Saint stands next to her, drinking from his smoothie all casual... except for his eyes. They're glued to Amelia. Huh.

She doesn't seem to notice. "Peanut butter delight. It has coconut milk as well, chia seeds, berries, banana, spices... you know, all the good stuff for pro athletes."

I take a whiff— I smell the peanuts and coconut milk, banana and berries. I taste it, and the hint of cinnamon bursts on my tongue.

"Mmh, It's good," I say.

"Thanks," she smiles. "I have to go deliver the rest, before I kidnap Saint for dinner with my brother. He surprised us both with a quick fly by in town."

We say bye and Ames walks away. Saint is about to follow when I stop him.

"Is she single?" I ask.

His frown competes with the best of mine. "No. She has a long-term boyfriend. Why do you want to know?"

I shrug. "Just putting two and two together. Suddenly wondering about your love life."

His eyes narrow but Saint doesn't add much.

"Didn't you just ask about Evie?" I raise an eyebrow. "Then give me a whole speech about it?"

"Revenge doesn't suit you, King," Saint says, before punching my shoulder and walking away.

I'm about to laugh, when the ping I set for Evie's emails comes from my pocket.

When I read her email, all humor evaporates.

Chapter 21

Evie

It's the end of the work day and I'm itching to leave. I want to run home, take a bath, lick my wounds, and forget that Logan remembers we had sex. That he's known this whole time.

I never forgot about you.

Fuck.

One minute. I can afford one minute to collapse before I go home.

I'm at my desk. I place both elbows on the wooden surface, rest my head in my hands, and groan. My screen is still on, the window with the email I sent Logan still open. He's going to hate it but, as long as he doesn't ignore it, I can live with it.

I got invited to the team's holiday gala. Things are going so well with the Logan project, the boss wants to maximize on the success and have it be the strongest first year a Strike quarterback has ever had. Selena wants me to push harder, and the fundraising party is part of that. But attending the gala will require a new dress and new shoes I can't afford, and possibly having to spend money on an auction and related donations.

In my world, that's a crisis. That's why I ran to Logan after the call with Selena and his agent. I needed his help.

Silly me, honestly. Reason number one hundred and three why I don't get close to people. It makes me believe I could ask for help and it wouldn't get me in trouble. Thinking I could rely on him threw a bomb between us instead. Now my one night with Logan is out between us, and handling whatever comes next is an extra thing on my plate.

"Seriously? All I get is an email?"

I jump in my chair. Logan stands at my door. I keep it ajar in between meetings, according to the organization's open door policy for us mid-level folk. He only had to push it with a finger to see me slumped over my desk.

I purse my lips. "All you need to know is written there."

"It's written in point form." His voice makes it an accusation.

"And broken down into a minimal outline to keep things clear and concise."

"Oh, I noticed." He comes into the room and stands right in the middle of my office, in all his height and wide shoulders. "One heading reads 'facts'. The other says, 'tasks'. You highlighted 'I'm not going to the gala' in orange. It's *underlined*."

I turn off my computer and stand. He tracks me from his place, dark gray eyes fixed on my movements.

My purse hangs from the back of my chair and I grab it. "All I need is a good reason to decline the invitation. Whoever has an idea first can email the other. My only request is that we coordinate the story, so they don't decide I'm not doing my part in the project."

I round my desk and make for the door, but Logan doesn't move. To go past him, I'd have to squeeze through the small space behind him. I'm too proud to do that.

"I'm going home now, if you don't mind," I say.

He scrutinizes me with those shark eyes of his as he steps to the side. "Is this because we've had sex?"

"Logan!"

"You send me a curt email. Refuse to go to the gala with me, even though Selena and my agent would love to see it happen. What's next? No more dates? Just because I know you have a tattoo? I know we had incredible chemistry together, but I didn't expect that giving me a few hours in a college dorm would change everything between us six years later."

"That's not— I just—" I cut myself off. "Fuck."

I close the door and lean back on it. Logan faces me, one of his epic frowns in place and his arms crossed.

"That's only part of it." I clench my jaw. "You didn't tell me you remembered!"

"You didn't either, Evie." He takes a step closer. "Neither of us lied. This wasn't miscommunication, if we both chose to say nothing. But it also means we both did this, so how am I the bad guy here?"

I hate that he's right.

"Will you ever, just once," I say, "fall for one of my distraction techniques?"

"Why do you need distraction techniques? Jesus, Evie. Tell me the truth. I know you're angry, but why?"

"I try not to lie. Distraction is all I have left when I don't want to answer, in an industry of pleasantries and networking."

"You're doing it again. You're answering that question so I forget the second."

I purse my lips. He pins me with the intensity of his eyes. I want to look away, hide from his inspection, but I don't. My hands are at my back, and I dig my nails into the door. They don't go far.

He takes another step towards me. "Why are you angry, Evie?"

We're close. His arms are an inch away from my breasts, and my nipples harden like they want to reach for his warmth. My body is a traitor, much more concerned with how this moment echoes that time at the bar, when he sauntered to me and told me we should test our chemistry before leaving the place together.

I could ask him now if he remembers like I do. If there are nights when he thinks of it and wonders what it would take to feel like that again.

My lungs work fast. Our eyes remain locked, and he's looking into mine with that lie-detector energy.

"Tell me," he says.

It's that voice that breaks my defenses. It's a request, the kind that pains him to ask for.

"I'm angry..." I gulp. "I'm angry because I'm scared."

His frown deepens. His eyes shift between mine, thoughts running through his mind. I let him study me, but I don't say anything else.

Eventually, his features relax. A notch still marks his brow, but it's not the killer frown he had until thirty seconds ago. My heart mirrors him, and it slows down, too.

A corner of his lips curls up. "Let me help you, Mystery Girl."

"What?"

He uncrosses his arms. One hand goes into his joggers' pocket. The other comes to me.

He tips my chin up with a finger. "Mystery Girl. That's what I called you in my head for years. You're still a mystery to me, Evie. One I want to unravel. Until then... the least I can do is prove you can rely on me."

"What if that scares me, too?"

My voice comes out thin. His thumb makes a pass over the curve of my jaw.

"Then I'll move real slow," he says.

***

We're walking out of the building together, on the way to the parking lot. I'm still a bit shaken from his declaration, and my stomach clenches in a mix of hunger and nerves.

"We need to talk," he says. "Let's go out for dinner tonight."

He wants me to trust him. I'm not sure yet I can do that, but we do need to talk.

I wear my jacket. The hoodie he let me borrow hangs from his arm.

"I don't know if that's a good idea." I stop with him, next to which I assume is his car. "People figured out my name on social media. It's one of the things I'm worried about."

"If they know your name, more content can't make it worse, right?"

"This is precisely why we need to talk. There's a lot to unpack, Logan."

He purses his lips. "All right. Come to my place, then. We'll order something. Talk in private."

I bite the inside of my cheek. I'm not sure that's better.

"Mystery Girl." His eyes twinkle with suppressed humor. "You're safe. I'm not going to jump you— unless you ask me to."

I tsk. "Don't call me that in public!"

"Only in private, then?" He chuckles. It's a good sound.

"Stop. I don't think we need to go anywhere. We can make it a quick chat."

He gives me a long suffering sigh. "Fine. At least it's not raining anymore."

We make it to my car, and he leans on my door. It's a modest, older silver sedan, and he makes no mention of it, despite being surrounded by sleek models and fashionable SUVs made to look like tanks.

I step closer, only to make the conversation a bit easier. With him resting on the metal door, I don't have to look up too high.

"So what did Selena and my agent say, exactly?" he asks.

"They're ecstatic with everything we're doing. That the fans and the press are obsessed with you, with the team. New fans are coming in, your agent is getting more inquiries for sponsorships— all the fun stuff."

His brows quirk. It's good news, and he doesn't understand my fears.

"Selena is excited," I add. "She said that the mix of great interviews with the TV crew, strong social media presence, and your social appearances outside of the weekly team responsibilities, are headlining the kind of season she wanted for you. That if I kept it up, she could see me getting everything I wanted."

"Evie— how is this a problem?"

"They said they want to support our efforts. That's why they're inviting me to the gala. I reminded them you and I are not dating, and they reassured me that they don't have an opinion on that either way. That they only want to give us more opportunities to keep doing what we're doing."

"I like to think I'm a smart man, but you're going to have to explain this further. Isn't this all you wanted?"

I shift on my feet, and pull my jacket closed a bit more. It's a cold December evening, and the breeze needles deep into my bones.

Logan isn't putting it all together. I might have to explain, using all my words, and opening up my chest in the process.

I bite my cheek again. He studies me as usual. I stay silent a bit longer. With no words, he offers me his hoodie again.

I shake my head, but the gesture helps.

"One thing is that my friends are giving me a hard time," I say. "They swear there's something between us."

"Do they know...?" He leaves the question hanging, but points between us with a long, straight index finger.

"No." I snort-chuckle. "No. But that's easier to handle than the fact my parents are asking about it. With them it's a lot more complicated than that."

I don't want him to ask about that, so I jump to add more. It's all the truth, so I hope he doesn't ask me more tonight.

At least, even if the next part is the hardest, he already knows about it to some degree.

"It's a lot for me, and we're only adding by spending more time together outside, especially something beyond casual outings. The worst part is the gala in ten days."

I have to say it. I need him to understand. It still stings.

It's one of those times when he knows to keep silent, because he'll get more out of me that way. I don't know how or when he learned this trick, but it works. He's good at reading me, and it's something I don't really enjoy, but I can live with for once.

I sigh. "I can't afford to go to the gala."

The wrinkles between his brows intensify. It's all I need to know he wants more.

Maybe I'm good at reading him, too. It's a small relief.

"You know I live on a tight budget." I suck on my bottom lip. "Where do I find a dress like that? With such short notice? Worst of all, how do I pay for it? And since I work for the Strike, will they expect me to participate in the auctions at the charity event?"

He stands, bringing him closer to me. His serious, focused frown is in place, and he goes as far as to open his mouth to tell me something I'm sure I don't want to hear.

"Logan— don't. Don't offer to pay."

He closes his mouth at first. His eyes narrow.

Eventually he finds the words and gives them to me in a monotone voice. "I won't offer, but you have to know I'm thinking about it."

"I knew you would, but I can't accept it."

"Why on earth not?"

"Can we just— not go there tonight? Please."

"You still plan to hold back?"

"Of course."

"Mhh. What did you call me once? Stubborn?"

"Takes one to know one, I guess."

I don't know what else to say, but I don't need to hunt for the right words. He puts his finger on my chin again, and he aligns my face to him.

I stop breathing.

"The conversation isn't over, Miss Moreno." His eyes drop to my lips.

"Let's see if you still feel that way when I start asking you a thousand questions back. I'm not the only one who holds themselves back."

He releases me, steals my keys from my hand, and opens my door for me.

He raises an eyebrow my way. "Maybe I will like it more than you think."

I like it when you bite back.

I chew on my bottom lip, to stop myself from saying anything else that could get me in more trouble than I am.

I climb onto the driver seat. He leans down into the space, the open door protecting him from the breeze.

He offers me my keys. "Do with that what you will, Evie. Good night."

He closes the door, I turn on the car, and drive away with my heart beating from somewhere behind my clavicles.

He stands there until I can't see him anymore.

I'm still thinking of the past few hours, when I get a call from my parents that derails every plan.

Chapter 22

Logan

We have a Thursday night game in Week 15 that we barely win. The defense had trouble again, and we weren't as strong as we could have been on offense. We hear all about it on Friday morning. By early afternoon, Coach releases us early with the expectation that we will use the time to rest and recover, before the gala on Monday night and the training he'll squeeze out of us the next week.

My first thought is to check in on Evie again, but no one responds when I knock at her office door. No muffled words make it out either. When I spy onto the parking lot, I don't see her car.

"Fuck," I mutter, before I jump in my SUV and drive home.

Mystery Girl disappeared again. She left me standing in the parking lot and, unlike years before, this time I didn't expect she would hide.

I haven't heard from her in days. She hasn't been around the building, checking in with my teammates and asking coaches about their children or pets. Two days ago, I came half an hour before the pregame hotel curfew, only so I could go to her office. She wasn't there. I've texted her, even sent an email, and I got no response.

I'd never admit it out loud, but I smelled the hoodie she wore, in a desperate search for traces of her. Lavender still hangs around the fabric, so I didn't put it in the wash. Not until I know she's okay.

Something's wrong.

My house has a big, nice garage, but I don't open the door right away and park on the concrete pad outside. I tap my fingers on the wheel, deciding my next steps.

I threw my phone on the console cubby earlier, and I grab it now to text her again. If she doesn't answer, I'll call her.

A notification shows I have several messages, but none of them are from her.

> Saint: welcome to the group chat, King.

> Dom: we held a meeting and the motion passed. You're in

> Leon: if you leave the chat, we'll just keep adding you back

The texts arrived ten minutes ago in quick succession. My brows keep the frown, but humor pulls at my lips after reading their words.

> Logan: do I have a say at all?

> Dom: of course. You get to say thank you.

> Leon: we need to keep an eye on our shiny new QB, and you're cool enough. You handled the intervention well

> Saint: we've learned to read between the glares.

Damián: and I'm inviting you over for a holiday dinner. With the BBQ several weeks ago, it will be the second time you get to come home and spend time with all of us. It was time

Logan: is this because your dog liked me?

Damián: Barkley is a great judge of character

Logan: send me the details for dinner. I'll stay in the group chat. I guess you're all cool enough, too

Dom: details incoming

I lock the screen and throw my phone into the dashboard cubby again. The tapping on the wheel returns, but it's a happier sound.

My chest is open. My lips are relaxed enough that I know a ghost smile rests there. This feels big. It's a major step into what I wanted out of joining this team.

I really want to tell Evie.

This time, when I grab my phone, it isn't to text her or call her. Ever since the club, I've had her address saved for an emergency. I don't even make it out of the car, before I follow my GPS directions to a different place.

At first, I have trouble finding a parking spot. Then, she doesn't answer when I buzz her place. A few people stare in my direction. Concern shadows their eyes when they look at me but I don't take it personally. I'm a big guy, wearing jeans and keeping the hood of my jacket up over my head, and standing for a long time by the locked doors. No one interrupts me, so I keep at it.

She still doesn't answer.

For a moment I wonder if this is one of those times when I'm pushing too hard. But worry has wormed into my guts, taking hold of my organs and pulling down like a fucking rollercoaster.

Something happened.

A large person with strong and masculine features approaches me, keys in hand.

"Can I help you?" He asks, eyebrows furrowed. The way his chin is tipped tells me he means business.

I face him. "My friend lives here. I can't reach her."

The moment he recognizes me, his face changes. A child-like joy fills him.

"Holy sh— are you—?"

"I'm Logan King." I offer him a hand. "Do you mind letting me in? I need to check in on my friend."

"Yeah! Yeah, of course."

We get into the building, which gives way to a small hall and a single elevator. From her old text, I know her apartment is on the fifth floor. I'm restless, wanting to run up the stairs tucked to the side of the space, if it means I'll make it faster. But her neighbor is staring at me like I'm a miracle incarnate, sent from the heavens to materialize in front of him to give him a powerful message.

Too bad my mind is blank. The only reason I gaze back is because I can hear Evie's voice reminding me of my social credit with the public. I shouldn't tell him to fuck off and let me go to Evie, though I want to.

I bite my cheek and search for better words to say the same thing.

"Uhm..." He takes his phone out. "Can we take a picture?"

"Sure, but I really need to run after."

"Of course! Thank you so much."

I don't know what face I make in the photo and I don't care. As soon as he snaps the picture, I nod and run up the stairs.

Her apartment is one of four, distributed around a plain room. I find her door, labeled with the number she mentioned in her original text, and ring the bell.

Ring it again when she doesn't answer. I'm starting to breathe faster, anxiety twisting my guts.

"Evie!" I knock on her door.

The peephole has a yellow tinge to it, and I tell myself there's light in her place.

I knock again. "Evie!"

The door opens, but no more than I need to wedge a shoe in there. Just in case she panics and tries to close it on me again. Her fingers curl around the wood, and most of her face becomes visible, but she doesn't talk. Two large, tired eyes stare at me.

"You're pale." My brows furrow.

"You're here?!" Shock constricts her words.

She shakes her head in disbelief. The messy bun on top of her head wobbles.

I frown. "I've texted you. Emailed you. Where have you been?"

"Why are you here? I can't believe it—"

"Are you okay? I've been worried about you."

That steals her complaints away. She quiets, and gazes at me with...

Is she tearing up?

My chest caves in.

I move automatically, trying to reach her, holding back from steamrolling her door open, but she blinks it all away.

"Evie, let me in."

She shakes her head. "My place is a mess. I am a mess."

"I don't care."

"I probably smell."

I place my hand on the door, like I want to push but I'm waiting for the green light. "I don't care. Let me in?"

"You have hyperosmia and I haven't showered in three days—"

"Evie. I'll prove to you I don't care. Here, let me sniff your neck."

I pull back my hood, like seeing me properly will help.

"You're being ridiculous!" she says.

"You're being silly, arguing with me like this. Please let me in."

Hesitation etches itself on her face.

I give her an exasperated look. "I have been surrounded by sweaty men ever since I can remember. Do you know what a high school locker room smells like within one week of the start of the season?"

She snorts, and her doubt slowly evaporates. I'm one or two words away from winning.

"Mystery Girl, I'm sure you smell much better than the guys after a game."

"Don't call me that." She sighs and opens the door.

I come into her place with measured movements, in case she gets spooked. But she walks away without paying attention to me and dives onto her couch. She cocoons herself in a large bed comforter, not giving me a chance to see her in her pajamas much, or take in the scent of her neck for evidence. That would have been such a great excuse to get close to her. Hold her, and make sure she's okay.

Her place is small. My wild guess is that the whole apartment fits in the combined space of my bedroom, closet, and bathroom. Despite her warnings, it's clean except for a few plates, mugs, and boxes on the counter. Past them, a small kitchen with minimal appliances and only a few cupboards.

No pile of scrunched up tissues, or medication bottles laying around. She doesn't seem sick. But for her to have skipped days at work, this must be big.

I stroll to her, hands in the pockets of my jeans. She sits on the one sofa in the living room, across from a medium-sized TV. The walls are light blue, like I remember from our video calls, and the comforter is dark blue around her.

The duvet covers most of her. I bend at the waist and peer into the small breathing hole she left open, only big enough to show her eyes, nose, and top lip.

I smirk. "You okay, there, Evie?"

"Mhh."

I almost smile at the sound. She sounds just like me.

"Did you decorate your whole place in the team's colors?" I ask.

"I decorated it with the fashion sense of whatever I could buy on clearance."

I gently pry the blanket loose, until I can see her whole face and the messy bun on her head.

"What's going on?" I ask. "Was it something I said?"

She deflates but doesn't cover herself further. "No, it wasn't you."

I sit next to her. "What happened?"

"Logan... I'm not good at opening up to people."

"I've noticed."

"You're not good at it either, you know?"

"I know. Tell me anyway."

She rubs her lips together. "Why don't you share about yourself?"

It's clear what she's doing. She explained her distraction techniques last time we talked. This is one of the walls she puts up, when she's feeling vulnerable.

If I balance the scales, it might make it easier for her to open up. I want to know her badly enough that I'll open up for her. If I'm asking her to be brave, courage on my part is a fair ask.

I sigh. "Since I was a kid, people rarely asked something about me. It was always about my dad, or football sometimes. Me? Not really. I learned to cherish the privacy of it. To be known is a two-way gift, and I'm careful with it. Not everyone gets to know me."

She watches me like she's the one putting pieces together now.

I lean closer and offer some more. "But being careful has a cost. I've spent a lot of time alone. I'm not close to my parents, and I never made true friends. That's why I've been trying so hard to get close to the guys. I think I found the right people, so I'm trying to remember how to open up, too."

"And you want to know me, too?"

I nod. "So what's going on?"

She chews on her lip for a while, before her eyes leave me.

She stares at her lap. "It's... my parents."

"Are they okay?"

She opens her mouth as if to tell me more, but then closes it again. She glances at me, as if to check my reaction to the little she has shared.

I don't say anything. In the past, silence has let her push through the struggle, until she tells me a bit more. I cross my fingers and wait, tracking the small changes on her expressive face, and counting seconds until she makes up her mind.

"Maybe I should start from the beginning?"

"Tell me everything, Evie."

She takes a deep breath. "My parents... they came here from Argentina when I was a toddler. By the time I was seven, I was making phone calls and reading government paperwork for them. They wanted me to focus on school, so I had a degree to back me up as our family grew roots here. But that meant that they tried to do things on their own, too, and those turned out terribly for us. They speak English, but get nervous around anything official. I still think people took advantage of them, encouraging them to sign things they shouldn't have, and we're still dealing with the aftermath."

Her voice isn't rough, but it's not steady, either. It's somewhere in between, with a sense of breathlessness to it, like she's trying to get it all out before she can change her mind.

I put a hand on her back and let her get through it.

She rubs her face. "Responsibilities multiplied as years went by. I grew up fast. Now I'm an adult who has no idea how to get herself and her parents out of this mess in time, before everything gets worse. We just got a letter from the bank and I just— I pulled on the emergency break. I'm so tired of taking care of people and having to juggle all the balls. My life can't move forward, because I don't have the energy to figure out where the lines are with people... or even within myself. Am I giving too much? I'd rather give too little, if that will keep me from having to take care of someone else. I'm too damn tired, you know?"

She stares at me, searching for an answer. Do I know? Hell if I do, but I nod, and desperately hope I understand. This is the final key, and it will open doors to things I cannot see yet, but which I crave.

A deep seated sigh leaves her. "I'm constantly chasing after rest. I fantasize about a vacation where I do nothing. Nothing but to breathe, eat, swim, and read in the sun. But there's always another reason to stress, another fire to put out. So I come home and spend time by myself, and I hope it makes a dent in this relaxation deficit I keep running. But sometimes— once in a while— I need more than a quiet evening."

I want to make that vacation happen. To start. I want to find a hundred ways to make it better.

"Do your parents help?" I ask.

I don't think she has many people in her corner. There's no reason I can't be the one to show up for her.

She nods. "They're trying. But they can't keep up with everything, so I keep stepping up. They're my only family, you know? I can't leave them to struggle. They don't have anyone else, either."

"So you only have them, too?"

The idea she's been so alone stabs me in the chest, right between two ribs, so the sharp tip scratches right on my heart.

"Yeah," she says. "The therapists I follow on social media tell me that helping my parents at the age I needed to be helped, crossed a few wires and now I can't ask for support. That it caused hyper-independence on my part. Difficulties with boundaries. You know, all the classics."

I'm alone by choice and trying to change it. She's alone because she's hurting, and unsure if she can change it.

I take a deep breath, and hope it soothes the scrape of the blade still stuck in my flesh.

I lean closer to her, shoulder to shoulder. "Thanks for telling me all of this. I'll take care of your secrets, Evie."

She gives me the first sign of a smile. "I think I believe you."

I push the comforter further down, until her neck and shoulders come into view. A bunch of her hair comes off her bun, and it falls down at her nape. A few tendrils halo her temples.

"Don't look at my hair." She pats the strands away. "It will ruin the moment. My dry shampoo is holding on strong but it won't take close inspection."

"You're pretty like this. You look... homely."

"Homely?" She gives me a pained expression, but humor weaves through it. "Isn't that a euphemism for plain?"

"To me it means you look—"

I interrupt myself before I can finish the sentence, but I hear the words echoing in my brain.

To me it looks like I'm home.

Damn.

"I look like what?" she asks.

"You look comfortable," I finally say. "Like there's no pretense."

I gulp, forcing the thoughts away for later contemplation.

"Uhm," she utters. "Thank you, I think."

Her deep brown eyes still look sad, and it centers me like nothing else. I can't have that.

"I have only one more question," I say. "It's a critical part in all of this."

I lift my fingers to her chin, and gently invite her to look me in the eyes.

She does.

I jump in and offer myself to the gods.

"Who takes care of you?" I ask.

Chapter 23

Evie

No one has asked me that before. That's why my heart stutters, and my lungs find it hard to keep their rhythm.

Who takes care of you?

I take a slow, deep breath to try to bring it all back to normal. It only works somewhat, but I stare into his deep blue eyes.

I gather the iron in my blood and I make steel out of it, and it strengthens my voice.

"I take care of myself," I say.

He leans a little closer. "That can't be easy."

"It's not, but I don't know another way. That's why once in a while I will get a particular piece of bad news— too many fires at once— and I crumble. I hide for a little while."

The whole time, I know I should keep going, but it's like my body has flamed out and it won't move, no matter what I do. So I take my sick days and turn off my phone. I disconnect the buzzer. Rot on the sofa for three days. It's not rest, because my brain keeps screaming at me that I should be doing something. That I should work and do more. But I just can't do more.

Eventually, the screaming wins the battle. I manage to pick myself up, and go back to the grind.

"It's fine." I shrug. "I'll get over it by Monday."

"What happened?" His voice is soft. Careful. "What triggered it this time?"

Like he could read my mind and he heard everything I didn't say, and he wants to know more, but he'll be gentle with it.

My chest swells. It's a feeling I've had before with him, when he undoes the layers of my answers, and finds ways to reach even deeper. It's a raw sensation, rooted in the discomfort of doing something new.

I'm going to answer, and that's something I never do... because I don't let anyone ask.

He asked.

I take another deep breath. "The day Selena and your agent invited me to the gala— that night, my parents called. The letter they got from the bank... well, things are... bleak."

In his usual approach, he doesn't say anything, hoping I'll add more in the space he leaves open for me.

"We may lose my childhood home." I stare at my lap. "We've had to negotiate a payment plan a few times with the bank. We haven't been able to keep up with the pace they want. We've been making inquiries to see if we can negotiate something else. The letter said they won't consider it."

He rubs his lips, like he's holding back thoughts. Overwhelm builds inside of me, seizing my throat and forcing me to stop talking. The frown that always marks his face almost disappears, and he surrounds my shoulders with an arm.

He pulls me close. "Let me help."

"Logan—"

"I'm not offering to pay the debt off yet, so don't panic. But I could loan you some—"

"*Yet*?! You can't— I can't— I couldn't do a loan—"

"Okay, I guess that's a no for now. It's fine. We don't have to talk about that yet—"

He sees my panic, and changes tactics before I can protest again.

"But what if," he says, "instead of hiding in your apartment and scaring the shit out of me, we get you to the gala? My treat. At least take that."

"Logan..."

"Take a break. Take some help. No one can do life alone."

I pace my breathing, in the hope it will keep my feelings in check. The emotions that underpin everything are still raw, and they bring a new ache to my chest.

Shadows cross his eyes, frustrations he's not sharing. I'm about to ask when he says more.

His eyes lock on mine. "Let me show you that you can let someone in. That someone wants to help. My actions are much louder than my words."

"Aren't you a loner, too?"

"I'm insufferably picky. Not the same. I didn't fit with my previous team, so I didn't get close. But I like the guys here, so I'm changing that. I'm in sports, Evie. Of course I know we all need a good team."

"So you'll let the guys close? Really?"

"Hey, don't sound so suspicious." His voice mocks offense. "I'm in the group chat now. I'm going to Damián's for Christmas dinner. I think I'm killing it."

A reticent smile appears on my face. "Fair. You win."

"Let a few people in, Mystery Girl. I'll handle the gala stuff. We'll start there."

I chew on my lip. Half my heartbeats drum to warn me, reminding me this is a risk. That I'm jumping off a cliff and I don't know if there's a parachute in this baggage I carry with me.

A nod is all I manage.

"Excellent." He pulls me closer. "Now I need you to know something."

I stare at him.

He smirks, dives for my neck, and takes a deep breath.

"Logan! Oh my god." I push away.

He keeps me close, strong enough not to strain despite my efforts. "You smell good, Evie. Maybe a little musky, but I don't mind it too much."

"Unbelievable."

"Fight me all you want. I like it, and it doesn't change what I think."

"Why would you say that?" I laugh.

"Because I want you to let me run a bath for you, but I don't want you to think it's because I'm sensing the fumes." His voice remains deadpan.

"Stop!" I say, but my laughter doesn't go away.

"I'm not even trying to get a peek. I have an amazing memory of that night, you know? I don't need to update the image in my head to remember the details."

"This isn't funny!"

"For once I have a weekend off, and only a half day on Monday. I can't think of anything more fun to do with my free time, than getting you naked and in the water."

"You're the worst."

"Incorrect. I'm the best. I'm so selfless I'm not even going to try to join you. I'm going to let you relax."

"Logan—"

"Remember how I like the guys so I'm getting close to them? I like you too, so this is what you get. You're stuck with me now."

Tenderness still swirls inside, when Logan tears me away from my sofa nest. He leads me to the bathroom, where he filled my basic, formed plastic shower-tub combo with water and bubbles.

"I had to use your body wash for the bubbles." He delivers me to the middle of the room. "I don't know how long they'll last. Now undress, get in, and call me if you need anything."

I don't plan to do any of those things until he leaves, but I keep him with me for a second longer.

"You've been bossy since I first met you," I say. "But I'm not complaining today. Thank you."

A corner of his lips tilts upward, but he says nothing. He nods and leaves, closing the door behind him.

I let myself melt into the water. I sink into it, holding my breath for a good fifteen seconds before I come out again. The sigh that leaves me takes some of my worries away, my chest lighter than it's been the past few days.

The space between the tub's edge and the wall is small, but the right size to rest against. I lean my head back and take a slow, deep breath.

Logan and I are getting close. Where I could have doubted it before, confused it for familiarity due to how close we work together, I can't lie to myself about it after today.

The way he showed up. The way he stayed.

The fact we're joking about our one-night-stand, but nothing has changed.

How in all his directness, he said with his whole chest that he wants to help, treat me to the gala— whatever that meant— and get close to me. He said I need to let people in, and he offered to step up in that regard.

I chew the inside of my cheek. It takes effort to keep my breath even, when it wants to race again.

What am I supposed to do with all of that?

If I tried to stop it, he would insist. Yet all I feel is weightlessness, because when it's hard to ask for what you need, having someone who wants to be there without being asked... someone who is willing to poke at your walls, when you're too set in your ways to invite them in... it's a gift.

Friendship may not be such a terrible idea. Trust has built between us. He earned it with his bluntness and consistency.

I let the warmth of that seep into me, right through my skin from the water around me. Time goes by unchecked, because this is something I've hungered for, and I'm letting myself count how long it will last.

My movements are minimal for a while longer. The water starts to get cold, and a shiver runs down my spine.

I sigh and blink a few times to come back to reality. I remain in the water for now and wash thoroughly, scrubbing my skin clean. It's time for my hair, ahead of emptying the tub and rinsing it all away with the shower.

Except I discover my shampoo is done. I forgot to replace the bottle earlier in the week, before I went into crisis mode and into my bog woman era.

I purse my lips and think. My options are getting out of the tub, half-drying myself, running for the bottle and coming back, and managing alone. Or I could call for Logan, since he's here in my apartment and could help.

He has seen me naked, even if it's been years since. I'll still do my best to cover up, but he told me to call for him if I needed anything. I don't have to make a big deal of it.

"Logan?"

I stir the water, to build the bubbles around me again. It works— minimally. Enough that I don't think I'll flash him by accident.

He doesn't hear me so I call again. I start to worry that he left without telling me, and I'm about to try for a third time, but he enters the bathroom before I can.

He doesn't hesitate, his movements assertive like we do this all the time. His eyes survey the scene quickly, and if I hadn't been paying such close attention, I would have missed the hungry look that flashes across his face.

He locks it down tight, and limits his gesture to raising a questioning eyebrow.

"I ran out of shampoo." I hug my legs, hoping it covers my breasts more effectively than the flimsy suds.

I'm naked in here, after all, and the brief desire he revealed settled too well in my lower belly.

I lick my bottom lip. "There's a new bottle in the hallway closet. Do you mind getting it for me?"

He nods and leaves, only to return within a minute, bottle in hand. The lid is open, and he brings it to his nose.

"Mmh." His brows relax to a nearly neutral state. "It smells good."

I take an arm out of the water and ask for the bottle. "Thank you."

He shakes his head, ignores my hand, and kneels next to me by the tub.

"I'll do it." He squirts a bunch into his hand and frowns. "Is this enough for long hair?"

Despite my thoughts earlier, my first instinct is to panic.

"What are you doing?" I ask.

"What does it look like?"

"You can't wash my hair." I rest my arms on the side of the tub, letting the formed plastic cover me.

I keep my arms close to me, letting them block the view of my breasts. The water is high enough that he'll only get to see the curve of my back, disappearing into bubbles at my mid back.

I'm hoping it comes across like a power pose, as if I'm a powerful CEO rather than a naked woman in a tub.

He shrugs. "I can, and I would like to."

"It's too much."

It's touch, and I'm starved for it. It's a whole new level of intimacy between us, when I'm just getting used to the idea of friendship. It might confuse my skin, and tempt me with being caressed by Logan again. Held and manhandled by him.

I can't accept touch, if I'm hoping for friendship. And it won't be friendship, if I ask for touch.

He may be good at reading my thoughts, but he doesn't this time.

"Too much, what?" He rubs his hands together, to spread the product between his palms. The arch of his eyebrow is challenging.

Carefully, he runs his hands over my wet hair. His dark gray eyes follow the movement, rather than inspect me this time.

A shiver runs down my back and I arch like a cat.

Touch, or friendship? It's hard to decide, when his hands are on me and they unearth tingling sensations all over. The kind that makes me think of bodies rubbing against each other.

The marks he left in my memory, that night we had together. They light up and blink steadily, like they're warning me something is changing, and I better pay attention. They want me to remember how good it felt to be in his arms.

I can't let myself crave his arms.

"You wouldn't do this for the guys," I finally argue.

If he's friends with them, I'm pretty sure he doesn't touch them like this.

His fingers stall at my nape.

He looks into my eyes again, hands cradling my head. "Preferential treatment for someone I've slept with."

"I'm serious, Logan."

His brows furrow. He works the shampoo into my hair, firm fingertips massaging my scalp.

I bite my lip not to moan in pleasure, and wait for his answer.

"I think I'm serious, too," he says. "It feels natural. I'm not questioning it."

I watch him for a couple of minutes. The concentration on his face, the sweetness of the gesture, and how it makes me want to melt into the water again and let him pet me for a while.

"Let's not question it, Evie." His voice is deep. "Can it be enough that I want to?"

With his fingers working magic on me, I can let it be okay for now.

Touch, or friendship? I'm not sure what I need from him the most.

I nod and sigh, and rest my chin on my hands. He washes my hair with care, and I pretend I'm not scared that I need both of those at all.

Chapter 24

Evie

After rinsing off, I change into fresh pajamas in my bedroom, to find Logan brought the comforter from the living room and made my bed. Only a couple of months earlier, I would have been embarrassed by it. Now that he sought me out when I disappeared— with his version of gentleness and dependability— I managed to simply take a deep breath and go with it.

I find my favorite oversized sweater and put it on. It falls to my thighs, practically covering my soft cotton shorts. My hair is still wet, but I comb it and let it air dry. With moisturizer all over my skin, I feel like a new person.

The bed didn't prepare me to discover Logan tidied my kitchen and living room, too. My stomach churns but, when I smell the food he got us for dinner, I tell myself it's due to how ravenous I am.

"I hope you like shawarmas." He opens a cupboard and takes out a couple of plates. "I found a place with great reviews nearby."

"That looks like Moonbake Shawarma. You're going to love it."

I don't have a dining table. We sit on my sofa. He smells the food before giving it a big bite— and moaning.

The sound reverberates in my bones. I stuff my mouth with food, so I don't say anything I might regret.

"Wow," he said after his second bite. "You were not exaggerating."

"It's the pickled veggies and that garlic sauce."

"It's all of it. This is delicious."

His frown is there, but something about his eyes show how much he's enjoying the meal. I'm not used to having company, and he's tall and muscly enough to occupy plenty of space. It does something to the very air of my apartment, and the contrast gets me talking before I know what I'm doing.

"You got bigger after college, didn't you?" I ask.

He glances at me. "Some. Mostly lean mass, a bit of height."

"It was my first impression, when I saw you at Selena's office that first time."

"Mine was shock." He swallowed another bite. "I think I knew just from hearing your voice, but when you turned to look at me—"

His eyes are cast to the floor as he reviews his memory of the moment.

I lick my lip. "I guess you didn't have time to prepare like I did."

He shakes his head. "But I recognized you right away."

"I can take that as a compliment, I think." I dab my lips with a paper napkin. "I was convinced there was no way you would remember me."

"Why not?" He raises an eyebrow at me and takes another bite.

If I catch him stealing glances at my thighs, I don't say anything.

"You're famous, Logan. I may not have known who you were when we met at the bar, but that changed just a few months later. Even when your old coach kept you on the bench for nine out of ten games, the camera managed to land on you regardless. Your life is too big to get caught in a random one-night-stand years ago."

You must have had many other partners since. That night was special to me, but I know it doesn't mean it was special to you.

I don't say it in as many words, but he's back to being able to read my mind.

"You left me with a million questions, Evie. I tried to get you to stay the night—you left while I couldn't ask for more. But I thought we had a good time. We had chemistry. We fit. We could have done it all over again, next time I came around town."

"I was only looking for one night. Nothing more. One time is fun. More is the start of something. You know I don't do that."

He squints in the way that tells me he's putting puzzle pieces together. "We had sex more than once that night. Does that mean we had something?"

"It's... that rule doesn't apply to that night. That's something I decided when you and I— I decided on it afterwards. One and done."

He cocks his head. "Did I leave an impression?"

I open my mouth to reply with banter, but it doesn't come out with the same ease as usual. The truth is he did, but I can't come clean with it.

"It doesn't matter." I keep my voice even. "It will lead nowhere, so maybe we shouldn't go down memory lane."

Maybe friendship is the answer, never mind what my skin wants.

"Why do you always insist on reminding me we won't date?" He frowns. "I know it's not in the cards. Neither of us is looking for a long-term relationship."

"Exactly. So no dating, no sex, no reason to—"

"That's where we differ. I agree with no dating but... why does it have to mean no sex?"

My diaphragm stalls. My whole system hiccups to a stop. He's serious, and the question pulls down his brows into one of his killer frowns.

He means it. He's been wondering the same kind of thing I have been. He's been offering friendship, and he's been thinking about sex, too.

It's too dangerous to contemplate for long, or with his keen eyes on me.

"Logan— we can't have sex and keep getting closer. There's too much between us now. It would change everything."

"You really, really don't want anything that gets you close to someone, huh?" He puts what's left of his food between us, wrapped in the waxed paper and bag in which it came.

"Call it commitment issues."

"No, I don't think that's it." He leans closer to me and peers straight into my soul. "I don't think you have an issue with commitment. It's not about choosing a single person and worrying about greener pastures."

He frowns, and I know something clicked before he says it.

A corner of his lip lifts. His eyes clear. "Everything you shared earlier— it makes sense, really. You don't let people close in case it will land you caring for someone else, when you don't know how to ask for it back."

Fuck.

I don't say anything. I'm in shock. Not even my food registers anymore. I still hold it in my hands, but my arms lay on my lap lifeless.

He continues as if he's not reading me like a book. "And because of that, you keep people at a distance. That's why you don't date."

One, two, three seconds later, his face clears. Too much glee fills his features.

"Evie, I think I finally understand you."

"This is unfair." With my words, I manage to gather enough presence of mind to put my food in its bag, and on the empty space next to me on the sofa. My brows furrow. "You waltz into my life and read between the lines of who I am— of who I show to the world— until I can't hide anymore. But it's unbalanced! I don't know you the same way. I was supposed to be helping *you* open up!"

It doesn't change his look of success. "That's fair. Moving forward, you can ask whatever you want. I'll answer."

"Oh, yeah? Then tell me more about your dad. Why do you hate the media? Why did your old coach not play you? Do you even like football?"

That takes away his humor. "It took me five months to get here with you. Cool your engines and give me a sec, okay?"

"Answer at least one question. Give me at least one."

Show me that if I choose a connection with you it won't be a mistake, because we'll fit this way, too.

His eyes narrow as he thinks it through. "I do love football. It's ironic, really, because I'm good enough at it that it lets me prove I can be exceptional at something— something that will make people pay attention. See me. But because it's what my dad did, people search for him in what I do all the fucking time anyway. Even if he's not the one training for me, or with the discipline to hone my skills like I did. He was great at this, but even if we're both quarterbacks, our styles are different. Not that anyone seems to care. So enjoying football— the physical demands that keep me in my body, the quick thinking, the way the world disappears— it helps me keep doing it, but it traps me in a career where I'm never free of him."

His sincerity rings in the spaces between the sentences. My body softens as I let all that in. If I choose friendship, we will fit, too.

I sigh. "And it's the media and the fans, the ones searching for him in everything you do. I get it now."

He doesn't smile, but a spark lights up behind his eyes. "Maybe you get me, too."

And yet I want his hands on me again. Both realities coexist inside, but the pieces don't connect seamlessly. My body responds like we might indulge and try to have it all for a little while, even if I know I need to choose.

Chapter 25

Logan

The next morning, I enter Evie's building again after she buzzes me in, my hands full. She's been waiting for me. Last night, we wrapped up our dinner quickly after one too many truths had been revealed. I said goodnight to her with a kiss on her cheek, because why not. Then I told her I had a surprise for her, and to be ready at two because I'd drop by again.

Two follow up texts have arrived since. One last night, and one this morning. She's been anxious about the surprise, and I've done my best to relax her, but I didn't reveal my plans. It's been a pleasure to tease her about this, too, when I know she can take it.

Someone is coming out of the elevator, and they recognize me instantly. Their face morphs into a caricature of shock, and I walk past them with a simple nod of acknowledgement. Despite the garment bags and boxes I carry, I manage to press the button for the fifth floor, and ride the small metal box by myself.

She's the first thing I see when I reach her floor. She waits for me, leaning on the frame of her open door. Her dress today is a simple navy t-shirt dress with white polka dots. It reaches down to her mid thigh, and I have to pull my eyes back up when I stare at her legs a tad too long.

Her eyebrows twitch. "What are you up to? What's this?"

"Hello, Evie. I'm doing well today, thank you for asking. Coffee? I'd be delighted, I appreciate it."

"Wow, okay," she laughs. "I deserve that."

She lets me come into her apartment, and I place everything on the kitchen counter. The boxes pile up four high, and four bags lay next to them.

"What's in those boxes?" she asks.

"Make a wild guess."

"What did you do?"

I open the top box to reveal stilettos like the ones she wore at the club, but with a vintage look like the shoes she wears at work. The zipper on the bag next to it doesn't need to go down too low, to reveal the gauzy burgundy fabric of the dress inside.

"Logan—"

"I took the liberty to snoop through your closet last night while you were in the tub. The outfit you wore at the club that night fit you like a glove— you looked beautiful. I figured I could use it as a reference for the dresses I promised, so I put it on your bed and took some pictures. I sent them to my tailor, one thing led to another, et cetera."

"You made no promises regarding dresses."

"Fine. I said I wanted to treat you to the gala. This is part of it."

"You can't Cinderella me like this." She frowns at me, but I see the sparkle of excitement in her eyes.

"I can. You agreed. You'll have to take it."

"Tell me why."

"Maybe I'm doing this for the pleasure of winning. Getting my way with you."

"Nope. I don't buy it."

I sigh and step close to her. We stare at each other. Her stance challenges me, her eyes asking me to convince her.

I put my hands on her shoulders. "I want you to get a chance to spend time with us. Everyone adores you. Everyone wants more of you. I want you to see that people enjoy you, not because of what you do, but because they just do."

"Sounds fake, but okay."

I don't think I'll ever get tired of the way she keeps up with our arguments.

There's no heat to them now. Only a tease. A challenge.

"You wouldn't know, because you haven't let them show you," I say.

"This is too much."

"It's not. Evie, come on. I am paid generously for my talents. You know how I negotiated that deal with Selena when I came to the Strike. I can do much, much more than buy you these dresses. I just need you to let me."

I trace a path up her shoulders until my thumbs caress the column of her throat. It's a subduing move.

I tip my chin and I gaze at her from under the ridge of my brows. "You deserve good things like everyone else."

"You know how I said last night you waltzed into my life? I should have said you *marched* into it. You're the whole battalion going into enemy lines."

I step closer. "You've never been the enemy. I like you too much."

Her pulse speeds up under my fingers. My heart hears the calling and matches her.

"I like you," I say. "Not because you're helping me with my media presence, but because who you are and who I am— we click. There's chemistry between us."

Something flashes through her eyes, but she doesn't share it with me.

She chews on the corner of her lip. "It's a pity no one knows how sweet you can be. Hidden under this... dogged personality."

"I'm not sweet, and I don't need them to know."

"You want to be exceptional at what you do and that's enough?"

"That's what I want from everyone. The fans, Selena, everyone else. But you? Saint and the guys? They'll learn this part of me the way you have."

"So you'll be grumpy forever."

"Why change what's working?"

She snorts.

I squeeze her shoulder. "Now go try on the dresses."

"So pushy." She's still biting on her lip— sucking on it. "I won't model them for you."

These aren't nerves. It's something else. Something... warmer.

My temperature goes up a few degrees.

"That's okay," I say. "Choose the one that makes you the happiest. The one that makes you feel the most beautiful. I'm happy to be surprised."

She takes a few steps away. "If you want to make yourself coffee, I only have instant at the moment."

"I'll survive."

"You're impossible."

"... to resist."

She breaks and laughs. It pulls a micro smile from me— and she freezes. She stares at my mouth.

"So unfair," she mumbles, her eyes fixed on my lips. "Thank you."

I nod, and stay there until I hear the click of her door closed.

She takes her sweet time locked in her room, but I don't mind. I sit on her sofa and turn the TV on. She doesn't have the sports channel, so I choose a random cooking show and get on my phone.

I sip from my coffee and check the profile she runs for me. A few videos with clips from games appear on the feed, but it's a remix of a thirst trap that has the most views. I rub my lips and allow myself the image of her filming me again, getting those eyes that tell me she wants me, too, despite her insistence that it won't lead to more.

The feeling intensifies when I imagine her editing this video, biting her lip and lusting over me, because no one will see her and she can allow herself the moment.

Fuck, I did not mean to get hard, but I want her. She believes that doing something about that means we can't get close. I'm torn as to how to prove her wrong. As long as we both know this doesn't mean we'll end up in love and getting married, we can take this further than she thinks. I'll be happy to demonstrate. If she lets me.

I take a few breaths to tame what's happening in my sweatpants. A hard-on won't help me at the moment. On the TV, someone is missing an ingredient they had to use on the dish they just made. I watch them assume the worst about their future in the competition and it helps.

Back on my phone, the hashtag for my name shows me a few fan made videos. In these posts I'm not looking for their editing skills, but I jump straight to the comments. I ignore the ones talking about me, and zero in on the ones discussing my love life. Because in other people's eyes, they involve Evie.

I'm still thinking of how he helped her out of the club tbh

She's in PR! This is all a PR stunt

Look up the video of her in the box a couple of games ago. She wasn't wearing his jersey

She looked invested in the game for that one time she was at the suite

Huh. Well, I might have to look that up, too.

"Hey." She sits on the couch next to me, wearing the same polka dot dress from earlier.

She pulls up her legs to face me better.

"How did it go?" I ask.

"Those gowns are gorgeous, Logan. The shoes fit, too. Thank you." She watches me closely.

A new glimmer shines in her eyes. Something has changed, but I'm not sure what.

I tip my head in acknowledgement. "I see you saw reason and will accept the dresses. I'm glad."

"Yes, I will."

My hesitation lasts only a few seconds. "How come?"

"I felt beautiful in those dresses. Like a person who does things for pleasure and not for obligation."

"Precisely what my goal was."

Yet there's something suspicious about the energy she's bringing into this.

Ever since she came back into my life, I've needed to understand what's underneath her skin. I've craved to learn what she doesn't tell anyone else. This new thing in her vibe— it's no different.

"What about lingerie?" I ask. "I thought that going through your undergarments last night was too much, so I didn't shop for that."

It's a push. A way for her to show me her hand, but it affects me too.

Heat spreads through my torso. Blood rushes to my cock again, and the needy organ is all too happy to remind me sex with Evie was the best sex I've had, and we'd be happy to try it again, despite how low our chances are that it will happen right this second.

The way her gaze remains steady on me— the wet tease of her tongue on her lips— she's thinking about it, too.

I'm done. I'm hard again. The gray joggers I wear won't hide it for long.

"Lingerie is my weakness," she says. "I have a few pieces. I have what I need."

Damn. I want to see her in every one of those pieces.

My voice drops. "Maybe I should have bought you some extra. Do you think I still have time?"

She told me last night that we can't have sex and be friends at the same time, but today... today she's testing if the statement still holds true. Because the dresses made her feel beautiful, and got her thinking about pleasure.

Fuck. That's what's under her skin. Something about trying on the dresses has her thinking of sex with me.

I lick my lip. If my gut is right...

"Stop looking at me like that," she whispers.

"How am I looking at you?" I let my eyes trail down her body, mapping every hill and valley, and recording every expanse of bare skin.

"Like you want to fuck me again."

Her eyes don't back down and yes. I want to fuck her again. And again.

I want her to tell me every one of her truths, and trust me like she does no one else. And I want to repeat that night we had years ago, more than once.

I lick my lips. "I'm imagining you in lingerie, Evie. I can't help what I'm doing with my eyes... or what's happening in my pants."

"We can't have sex—" she tries again.

"I accept your hesitation. In that, I will never push— unless you ask me to."

I stand. My cock strains against the gray fabric, barely kept in place by my boxers. Her eyes drop to the hard length of it, and her lips part with lust.

"But it's been a while for me," I say, "and thinking about you dressed in flimsy lace..."

And watching me. Wanting me. Arguing with me. Fuck, everything she does makes me want to have her again. Get her to push back, too.

I want her to eventually melt. Tremble in my arms with the intensity of sensation.

It takes every fiber of restraint I possess not to break and ask her to say yes to all of it right now.

I place a hand on my erection— it's not a self-pleasuring gesture, but an acknowledgement to how my body responds to her.

I fist myself over my clothing, a sort of *calm down, boy*.

"I will not do anything you don't want me to do," I say. "So until you know what you'll take from me, I'll wait."

Her chest rises in a steady, fast rhythm with the force of her breathing.

"I'm going to go," I add, "before the images of you in lingerie have me finishing in my pants."

She stands in front of me. While her nerves and doubts yesterday made me want to soothe and stand close, hoping my warmth would comfort her and melt her defenses in equal measure, this new Evie hits different. Her self assurance makes me hard at a whole new level.

"Evie..." I clench my jaw so I don't grab her and kiss her.

"If we have sex, friendship will be off the table. Do you understand that? I can't cross those lines. Especially not with you, when we're just now getting close."

Her eyes go back to my painfully hard cock.

I come close and tip her chin up with my free hand, forcing her to lift her eyes at me.

To be the one to take her with all her determination. To be forceful, until she melts for me and me alone. To be the one she trusts with her tenderness, too.

To be the one who gets to do it all.

Precum leaks from my cock without any warning.

"You have no idea the things going through my head," I say. "Especially now that you're trying to make me choose between friendship and what we could do together in bed."

"I can't have both at the same time."

"Is this our new game? Seeing who breaks?"

"It will keep the gala interesting."

"You are going to break me, but it won't be about getting me to smile."

I gaze at her lips for an extra long moment, before I go through that door and think for hours.

On Sunday I send her an express delivery of lingerie.

Evie: how often do you think about it? Us together that night?

Logan: all the time.

Monday morning comes, and she texts me once more.

Evie: let's not question it. Let's just have a good night tonight, and see where it goes.

Chapter 26

Evie

I walk into the events hall with my heart beating fast. A hundred different thoughts run through my head. It's the first time I join people from the organization for a big, social event like this, and I don't trust myself with any of it. Things are shifting, everywhere, and I may still give too much and get too little, and not realize it until it's too late. I may still stretch myself thin, fighting in the quicksand.

And Logan— I need to find the limits I will hold on to with him, too.

The large room is packed with people. Everyone mingles and enjoys cocktail hour in their fancy costumes. Drinks in hand, they sprawl through the open section at the front of the hall, and among the dining tables scattered at the wings. At the center of the room, a large indoor water feature runs softly like a creek. It holds a medium-sized tree that has been shaped to look old, with moss on natural rocks and lighting effects that make it seem like it's the remnants of an ancient, magical forest. The rest of the hall is decorated along the same lines, with shimmering silver tones and blue lighting everywhere— the echoes of the Strike's uniform— with vines up the walls and long drapes falling between them.

We have stepped into a fantastical land of possibility.

"Evie?" Dom grins at me, an arm around a beautiful, white-presenting brunette.

I grin back. "Hey, Dom!"

He gives me a quick hug and he introduces me to Mabel, his date for the night.

"Are you here alone?" he asks me.

I blink. Logan and I will spend time together tonight. He got me this beautiful dress as part of convincing me to attend, and we have unfinished business. But I don't know if that means he's my date to the gala.

"Come with us, then." Dom doesn't wait for me to make up my mind, and makes a calling gesture with his head. "Everyone will be happy to see you."

I follow him through the crowd, smiling and waving at other players and admin I usually only see at the Thunderdome. Dom takes me to a spot near the fountain, where the usual suspects gather.

"What a wonderful surprise!" Saint kisses my cheek. A diamond earring blings on his earlobe. "It's lovely to see you here."

"You look beautiful." Bear's deep bass voice is as friendly as usual.

Nat and Damián give me quick hugs.

"That is a gorgeous dress." Nat smiles at me.

She wears a floor-length dark green piece, which makes her lavender hair stand out. I gaze down at my gown, and slide a hand down the soft, champagne-colored material. It's ruched on top in an intricate pattern, which spirals into a soft knot on top of my heart. A magical, hidden structure allows me to wear it with no bra. Two cap sleeves hug my shoulders, delicately embellished with jewels. The skirt falls to the floor, hiding a pair of stilettos that are so gorgeous I salivate at the mere thought of them.

"And aren't these shoes incredible?" I ask, lifting the soft fabric to show her my new prized possession.

"Wow. Those are incredible," she says.

"You look incredible yourself, of course," I add.

"I need to know." Saint gives me a dimpled grin. "What do we owe this miracle to? Or should I say, to whom?"

Neither he or Bear seem to have dates with them tonight.

"Selena, actually." I wear my hair up in a loose updo, and I move wayward tendril out of my eyes. "She wanted me here for the project with Logan."

"Since we're talking about our quarterback..." Bear gazes at me with a playful gleam to his eyes. "Did you know he recently placed a bet on the Hypercubed that he'll get you to wear his jersey?"

"Did he, now?" I shrug. "We'll see about that."

I know I told him to do it, but depending on what ends up happening between us, it might be a bad idea all over again.

"You've worn his hoodie before." Dom joins the game Saint and Bear are playing. "His jersey wouldn't be much of a stretch."

I maintain my nonchalant air, even if nerves flutter inside.

"That was out of necessity," I argue. "It was raining."

"I personally think it should still count." Logan's voice reaches me from my side. "It has never happened before, has it? You've never worn anyone else's name, despite working for the Strike for years."

His hand lands on my lower back.

I stare up at him. His frown isn't more than a notch on his brow, but his eyes are intense— heated on me. Little flames spark to life on my skin. My lips part. The air has thinned, now that he's around.

He looks unbelievable, with his imposing height and those supernatural, dark gray eyes that fit the theme for the night so well. His entire outfit is monochromatic, in shades of a hard-to-define color, somewhere between a dark petroleum blue and black. Everything is made of matte fabrics, except for the lapels of the jacket and his tie, which shine in a silky material. My eyes travel from the one button at his solar plexus up and it hits me— his tux is the color of his black hair in the sun.

"Hi." The shy word escapes me.

We lock eyes again, and I'm embarrassed to realize I'm a little breathless.

"Hello, Evie." His voice is deep. He takes a small step back and gazes down my body. "You look stunning."

"Thank you." I gulp. "The dress has something to do with it."

"It's you," he says.

I study his look like it's not seared in my mind already. Butterflies invade my belly all over again.

He steps right next to me, and I face him.

He leans close to me and speaks to my ear. "The way you're looking at me says you like me in this tux."

I open my mouth to respond, but stop myself just in time. The words forming on my tongue cannot be allowed, especially not here.

I would like you out of it, too.

I'm barely aware we're surrounded by people, but the thread of consciousness that keeps the fact on my mind saves me from saying more than I should. I blink several times instead.

"Cheers, everybody." Saint draws our attention by holding a cocktail glass up.

It steals me from the moment, bursting the bubble in which only Logan and I seemed to exist. Two servers stand by the group, offering drinks to everyone.

I had not noticed. Now everyone holds a drink, except Logan and I.

We each take a glass of our own and join Saint, who stares at us with a knowing gleam in his eyes.

"To a great season," Saint says. "And for all the reasons we have to be here together, tonight."

My instinct is to drown the glass, and hope it puts the butterflies to sleep. I force myself to only take a sip of my drink as a gesture, but I cross my fingers I'll keep the winged insects in a cage anyway.

The group sits at a table and eats through the meal, while speeches go on at the stage. A few of the coaches, the GM, and others take to the dais to talk about the team and the progress this season. Attendees cheer and applaud at the right spots, and the mood is generally positive. Everyone at our table is mostly quiet while this goes on.

Even though the same can be said about Logan and I, the way we gaze at each other suggests we're not really paying attention.

Sometimes I catch him looking. Sometimes he catches me.

Sometimes, our eyes lock and we gaze at each other for several seconds, like we can communicate telepathically.

If he's ever been truly able to read my thoughts, this is a time when I equally want him to, and I'm scared of what he would do if he knew what's going on inside my head. The way my skin tingles when his eyes stay on me for too long. How I'm winded, because his solid presence next to me has my chest working too fast, too shallow. The fact that the heat pumping in my veins has me wanting to tear this gorgeous dress off my skin or, better yet, how I want him to do the honors and free me from this gown— with his teeth.

I take a big gulp of my white wine as Selena takes to the stage. She thanks the people who introduced her, as well as the previous speakers. It takes some time, but eventually I manage to pull my eyes from the quarterback and cast them toward the dais.

Selena's dark brown skin glows in the lights. Her charcoal embroidered dress must have jewels attached to the fabric, because it twinkles as much as her eyes.

"And what a first season for this new era," she says. "I am so proud of everyone working for the Strike— no matter the level, no matter the department. Everyone is part of the team, and I thank you all for your hard work."

Selena is within Logan's sightline, but he doesn't pay attention to her. He licks his lips, while his eyes remain on me.

I can feel my own heartbeat.

"Speaking of the team— what a group we have this year," Selena continues. "The consistency in the plays, the cohesion. Every time Coach Clark and our General Manager, Mister Williamson, and I meet— oh, how proud we are of the push we've made this year to bring the Strike out of the shadows. To bring our new quarterback to our midst, Mister Logan King."

People applaud around us, but the quarterback doesn't react. He continues to gaze at me, his frown wrinkling his forehead.

It's the intensity of a few months ago. He studies me closely and tracks every one of my movements, like he's an apex predator and I'm his prey.

Shivers run down my spine.

"They're talking about you, Logan," I whisper.

He licks his lips and watches me for a second longer, before tearing his eyes away and looking toward the stage.

Selena grins at him. "We all know his reputation as a... shall we say, solemn player. But his work is sharp and with his drive this season, the new king of football is helping us reach every single marker we had... and more. The playoffs are just around the corner!"

One of his ghost smiles appears on his lips. I know what this one means. This is Logan, pleased. This is one of the moments he came to the Strike for.

I grin. He glances at me.

The power in his stormy eyes could bring me to my knees.

Chapter 27

Logan

Selena goes on to talk about other players and the hopes she has for us. Dinner ends with the silent charity auction. Everyone grabs a drink and ambles through tables full of donated pieces of art, charity organizations set ups, and other prizes designed to make every guest spend money. Whenever Evie gets distracted by someone excited to see her at the gala, I handle it by putting her name and my billing number together on a donation, so it appears under her name but I pay for it. I don't know if and when she might realize, but it's fine.

Evie stands a couple of tables away from me. I gaze at her, who grins at someone I'm pretty sure is in the front office as well. My heart skips a beat— again. She looks delectable in this dress, just like I knew she would, and I can't stop thinking of the way she smiled at me when Selena praised my work.

I've known for a while that I want more with Evie, even when I couldn't define what that was. That's not a problem anymore. While the owner highlighted how close I was to achieving everything I wanted out of this season and promised even more, an insistent thought tolled in my head until I couldn't think of anything else.

I am close to getting everything I want, but I want Evie more than anything.

I study her, with her graceful, open movements just a few steps away from me. She laughs, and the sight catches in my chest.

"I give it a month." Saint shows up next to me, his eyes on Evie as well.

I raise an eyebrow at him. "A month to... what?"

"Until you two start dating."

"We're not together." I shake my head. "Neither of us is looking to date."

A frown gets added for good measure. Even if I'm having trouble remembering why I said I wasn't interested in dating at the moment.

"In fact," he continues as if I hadn't said anything, "I'm considering putting it on the Hypersquared board."

"Don't you dare." The words come out through my teeth. "Not that."

"Fine." He shrugs good-naturedly. "I won't. But be good to her, okay? I think she would be good to you, too."

"You have no idea what's between us." I keep my tone stern but even. "Or how good we could really be to each other."

"I know she has a generous heart, though protected. I can see you care about her, too." He puts a hand on my shoulder. "All I'm saying is I'd be happy to see you both happy."

"Why are you telling me this now? I thought the intervention already happened."

"Because if you haven't seen it yet, there's a new video in the group chat. Nat was recording the hall when you arrived, and ended up filming you and Evie and— well. It shows a lot of what's going on. Just like the way you keep seeking each other out tells me a lot."

I bite on the inside of my lip and gaze at Evie. She casts her eyes at me. The connection grips me by the guts. Her features soften. I have to take a long, deep breath to keep myself in check.

Fuck. I want a lot with Evie. Everyone seems to see it.

Saint sighs next to me. "Not all of us get a chance to pursue who we really want, Logan. Play this right, and you might get the biggest prize of all."

I wrap up a conversation with some of the guests at the gala, and make my way to Evie. I find her near the center fountain chatting with Bear and Saint.

She laughs at something Bear says. It illuminates the room, and a few of the light rays spear through my organs.

I step close to her and I can't help it, I put a hand on her lower back. The dress is soft and soothing under my hand, and I need the connection.

She gazes up at me, the million fairy lights in the room reflecting in her eyes.

I'm so gone.

"Logan." She grins. "These two bandits here tell me there's a video you have to show me."

"Mmh." I frown. "I've heard about the video, but I haven't watched it."

"It's only fair if you two watch it." Bear's smile whitens the scar on his top lip. "That was the council's decision— if we watched it, so should you both."

Evie raises both eyebrows. "Should I be worried?"

"I don't think so." Saint's dimples show, even though his smile is minimal. "But text me if you want to brainstorm what it means."

"That sounds like a trap." My eyes narrow.

Saint raises a cheeky eyebrow. "Hey, some of us are jealous because we've tried for years to get Evie to spend time with us and we couldn't."

"Jealous?" Evie laughs as if it's a joke.

I know it isn't.

"Everyone is happy to spend more time with you," I say.

"But as much as I want more time with Evie, I should get going." Bear checks the expensive watch on his wrist, which doesn't do much to hide the tattoos peeking out of his shirt sleeve and crawling to his hand. "I should get going."

"I'll go out with you. Bye, guys," Saint says to Evie and I. "I hope you two have a wonderful night."

I narrow my eyes at him but say nothing.

"Can I give you a hug, Evie?" Saint asks. "It feels wrong to say goodbye and walk away, just like that. It's okay to say no, of course."

"Aw, you're sweet." Evie steps away from me and walks into Saint's arms for a quick hug.

Bear opens his arms too, and she walks into them with a laugh. He squeezes her until she groans.

"Wow, Leon! That's what I call a hug."

The big bearded man grins. "I reserve it only for cool people, so obviously you get one."

I frown. I'm not jealous per se— the guys are not trying to seduce Evie— not that I am either— or not the way Saint keeps suggesting— as of now, anyway. Bets are off for what might happen later tonight.

The point is, they hug her in ways I haven't gotten to hug her yet, and there's something about it that scratches at my brain.

I nod my goodbyes to Leon and Saint, and they walk away.

Evie turns to me. "So, the video? Are we watching it?"

I study her. No traces of the past few days show on her face.

"We haven't had much of a chance to talk today," I say.

She cocks her head and gazes at me with humor in her eyes. "You want to chat?"

"Among other things."

"Like what other things?"

"Watching the video."

"What else?"

"Did you see there's a terrace behind those vines?" I point with a gesture of my head. "It's a nice set up to film some extra content."

"Will you do anything to get me alone, Logan King?"

Her smile is definitely flirty. It does things to my lower belly, and to the flow of my blood.

I raise an eyebrow. "I don't know. Have you decided what you want from me?"

She stares at me for a few seconds. "Quality social media content is a good start."

I cock my head toward the vines obscuring the large glass doors. "After you."

She starts filming the moment we step outside. It's a classic set up, like one might see in an old stately home in Europe. The terrace is built in white stone, bound by ornamental columns and barriers at waist level. They open into a short staircase leading to a manicured garden, big enough for an outdoor party in warmer temperatures. Large terracotta pots hold plants and flowers spilling down from wide mouths, and hedges of deep green delineate the solid structures.

With hands deep in my pockets, I stroll toward the stairs and gaze down to the garden. She comes close and circles me, recording me from different angles. Whenever she crosses in front of me, I track her with my eyes but don't move.

"You look handsome," she says. "They'll eat it up."

Her attention is my kryptonite. I take off my jacket and, hooked from my fingers, I let it hang around my shoulder.

I don't look at the camera. I look at her, and the way she licks her lips.

She stands still, phone still pointed in my direction, like she wants to see what I'll do next.

I walk to her.

"How would you like me?" I ask.

"Loosen your tie."

Heat sparks to life in my belly. I bring my hand to my neck, pull at my tie, and open the button behind it. All the while, my eyes remain on her.

"Go all the way," she says.

I take a step closer to her. Her lips part. With my free hand, I loosen the knot further and pull again, until the strip of silk falls from my shoulders. I make a show of dropping it on the floor, before I run my fingers through my hair.

I take another step and gaze at her. "Do you like to see me following your instructions?"

She takes a deep breath and doesn't respond directly.

"Undo a couple of shirt buttons." She bites her lip.

I drop my jacket to the floor and do as told. A smattering of goosebumps appear on her skin.

It's winter, and she should be getting really cold outside in only her dress. If she's feeling anything like me, she doesn't notice the temperature, because heat builds quick inside.

I want her to feel like me.

"How do you want me?" I ask again. My voice comes out deep and roughened up.

I'm getting hard. All because she's looking at me with ardent eyes, and using the camera as a shield.

"How far will you go?" she asks.

"As far as you like... as long as you let me take control back."

"I meant with the game."

I arch an eyebrow. "The one you and I play?"

"The season. Playoffs. Fuck." She straightens and drops the hand holding the phone to her side. "I can't use that on social media."

"Is that really what we're doing here?"

I come close enough that she has to dip her head back to keep her eyes on me. I'm not sure if she's still recording, but I don't mind either way.

"Tell me how you want me, Evie."

"Logan..."

"Tell me you want me."

"Of course I want you!" she finally admits. "But whatever incredible sex we might indulge in again, it can't get in the way of— of—"

"It doesn't have to get in the way of anything. We can feel good and make this whatever we want it to be. Including friendship at the end."

"You can't offer me that and be all nice to me in your own ways, to then take it away, Logan. That would be cruel."

"I don't intend to. I'm a greedy man. I want it all. To do the things I'm craving to do to you and when we're done, let it change to something different. Something good. I never make promises I won't keep. If you want me to promise, I will."

"Logan—"

"Have I ever given you a reason to think you can't trust me?"

She doesn't answer, but her head moves from side to side. Her pull back is enough to trigger something in me. Emotions rush like a tidal wave in my chest, and only fierce determination can tighten my muscles and turn them into a sea wall.

"Dammit, Evie. I'm here shaking with the need to kiss you, fisting my hands so I don't grab you and say, 'fuck it. I need you'. I'm holding back because, as much as I want you, I want you to say yes to me even more. But only if you mean it. So I can't push. I can only wait, and it's killing me."

Her chest works faster. The neckline of her dress digs into her breasts, and all I can think is that I want my hands on her again, all over, all night.

"Evie." I groan. "Tell me what you want."

She gulps. Her lips press close together. I'm about to break.

"Say— 'fuck it'." She takes a step closer, and now we're a breath apart. "Say 'fuck it', Logan. I need you to push. I want you to."

I narrow my eyes and search her face for signs. All I see is determination that mirrors my own. A want that echoes what I feel.

"Fuck," I say. "Do you mean that?"

"Say 'fuck it' and kiss me. Break for me."

Resolve shines in her eyes.

I break.

"Fuck it," I say.

I pull her close. The world disappears. I kiss her.

I'm lost in her. All at once, adrift. Her lips on mine again are all I know. Her arms entwine around me, and there's nothing shy about the way I grab her ass and crush her against me. She moans— I do too.

It's a kiss six years in the making. It erases the moment I woke up and she was gone. It repairs the kisses I wanted to give her and couldn't. Her tongue drives me wild, like it did in that bar all that time ago. Both moments exist at once... us back in that small dorm room, and us today in fancy clothes as the gala dwindles.

"Promise me, Logan," she pants. "Tell me this isn't a mistake."

"It's not a mistake. I won't let it be."

She kisses me again. I'm hard against her, and she leans on me like she's one second away from climbing me.

"Take me home," she says, and I take her away by the hand, leaving my suit jacket and tie forgotten behind.

Chapter 28

Evie

The car rumbles as it takes us to my place. The privacy window is up, and we're alone in the back.

We watch the video on my phone. We tell ourselves it's all unresolved sexual tension. All we need to do is resolve it.

That's why I straddle his hips, his hands on my thighs.

"Evie." He groans. "Torment me."

I roll my hips and his head drops to the edge of the backseat headrest. I kiss his neck and close my teeth on him.

"Fuck. Yes," he grumbles. "Like that."

"I can't mark you," I say. "Or everyone will ask questions in the locker room."

"Do I look like I fucking care? Mark me, Evie. They can ask. I don't have to tell them anything."

He forgot his jacket and tie. His shirt buttons are still open and I pull the fabric further apart— I need to get to his skin. I bite a hard clavicle, but avoid leaving long-lasting signs.

He mutters something I can't decipher. His hands push up my dress, until he catches what I've hidden underneath all night.

"Garters?" He asks, his voice rough. "Why?"

"They make me feel good."

He kisses my neck, then speaks directly to my ear. "They make me feel good, too."

"And just in case we ended up like this— I thought you might appreciate it."

"I appreciate it. So much. You have no idea."

The silky fabric of my skirt sits scrunched up around my waist. His fingers trace the clasps, suspenders, and detour into the territory of my underwear.

He takes a deep breath. "I can smell you getting wet."

"Holy shit."

"It's a good thing. A mind-altering thing."

It's clear on his face. His rapid breathing. The awed tone of his voice.

I nibble on his earlobe. Bite a tad too hard in punishment. "What does it make you want to do to me?"

His hands make paths up my body. The structured bodice keeps everything in place, but it robs me of his touch. I dry hump him in retaliation. He's hard as a rock against me, despite the layers of clothing separating us.

"Fuck, Evie. I want to use my muscles on you again, just like we did that night. It has never been as good as it was that night with you. I want that again."

"Tell me. Torment me, too. Promise me more of it."

"I want to have my way with you." His fingers trace the neckline of the dress. "Make sure you bend to my will. And I want you pushing back, like you're arguing with me about this, too."

I continue driving us wild with the movement of my hips. His fingertips caress my skin, digging deeper into the stretch of soft flesh up my chest, and past the ghost of my collar bones.

He wraps a hand around my neck. "I want you to let me test your limits, so we discover the edges of what we like— together. I want you to demand things of me, like how far we'll go. Tell me exactly what you want from me. Be vocal about all of it."

I pant. I seek friction, needing his cock pushing against me.

"Don't tell me you want me unless you do," he says. "Don't tell me to keep going unless you mean it. Any sign you're not loving every second of it— the tussling and the words and all of it— all of me— I'll stop, Evie."

I bite my lip. My hands end up on his shoulders, and I dig into the hard muscles there.

He squeezes my neck tighter. "When you push back— I need to see fire in your eyes. When you scratch me and bite me— I need to know it's because you need me to pay for how good I'm making you feel."

"I'll make you pay."

"The moment that changes— I'll tear myself away, no questions asked." He kisses me. "I'm not interested in real pain or in your submission. I want to learn how far you'll fight with me in bed, and how much you'll love my strength when we're enjoying each other's bodies. What I want— What I need is to know how long it takes for your body to sweeten under my hands."

A knock on the window freezes us.

"Shit." He squeezes his eyes shut.

The car is not rumbling anymore.

I look out the window. "We're at my place."

The driver stands next to the vehicle, giving us his back and the privacy we need. Chances are he didn't see much, since the windows are tinted, but it doesn't take a genius to guess why we wanted to conceal our activities.

Did he hear us? I'm not sure how much I care, not here in the car. But outside...

Logan groans and pushes me to the side. It's a small sign of everything he'd been promising just a minute earlier. He digs a hand into a pocket and pulls out his wallet.

"A big tip should help," he mumbles.

He gets out of the car, gives the driver a few bills I don't see, then helps me out of the vehicle. His erection can't be hidden, but he doesn't seem too concerned.

As soon as we're in the elevator, he's on me again. He kisses me. His lips trail down my neck.

"What if there's a camera in the elevator?" I manage. "My neighbor... he... aaahh."

"Can't speak, my Evie?"

I take a deep breath, fighting to keep my thoughts coherent. It's a hard task, when I'd much rather focus on the way his hands grab my hips, then my thighs.

"Fuck," I say and try again. "My neighbor— he posted on social media about seeing you here. People in the building are... aaahh... well."

"Mmhhh. Keep trying."

I shudder. "They're on high alert."

"I don't give a fuck."

We reach my floor. I'm trying to rescue my keys from the tiny purse I carried all night, barely big enough for my phone and a couple of minimal needs like ID and credit card, just in case. It's strenuous work, when Logan is at my back, mouth hot on my neck and hands all over my body.

"Damn, you're desperate," I say.

He doesn't respond with words, but turns me around with firm hands on my hips. His kiss is hard and demanding, this time. We're back in the bar, close to dry humping in the hall. I melt against my door, but he keeps me standing with the weight of his body, and one of his hands up my dress and around my thigh.

"Logan— my neighbors. They will see."

"Let them."

"Logan." I push back from his shoulders.

He lets himself be pushed back, and stares at me with a feline smile in response.

He's a panther on the prowl. A hawk knowing he found his next meal.

"Yeah, like that." He presses me against my door again. "Match me."

"Mark me— where people can't see."

"You'll carry the medals of our time together under your clothes?"

"Every day, for as long as we're into it."

"Open the door and I'll show you where I'll mark you."

We get inside, I slam the door closed by accident, and he pushes me against the wall. The kiss is immediately intense. He trails it down my body, hands hard on me.

He kneels. "Hold this."

He pushes the fabric of my skirt up and I fill my hands with it.

"Fuck, these are sexy." He bites on a garter suspender and pulls it.

He releases it and it slaps my skin.

He pokes forward with his nose. "I don't need to touch you to know how wet you are."

He trails fingers above the silk of my underwear.

"I didn't buy any of this for you." He pulls the strip to the side. "I could tear it."

"Don't."

"Mmhh."

With a firm hand, he lifts my leg. My knee bends at his shoulder. He rubs his face to my thigh and gives it a little bite. Sucks on it. It's the first mark he's leaving on me.

I'm panting. I run my fingers through his luscious hair a few times, as he soothes the patch of skin with his tongue. I grab a firm handful of black locks and pull him toward my pussy.

"Ah." It's a short, dry complaint to the way I'm handling him, but a small smile tells me he likes it. "Of course."

He kisses me over the silk for a few languid seconds. Soon, he pushes my underwear aside, and sets to explore my labia with his tongue.

I moan. He works me with his mouth until I'm about to buckle and fall to the floor. My eyes close and my head lands hard on the wall. His tongue makes insistent passes on me, teasing my clit until I'm gasping for air.

It's too much. I pull from his hair again and make him stand. The gesture has him letting out a complaining sound, but he follows my direction. It's powerful, this sense that I can be rough with him too, and he'll allow it. That he'll enjoy it. I demand a kiss and he takes over my mouth. My taste is on him.

I twist and turn and push him back on the wall. A gust of air leaves him from the impact.

"Fuck. Evie—"

I kiss him again. His hands search the bodice.

"Where the fuck is the zipper?" he asks. "I need more of you."

I take a step back and find the secret tab on the side. I take another step back as I slide it down, another.

"Come find it," I say and turn to give him my back as I walk to my room.

His chuckle is dark.

I'm by the side of my bed, lights on, by the time he reaches me. Still fully dressed, he maneuvers me down to the bed with strong hands. I have no choice but to follow his demands, this time.

Logan goes back to his feet, but leaves me on my back.

He pulls from my dress until it's off me. "We're keeping the garters. And the shoes."

Everything but the garter set is something he gifted me, and he looks at it all with a tiny curl to his lips.

"Undress, Logan." My voice is firm, fueled by the furnace I carry inside.

He smirks and comes back to me in bed. "Not if you're not going to help me."

"Fuck."

I pull his shirt open, with no concern for anything but getting my hands on him. Buttons fall like rain on me. I push the fabric away until it's over his shoulders and I can't move it down his arms any longer.

"Shit." He crushes me under his weight for a few seconds while he takes the rest of it off.

"Oomph. You're too heavy."

"You'll take so much more from me." But he puts his weight on his elbows, and uses the new angle to play with my breasts with his mouth.

He kisses my ink. Licks it. Kisses it again. "Somehow— I think I missed this tattoo."

My nails dig into his shoulders. He moans, and the reverberation travels through to my skin. It's not long before he stands up.

He undoes the button of his pants. "Condoms?"

His torso is chiseled, with a definition I remembered through the years. Wide shoulders and a narrow waist, that I can't wait to have in my hands again. Years have sharpened the edges, and he somehow looks even better than he did back then.

I lick my bottom lip. "In the closet behind you."

He finds the box, throws a strip on the bed, and takes off his pants. "Turn around."

"Make me."

He scoffs, like a part of him is surprised at the challenge. The way his eyes glint tell me he liked it, too.

He climbs on top of me, keeping himself high so his body cages me. "Say that again."

"Make me."

The wrinkle between his brows is intense, as are his eyes. He has no trouble keeping himself up with just one hand.

He takes my face with hard fingers, and squeezes just tight enough my mouth parts. "Say that you want me to prove I can handle you."

"Prove you can handle me and I might say whatever you want me to say."

"Evie." My name comes out through his clenched jaw.

He sits back but I don't get to see much of it. He grabs me from the arms and forces me face down. Next thing I know, he's biting my shoulder, then kissing down my spine. I buckle, and he keeps me in place with firm hands on my shoulders.

The sensations burn, somehow intense enough to feel like pain, but so en-twined with pleasure I'm moaning and grabbing the comforter in my hands. My back is more sensitive than I ever knew, and I'm about to beg for a reprieve.

"I'd fuck you like this," he says. "Buckling like you're in need of training."

"Do it," I say.

"I'd bury myself in you, and let you ride my cock like that." He bites my ass.

"Logan. Do it."

He bites the roll of my hip. "You'll have to beg for it next time."

"I won't beg," I say, even if I almost broke just a few seconds earlier.

His chuckle is dark again. His touch leaves me all at once.

I groan. "What are you doing?"

It sounds like a complaint— it is. I turn and see him rolling a condom on. Before I can decide what I want to do, he pulls me from my legs, turns me so I'm on my back again, and brings me to the edge of the bed.

I dig one of my heels into his shoulder and force him to stop. "Logan King."

From outside, it might look like we're not on the same page. Here, in my room, with the way he gazes at me, and the way my body responds to him, we're writing the same book.

He straightens. "Evie Moreno."

I study him. Damn, but his whole body is glorious. His thick legs, shapely shoulders, and the longish hair I want to pull at again. His eyes look hazel in the yellow light of my bedroom, and his white skin tan all over. His cock juts forward, impressive and tempting.

He wraps his long fingers around my ankles but waits.

"Did you think of me all these years?" I ask.

His hand becomes a vise. He brings my ankle closer to his face, and kisses the soft patch of hosiery next to him. His eyes remain on me.

"You would come to me out of the blue." His kisses trek up my leg, a slow progress designed to torment me.

His hand caresses my stocking-covered skin. It lights me up.

I dig my free heel on his thigh. He groans.

"Evie. Whenever someone asked me about winning the college championship— I would think of you in your college's colors."

He steps close to my ass, half-hanging from the mattress. His cock rests on the juncture between my legs. With slow movements, he grabs my other leg and brings it up so my legs are together, ankles on his shoulder. His erection is now trapped between my thighs, hot and pulsing.

He moves back and forth, slow at first. His cock slides with mild friction over the silk of my lingerie.

"Sometimes," he says, "I'd be in the middle of a game, sitting on the fucking bench and itching to get on the field." He closes his eyes, like he needs to focus to bring the memory back. "With no warning, I'd be back in that dorm with you. I would wonder what your name was, where you lived."

His movements grow faster. My need for him grows, my insides calling for him to fill me.

"But my favorites..." He releases my legs, lets them fall wide open, and drops low to kiss me. "My favorites were when you'd show up while I used my hand on my cock."

He stays close to me, holding his weight on one hand, while the other snakes between us to move the strip of silk separating us aside.

He uses the side of his large hand, even the knuckle of his thumb to rub my clit. "I would imagine something like this. Me getting to touch you like this again, getting you ready for my cock."

"Do it, Logan."

"Mhh. You're wet."

"Come on. Fill me up. Stretch me." I don't care that I sound a bit desperate. I am.

"And the need in your voice..."

I'm writhing, trying to break him. "I'll get my dildo and do it myself if you don't hurry up."

"You think that's a threat?" He keeps using his hand on me, and I moan. "I'd love to watch."

He's thrusting on nothing, his cock rubbing against my thigh. I pretend I'm reaching for my bedside table. He lets out a dry chuckle, pushes me onto my back, and enters me at once.

He groans. I whimper.

"Me first," he manages through grinding teeth. "I'm going to make you come first. Before we do anything else."

He pumps in and out of me in a powerful rhythm. My arms flail as I seek purchase on the bed. He grabs me from the soft flesh on my hips to keep me in place.

"You like that?" He rasps.

"You're not going to make me come," I say.

Our eyes lock. He doesn't stop thrusting, sensitizing every nerve ending.

"The fuck I'm not," he says.

"I never let anyone make me come." I grab the comforter hard with one hand, and slide the other to the point we meet.

"Fuck. Evie."

I tease him and me in the same move, to end on my clit rubbing circles.

"It's a point of pride." My voice trembles. It reveals how good this all feels, with his cock inside and my hand on myself. "I do this for myself, too."

His hands grab me harder, his fingers digging into my flesh. I know he'll leave bruises, but I don't complain. Waves of pleasure coalesce in my lower belly, when he lifts me and holds me up, using his big quarterback hands and strong muscles, to keep me up in the air and fuck me harder.

"Take your hand off yourself," he growls. "I'll make you come."

"No."

"Evie. I swear."

"You wanted me to be a brat? I'm not going to give you the power to make me come."

"Too fucking hyper—indep—endent." The word breaks with his thrusts. "Come on. Let me be the one."

"I'm not letting you."

I'm about to come.

"Evie. Goddammit. I want to. I have to."

"Then take it. Say fuck it, and steal an orgasm from me."

He drops me back onto the mattress and pulls my hands up above my head. I try to fight him back, but he's too strong.

He kisses me— hard. "You're going to break me."

"That's the idea."

He changes the angle in which he enters me. I've never had a partner do this and I gasp— he's not thrusting, but rubbing my g-spot with the head of his cock.

"You're not allowed to touch yourself." He bites on my bottom lip.

I bite him back— harder. "You're going to have to stop me."

He whimpers. My orgasm builds, keeping me at the edge again.

"I know you want to come." His words are ground through his tight jaw. "And I'm the one making it happen."

"You said you want to make me come. Then make me."

"You said no one has made you come."

"I'm not letting you be the first."

"You want me to push on this too." His eyes are glassy with heat as he searches my face.

The roll of his hips is a constant stroke where I want him most. I work my hips too, dancing with him to the pace he sets.

I whimper. "Come on. I'm close."

"Still so desperate for me."

"Make me come."

"Do you like what I'm doing? Do you feel the way I'm using my cock to steal an orgasm from you?"

"Fuck. Logan."

"That's right, you do. But you're too proud to admit it, aren't you?"

"Aren't you going to prove you can handle me?"

"I'll make you suffer a little longer first."

I struggle against his hands, but he's strong and I can't get free. I love the feeling of it, how it pushes me to abandon the limits I beheld myself to, and which don't serve me anymore.

He pins me down and does something with his hips to drive me wild. "Look at me."

It takes me a second to process his words.

"Look at me. Now," he demands.

I open my eyes. Dark stormy clouds stare back at me.

His nostrils flare. "Do you want me to free you and let you come at your own hand?"

"I'm so close."

"Answer me. Tell me you want me to pin you down and steal an orgasm from you, or I will stop."

He stops moving.

I wrap my legs around him to keep him in place. "No. Don't."

"No, what?"

"Don't stop. Fuck me. Pin me down and steal an orgasm from me."

He thrusts again, hard. He manages to hold both my wrists in one hand, and he snakes the other one between us.

He rubs my clit, while keeping the angle where he rubs the right spot inside of me.

"Holy shit," I say.

"That's it." he groans. "I'll fuck you right until you give me all your orgasms willingly."

"Logan—"

"Until you're begging for more, because no one else can do it like me."

"I'm going to come."

"Come for me. Let me ruin you for everyone else."

"Fuck—"

My body gives up the fight and I don't resist. I come. His words take me over the brink, my mind blank, and my muscles shaking of their own volition. My breath catches in my throat as I tremble under him.

"Yes. Shit, Evie. Yes. Squeeze me tight." He hammers in and out now. "You're ruining me for everyone else, too."

He comes, like having me at his mercy is the thing that makes him shatter.

Chapter 29

Logan

I'm still not fully back into my senses. I'm still inside of her, still pinning her down. I can feel her breathing under me, fast at first, slow and steady after a little while.

I open one eye. The other. She gazes at me, a degree of humor and something else in her eyes, but she's quiet.

I blink and study her face.

I frown. "Evie..."

Questions build on my tongue. Her calmness— there's something off about it. It brings me back to my body, with the knowledge I have to be careful at the coattails of my awareness.

"You okay?" I ask.

I pull away and search her eyes. Most of her hair came loose from her hairdo, and I caress a few tendrils away from her face.

"I'm okay." She gives me a small smile, but it looks sincere. "Just... surprised."

"In a good way, or..."

She sucks on her lip. "It was good, just..."

"Talk to me." I keep caressing her face, even if there's no more hair that needs tending.

She sighs and hesitates for a bit longer, but eventually relents.

Her eyes steady on mine. "Tell me again no part of this is a mistake."

I tell myself I need to accept her worries. That she has reasons to feel this way and I can be patient, I'll show her she can trust me. I crave her trust, and it needles me that she doesn't believe every word out of my mouth.

I'll give her the words again, as many times as I have to. It'll buy us time, if nothing else, to prove it to her.

"It's not a mistake." I make my voice assertive, yet gentle. "I meant it earlier—when this is out of our system, we'll still get to be friends. Just friends who had to fuck each other into it."

She laughs. The sound eases something inside of me.

She's still smiling when she speaks again. "So we'll do this until we're done and once that tension is gone, we'll be free to be friends?"

Her body softens under me. Her relief puts a small smile on my face.

"That's the idea," I say. "We'll do this until we're satisfied, the way we didn't get to years ago. Then we'll go for brunch like nothing happened."

"Brunch?" she laughs again.

I get up and, unashamed, take off the condom, make a knot on it.

I smirk. "Or dinner. I'm not picky."

She gets up next to me and stretches. The sight is very much like that first night at the dorm. It comes with a warm feeling that settles quietly into my chest. I slip over to the bathroom, before returning to her room to put on my boxers.

"Are you telling me you're hungry, Logan?"

"I could eat."

"It's getting late. I have work tomorrow, you have training... you have nothing to sleep in..."

I straighten. "Really? Evie. You escaped in the middle of the night years ago. Now you're implying I should go home?"

"You... want to stay?"

"Yeah. Let's do this right. It's going to feel good to sleep together."

"What would that entail, in your opinion? Doing it right."

"Drive us to my place. I'll tell you all about it."

I convince Evie to come stay with me, and to bring a change of clothes for the morning. She compliments my house, and we eat some of the food Ames sends me weekly.

Later, we get into my bed. It's past midnight and we have to go to the Thunderdome early in the morning. I expect her to want to go to sleep right away, but she doesn't.

She lays on her side and stares at me across the bed. "Is this weird?"

"It's only weird if we let it be weird." I reach across the mattress and caress her arm.

"Okay. It won't be weird."

"I'm happy to soothe your worries any time."

She chuckles. "Thank you so much. You're always so comforting."

"I've been told that's what friends are for."

"I'm starting to believe I can count on you."

She's joking, but there's something about the look on her face that tells me she means it, too.

I close the distance between us and give her a gentle kiss. "Wonderful. Now close your eyes and rest easy."

"A kiss goodnight?"

"Why not?"

"Just wondering. We'll do that until we're satisfied, too?"

"Sounds good to me." I tuck the sheets around me until I'm cozy.

"And we'll go to TD tomorrow and act natural," she adds. "I'll go for lunch with my parents on the 24th— it's a short day for me— you'll go to Damián's for Christmas dinner."

"And we'll find moments for sex, amidst everything else." I stretch an arm across the bed and pull up the blanket to her neck, tucking her in for the night.

She sighs. "Don't disappoint me, Logan."

I don't intend to.

Chapter 30

Logan

It's been an easy week. I ended up sleeping at Evie's place one night, and she came back to mine another time. The team's schedule is always a little funny around Christmas, but the guys and I are ready for dinner together at Damián's home. I even got a treat for his pet. Barkley the Dog will continue to love me and vouch for my character.

It's still a couple of hours until it's time to go, and I'm feeling restless. Evie is visiting her parents and I'm alone at home. I need to kill time, but there's a feeling in my chest I'm not sure what to do with. After some inspection, I think this feeling means I'm missing Evie.

Interesting development, but I don't make much of it. Evie and I are having heart-stopping sex, and I enjoy her and her company, and it makes sense that I want her close all the time.

But now I'm left with empty time, and empty space around me in the shape of Mystery Girl. Like all those years when I'd think of her randomly, and the ghost of her would materialize next to me. I could get an extra workout in my gym, burn through the hormones... but I write a text instead.

Logan: Hey. How's lunch going?

Evie: It's good. Home food is good for the soul.

Logan: What did you have?

She sends me a picture of what looks like a thin cut of meat, rolled up and stuffed with greens, red pepper, carrot, and boiled egg.

Logan: Looks great. What is it?

Evie: Matambre relleno

Logan: I'm hungry now.

Evie: How long until you head up to Damián's?

I'm resting on the kitchen island with a smile on my face. I frown. Talking about food I can't eat, with a friend I want in my bed, isn't usually the kind of thing that turns my lips upwards.

I call her.

She responds at the third ring.

"Hey," she says in a muted tone.

"Am I interrupting?"

"No... I came outside."

"Please tell me you're wearing your jacket."

"What?" she chuckles.

It warms me up and steals another smile. With no one to see it, I let it be.

"Evie, you have a bad habit of going outside in the winter without a coat."

This time she laughs. "I'm good, thank you."

"Will you stay there much longer?"

"I don't know. Maybe. If I get the feeling they're about to spiral into despair over how close we are to losing the house, I may make a quick escape. I'm doing everything I can, you know? I can't handle emotional rescuing on top of that, not on Christmas Eve."

"Mmhh. Can I help with that somehow?"

"Logan..."

The line goes quiet for a few seconds. Through the months, I've learned to hear the things Evie doesn't say. I imagine the way she's looking at me, as she finds a way to reject my support again.

I sigh after a moment. "Maybe one day you'll let me help with this. You'll explain why this is so difficult for you, and I'll get to show you I still want to do it."

I'll do anything and everything I can to help her in this. Rather, as much as she'll let me. I'm still figuring out how much I can offer without prompting her to dump me.

"Maybe one day," she whispers.

"Now, can I at least assist your escape this evening?"

"It's fine," she says. "I can make something up— a fake commitment I forgot to mention or something."

"Come to Damián's with me."

I don't think twice before the words are out. The line goes silent once more. In the quiet, I hear her worries, and they drop heavy into my stomach.

I sigh. "It will be nice. I'm sure Damián has invited you before."

"He has, but..."

"What did we say? You're going to start letting people in."

"So bossy! If I go, I would be crashing the dinner and then—"

"¿Hija?" A masculine voice I don't recognize comes through the line. "¿Querés tu abrigo?"

"No gracias," she says. "I'll be right there."

A second goes by and she talks to me again. "Sorry about that."

"No need. I'm happy to listen and wonder why you don't speak in Spanish to me."

She laughs like it's a joke. "In any case. I don't know about Damián. I didn't even drive here and I don't want to cab there—"

"Is your car okay? Nevermind. Tell me later. I'll come pick you up."

"Logan..."

"I will text everyone. I'm in the group chat, remember? They will be expecting you."

"You're so proud of being in that group chat."

"Damn right. So I will use my privileges to make sure they're happy to see you."

"The way you phrased that though..."

I trace a mindless pattern on the cold stone under me. My eyes gaze out the window to the large yard, and the covered hot tub in its forever place on the deck. It promises a nice, relaxing time. I have to get Evie in there with me, soon.

"You know what I've learned of late?" I ask. "How much you actually like it when I push."

She laughs. "That's inside trading! That's illegal!"

"I've suspected it for a while, but the way you begged for it after the gala confirmed it."

"Logan!"

"You know you begged. You beseeched me, imploring that I would push and make you come—"

"¿Estás hablando con Logan King?"

Evie gasps on the line, like her dad just caught us getting naughty on the phone. And we were, just not in a way anyone is privy to.

"¡Papá! Were you listening? Increíble. Límites, okay? We talked about it."

"Límites?" I muse. "*Limits*, maybe? Is that *boundaries*?" I rub my lips, the need to chuckle building in my gut. "Tell him you're talking to me."

She ignores me. "Papá. Please. This is private."

I grin. "Tell him I'm picking you up in a bit and I'd be happy to say hi. Social credit, right?"

"Papá— ya voy." Her voice is firm, like she's reprimanding her dad. "Logan— Shush."

It's the same tone she uses with me. What sounds like a sliding door closing comes through the line, but I'm too busy laughing to imagine the rest of the scene too hard.

"Are you serious right now?" she demands.

"Not at all." I laugh some more.

"This is how I hear you laugh? When I can't see you?"

"All I'm hearing is that you want to see me."

"I want to see you laugh."

"And you want to see me tonight. Don't fret, Evie. I'll pick you up, and we'll spend the night together."

"If you come pick me up, my parents will want to say hi."

"In what world do you think that would stop me?"

———

I knock on the door and wait on a small porch. Evie's childhood home is a modest place, probably not more than a couple of rooms and the living spaces. The front yard is minimal, and the outside needs a new paint job. Radically different from the home I grew up in, or the place I live in now.

I imagine Little Evie growing up here, and something in me melts.

The door opens and three faces appear, only one of which I recognize.

The lines on Evie's mom's face are subtle, and her hair has more dark to it than white, but she has tired eyes. Dad's face lines are deeper, and his scruff has more white than his head, but there's glee written all over.

"Good evening." I offer him my hand and the bottle of Argentinian wine I picked up on the way. "I'm Logan King."

"I know who you are!" The words come out with a strong accent. "Welcome, welcome! Thank you."

Evie makes just enough room for me to shake her dad's hand and hand him my gift. She looks at it with signs of consternation in her eyes.

"We're not staying, Papá," she says.

I shake Mom's hand and give her the flowers I've been hiding behind my back. "A pleasure."

"Are you serious?" Evie mutters my way.

I keep my eyes on her parents.

"Ay, sos un encanto," her mom says.

I don't know enough Spanish to understand, but her pleased face tells me plenty.

"This is Luisa," Dad says. "And I'm Ismael."

"Un gusto." I have an accent when I utter the words, but it works.

Evie watches me in shock, while her parents grin and get excited.

"¿Hablás español?" Luisa asks.

"Not really," I admit. "I learned some in the past, but not much."

"I'm impressed!" Ismael says.

"Since when are you so charming?" Evie accuses, and steps down to the porch, pushing me away from her parents in the process. "Thanks for lunch. It was delicious."

"You can join us next time, Logan." A playful glint shines in Luisa's eyes. I've seen it in Evie before. "We've never met someone from our daughter's work before."

Evie doesn't let me answer. "Byeee! Love you."

She looks at me when she says the words and I know she means it for her parents, and yet...

"I said my goodbyes already," she tells me. "We can go."

I'm stuck in her easy *love you*, which is *not* for me, and I...

I blink a few times. "Let's go."

It's fine. That was a blip.

I shake Luisa and Ismael's hands again, and follow Evie toward my car, parked nearby on the street.

"I didn't get to say hello to you," I say, and kiss her temple.

"Stop! They're looking through the window, I'm sure."

I retreat, but it pulls at me in a way that doesn't sit right.

Chapter 31

Evie

Damián takes Logan and me to the kitchen in his lovely home. It's cozier than Logan's, like a family has been living here for years. Plants sprout in every corner, even on a wall arrangement that makes for a stunning design feature. All the furniture fits a classic yet homey style and, with Barkley running around excitedly saying hello to everyone, it feels like I'm invited to family dinner.

It's a new experience, and my heart beats extra hard at the idea, but I don't show it.

I bend down and give Barkley the treat Logan gave me for the pet. "Hello, hello, you're so cute. So cute. Cuter than the pictures!"

"I'm glad you're finally meeting him," Nat says. "He's such a friendly pup."

"Isn't he more than a year old now?" Logan asks.

"He will always be a pup in our hearts." Damián grins and offers us drinks.

Dom is there already, as is Leon. Saint is the last one to arrive and he does a double take when he sees me.

"Evie! I read the chat and yet I didn't believe it." He gives me a kiss on the cheek. "If I had known that a badass frown would get you to say yes, I would have been grumpier with you all these years."

"I really don't think that's necessary," I say. "The fact he's pushy has nothing to do with the frown."

"You're telling me that I should have been pushy instead?!" He complains.

We all sit in the living room, sipping our drinks and eating finger foods, while the main course finishes cooking in the kitchen. Logan sits next to me, and I pretend I don't notice the way his arm rests behind me on the back of the couch.

There's something possessive about it, like a claim he's making that I don't know how to interpret. Or that I'm afraid to acknowledge, one or the other.

I pet Barkley's head, casually resting on my thigh. "I don't know why you guys complain so much about me keeping my distance before."

"Why wouldn't we?" Dom asks. "We're a friendly bunch, but selectively friendly. We took our time getting King to join us, both because he used to be so grouchy and because we were taking his measure but, you? We've been trying to get you in the inner circle for a few years."

"*Used* to be grouchy?" Logan complains.

"It's fine, King." Saint's dimples make an appearance. "We like you just as you are."

"Well, I'm here." I smile. "And happy to be."

"Good," Leon says. "Maybe next time you will accept our invitation, rather than letting Logan be the one to convince you."

"No one has the same kind of magical powers I do." Logan's joke is monotone, but we all laugh anyway.

The same easy conversation fills the room throughout dinner. They joke and dare Logan to dance for every touchdown they get until they're done the season... and in the postseason, if they manage. When they learn I won't be at the Christmas game, they are vocal in their displeasure.

"You have to come," Leon says.

"Pen is attending this time, too." Nat adds.

"We'll even make Logan make a heart with his hands like this—" Saint demonstrates—" and we'll make him point it at the box, to confuse the fans even more."

"I'm not dancing, and I'm not doing the heart," Logan says.

"We'll find a way," Leon threatens, and we laugh.

If it's part of a bet, I'd love to see it.

"You have to come, Evie," Dom argues. "It won't be as significant when we bend the King's will and he makes a heart toward the box, if you're not there."

"He can make the heart regardless," I say.

"*The* King, huh?" Logan mutters. "The King will still win the crown, once I beat Damián's pinball score, and I get Evie wearing my jersey."

He gives me a complicit look to remind me we plan to collude on this, and it's too late to change my mind.

"Only if you dance, Logan," I say. "You have to dance."

"You say I have to dance," Logan argues, "and laugh when you can see me, and make hearts at you... what am I getting in return?"

"Me wearing your jersey."

"I want more." His voice is deep, and determination takes hold of the room in its wake.

If there are insects bigger than butterflies, then those are the ones invading my stomach at his words. Their wings tickle my insides, and my heart races in place.

Leon clears his throat. "The jersey is a big deal. Don't be greedy, Logan."

"I'll be greedy every day, forever," Logan says. "Why wouldn't I be?"

"I don't know," I tease. "Maybe because of a sudden need to be humble?"

"I haven't been tackled *that* hard," Logan says, and we laugh.

By the time dinner is finished, I'm starting to believe that Logan might have been right, and it might be okay to let them all in.

Later in my bed that night, he pushes me to my stomach, pulls me up from my hips to get me on my knees, and enters me in one big thrust.

"Fuck," I mutter.

He slaps my ass. "Rock back and forth and ride me back."

"Too bossy," I grumble for the millionth time, but I do as he says.

His fingers dig into my soft flesh.

"You feel so good," he groans. "I'm not going to be done with you for a while yet."

I don't know if he means he's going to throw me around some more tonight, or if he means the time we're having sex for. Ruthlessly, I push it away from my mind. My body feels too good to ruin it with misgivings.

I brace myself with an arm on the wall at the head of my bed, and use the other to touch myself.

Logan drops his torso to my back. He holds that one hand away from me and speaks to my ear.

"No," he says. "This one is mine, too."

He adjusts his angle and lifts my torso up. He moves in and out slowly, the head of his cock rubbing the right spot inside. Tremors tease my lower belly, as he lifts both my arms and guides my hands to his nape.

He nibbles on my earlobe. "Hands in my hair. I'll be the one touching you."

I pull the silky strands between my fingers and he hisses.

"Make it worth it," I demand.

"You know I'll make you feel good." His hands travel down my body, stopping at varied intervals to grab and squeeze. "It's why you're letting me have you more than once."

I didn't realize he remembers this, even though I said it in passing. That I never sleep with someone more than once. It brings a nervous flutter to my stomach and I push it away, too.

His large hand curls around my mound and all unease disappears from my mind. Two fingers find my clit, and I gasp.

"Yeah, make those sounds," he says. "Show me how much you like the way I touch you."

"Then make me forget myself, and steal those sounds from— me— too."

My lungs hiccup and it breaks my demand.

He chuckles. "That's right. Like that. Fuck."

Heat continues to rise in my blood. He thrusts faster again, his fingers playing with me until I'm writhing against him.

"Come for me, Evie. I need to feel you tremble in my arms."

He holds me up with his thick, strong arms. I arch my lower back to have him reach deeper.

"Harder," I say.

"I'll give it to you harder." He pumps in and out and uses his fingers on my clit with an insistent rhythm. "But you have to give me one."

"More."

His arms grip me tight. I can't move. I can only take what he does to me.

"Yes," I whimper.

Muscles clench inside and I come.

"Evie. God. Tremble for me."

In the haze of my orgasm, I can only register the way he groans and the way his pace loses its rhythm.

We decouple slowly. Soon we're in my bed, my body soft, and he pulls me to him. Only one lamp is on.

"Come here," he says.

"What time do you have to be at TD tomorrow?"

"Curfew is at two. We travel in the evening."

We're both still naked, covered only by my sheets. He wraps an arm around me, and his finger traces lazy patterns on my shoulder. The warmth of his body is perfect, and I let myself melt into it.

I sigh. "Are you staying here tonight, or are you going home? You'll have to pick up your bag in the morning at the very least."

"I was hoping to stay, if you don't mind."

"I don't."

The moment feels so good I let him pull me closer, until I have to entangle my legs with his. I close my eyes and take a deep breath.

"Good," he says. "I know you're still feeling skittish."

"Skittish?"

"Yeah. You know I have you figured out."

I snort. "I thought I was *Mystery* Girl."

"You were, but not anymore." He kisses the crown of my head. "That's a good thing."

"Mmh." The syllable echoes Logan's typical sound. "I need to figure you out, then."

"I'm an open book."

"Suuure. So why did your coach never play you with the Hunters? You were the backup for years. You should have gotten a shot."

He sighs. He doesn't add much for a moment, but I don't push. I can hear the way thoughts run in his head and, in my mind's eye, his ever-present frown is a deep line.

Logan sighs again. "I have to start by telling you about my dad."

"I'm all ears."

"He's... not bad as a dad but also not great. Absent, more than anything. Too busy being one of the best."

His heart beats a bit faster under my cheek, and it's the only sign I get that this is a big reveal for him.

"We text sometimes," he continues, "nothing major. But when I went to the Hunters, he wrote to warn me, because Coach McLellan hates him. Apparently, the Coach was convinced my dad got him fired from an old team. He insisted my dad wasn't as good as people thought, and didn't deserve the accolades. At first, I thought I would enjoy playing for someone who didn't worship my dad, because then I might find my own success. But then, well... I realized his grudge extended to me. He wasn't willing to give me a chance."

"So he took it out on you? How unprofessional, and what a waste of your time— and your talent."

"McLellan wasn't open about it, so I couldn't address it. He insisted I wasn't ready, that I needed extra practice, and the team couldn't risk the games by giving me a chance. He and the GM fought a lot about it, but without a chance to prove myself, I didn't have the power to demand anything."

"That sucks. What a waste for everyone."

"And the head coach— he also blocked the veteran starting quarterback from mentoring me properly." He takes a deep breath. "Don't tell Selena, but I was itching to leave. You may call it desperate. I would have accepted less money than we settled for."

I chuckle. "I bet McLellan regrets what he did, now that you're killing it with the Strike."

"Eh, he's probably saying it's because of his leadership and the decisions he made."

"Well, fuck him."

He chuckles. "Satisfied with my answer? I think it's my turn to ask something."

"A question for a question? Fine, then. Go ahead."

"Mine is very important. I've been wondering about it for years."

"You're just building suspense now?"

He paused, drawing out the seconds. "Did you keep the shirt you took that night years ago?"

I blink a few times, embarrassment tingling in my throat. "Uhm... why would I get rid of it?"

"That's a yes." He squeezes me tight. "Did you wear it when watching a game at home, so no one saw who you really cheered for?"

I laugh. "No. I wear it as a pajama shirt sometimes. It's big and cozy..."

"And it reminds you of me. Admit it."

"When did you get so cocky? Damn, Logan. I thought your grumpiness was your only personality trait."

"I got cocky when you admitted I'm the only one you've slept with more than once."

"Except for that one boyfriend I had, but yes. Every other guy has only been a passing distraction. You are different."

"Mmmmh." The sound is full of pleasure this time. "Tell me more."

"This qualifies as a question, Logan. Ready to bargain? I'll ask more."

"Absolutely. Now tell me how I'm different. Don't spare any details."

I smile, because he's so openly seeking praise from me. It's easy to share it with him, because he's showing me how playful he can be, and I'm certain he doesn't show it to anyone else. The least I can do is offer him the truth.

"With you I'm taking a risk." I rub my lips. "With you I'm indulging because us being together feels really good. If I'm doing it once, why not do it more? We agreed on doing this until we're done."

I trace the gentle hills of his chest muscles with a finger. His hands are still on me, and his unmoving fingers rest like a blanket on my skin.

"I was wrong," I say. "When I first saw you at the college bar. I assumed you'd be uncaring. Detached. It's what I was looking for at the time and now, since I've gotten to know who you are under those severe frowns, I realize this is what I was really looking for."

I gulp. He takes a deep breath that I feel right beneath my face. His heart drums a steady beat I can hear loud and clear.

"This is what I needed," I add. "All of it. All that you've shown to me. So I'll make an exception... as long as we remain friends afterwards."

With slow, assertive movements, he shifts until we're both on our sides. In this position he can look me in the eye and, in this light, his eyes are dark blue.

"I'm not breaking my word, Evie. I will not take what we have away, once we're done with sex."

My heart is the one beating fast now. "I hope you understand... it's hard to trust that, because if I do and then you break that promise... the pain of believing I had it but it was a lie— to discover I never had it but I now know how it feels— that's worse than not having believed in it at the start."

"You don't have to believe me right now," he says. "Keep your eyes on me. Collect the evidence. As long as you give me the time to prove it to you, I know I will convince you."

I search his eyes. His confidence settles in my chest like truth.

"I'll save my question for another night," I whisper. "Tonight, I'll just believe you."

"Good." He turns off the lamp. "I want my words to stay in your mind for the next few hours."

He puts an arm around me and gives me a sweet kiss.

"Maybe while you're asleep," he adds, "a door will open into the fortress in your mind. Maybe, tomorrow you'll wake up and you'll find you believe me at last."

He falls asleep after a while, but I stay up studying his handsome face in the moonlight.

Chapter 32

Logan

We're a couple thousand miles away from home, ready to play our Christmas week game.

The day starts wrong. We're playing the Hunters on their turf. In the pre-show interview, someone asks if I worry that playing my old team will weaken my plays, when Coach McLellan knows all the best ways to undermine my strengths. My instinct is to frown, growl, and do nothing, but I manage to give a decent answer— placating words and a whole lot of nothing. But it gets me in a pissy mood. My best hope is that at least Evie is proud of the skills I've learned in our months together.

When the Hunters keep sabotaging my shots and tackling me with a bit too much force, I have to use every sports psych technique I know not to let my anger overtake me.

We lose the game after an interception Dom and I could have prevented. Hours and hours of reviewing tape, down the drain with ten seconds left on the clock. My answers in the postgame interviews sound poor even to my ears, and if I crack a molar from grinding my teeth through it, I wouldn't be surprised.

Late that night in my hotel room, I lay in bed and massage my brow, hoping it will soothe my frown. I've been overdoing it today, the more things devolved. The only thing keeping me from having to run to the gym to burn the frustration off, is that once I finally got on my phone, I found a picture Evie sent me wearing my college shirt and a text reading, *call me tonight?*

Instead of trying and failing to manage my frown, I tap on her name for a video call and wait.

"Guess what," she says for a hello. "I just realized I'm wearing your jersey which has your name on the back."

She answered while going through the hall toward the bathroom, and now turns in such a way she can show me her back in the mirror.

"See?" she asks. "You won the bet."

My chest softens. My limbs warm up. It's good to see her, and the fact she's trying to make me feel better again only adds to it.

Damn, it feels good.

I smirk, though my brow loosens up. "I wagered a lot of points for that one. It will have to be a current jersey during a game, I'm afraid."

She sighs and returns to her couch. "Oh well, I tried."

"Besides, to prove it I would have to show the picture of you at home wearing this well-worn shirt with my name on it. Eyebrows would be raised."

"I guess that's true. We're still telling people we're not dating, right? If they're suspicious already, this would only make it worse."

I chew on the side of my cheek. Evie and I are having a good time while it lasts. I hadn't considered how that coexists with telling people we're not dating.

The frown returns to my brow. I silently count. Evie and I have been together seven times in the past couple of weeks. That's three more than I've ever sought out with anyone else.

Mmhh.

"You've never been intimidated by my grumpy ways, have you?" I ask.

It's a rhetorical question. She has never backed down from an argument with me. I've faced multiple types of responses to my general disposition over the years. More than once someone has argued back. What's different with Evie, is that with her I enjoy it.

"What?" She laughs. "No. It's never bothered me."

"So that's not why you try to lift my mood after we lose a game."

"Oh, no. That's just who I am. It must feel awful to lose. Grumpy I can take, but I don't want you to feel awful."

The idea of Evie caring like that for me brings a new kind of warmth to my body. Her smile on the screen settles easily into my welcoming chest. It's the kind of gesture I want to see over and over again.

"It feels awful," I say. "Every time. But it's part of the job for me to handle it."

"But you're going to the playoffs! You didn't forget about that, did you?"

I didn't, but it does wonders to my mood that she's the one reminding me of it.

"Congratulations, Mister Quarterback to the Strike! You did it!"

"But we lost the game. To the Hunters."

"And the Pirates lost their game too, which put you in position to skip the wild card weekend and yay! You made it!"

I allow a small curl to my lips. She's adorable. Too fucking adorable.

"Thank you," I say.

"Oh, but where's that full smile? You're in the playoffs! It's what you wanted."

I offer a fake grin, heavy on the grimace.

She laughs. "You're the worst."

"I want rings, Evie. Playoffs are the bare minimum."

"You and your ambition. Is that what's robbing me of your smiles?"

"Mhhh. What I'm hearing is you're greedy, too."

It's fun arguing with her, and she can take it. She cares enough to want to lift my spirits, and she wants my rare smiles.

I want her close. I want her again and again. I'm nowhere near close to being done doing what we're doing. I'm not done wanting her... everything.

My brows pull down— hard. My heart skips a beat.

Once upon a time, dating was never an option. I was never interested in the performance of it. But with Evie I haven't faked anything, and the want is there.

The need. The longing. It's still there. If nothing else, it's grown. I missed her this morning when I woke up alone. I have her on my screen, and I want her in my arms.

If that means I want to date her, I'm in a lot of trouble.

I've never asked this question before. I don't know what the answer is.

Double the trouble.

But I know I'm not done wanting her everything.

"Fuck," I mutter.

"Hey, there's nothing wrong with wanting you to give me special treatment."

"I give you special treatment," I admit. "I'm sexing you up and no one else."

It's the truth, but I doubt she'll understand how significant it is. To me, it's more evidence for my broken brain to consider.

I have no interest in having sex with anyone else. Meanwhile, just holding her hand would fix this day. She's hundreds upon hundreds of miles away, and her smile on a small device does plenty in that regard on its own.

Dammit.

"Doesn't count," she says. "I'm also not having sex with anyone else."

"Does that mean we're exclusive?"

If I'm going to even entertain this, that's a necessary question.

And does that mean we're dating?

"We are," she nods. "Sure. If not on purpose, by default—"

"No defaulting. We're exclusive. On purpose, now that we're talking about it."

"Fine. Until we're ready to move on."

My blood chills in my veins. Gooseflesh takes over my skin.

I may not want to move on.

Fuck. Now, what?

"Mhh."

"The point is," Evie insists, a smile on her face, "I want you grinning at me. I want you to laugh when I can see."

"Then come out for dinner with me tomorrow. Bring a bag, and come home with me."

I'm running out of curse words to express how good it feels to act like we're dating, and how shocking it is to my system at the same time.

"One of our not-a-dates?" she asks.

"If that's what we're still calling them."

"Sure." She shrugs. "I saw your pregame interview. You might benefit from a refresher."

And now I'm unhappy. I wish I could find humor in it.

"Always so accommodating, Evie." I shake my head.

"I'm not going to get that promotion otherwise."

"Come on. You like me."

Tell me you like me.

I think she does. I hope she does.

She sighs. "I do, but don't let it get to your head."

But the problem isn't if I let it fill my mind and I think too much about it. The problem is if I let it get to my heart.

I get through all of Monday without panicking much. My latest discoveries about my feelings for Evie could push me there, but I keep them in check. During training, Saint and the guys ask twice if everything is okay. Apparently, my frown is particularly severe in the video room, but I don't share my thoughts. They already suspect too much, and I cannot reveal any of this until I know how the fuck I'm going to handle the situation. Evie might appreciate it when I push her out of her comfort zone, but I can't push her into considering changing the rules and arguing about dating.

Or can I?

The question stays with me all day.

The restaurant Bear recommended isn't as fancy as the last one Evie and I visited, but Leon vouched for the food and the service so I give them a call. I ask for a private booth and, later, I sit there to wait for Evie.

The light in this place is moody, halfway between the fancy restaurant and the club. The booth is furnished with tufted black leather, and framed in a dark wood that echoes the table. For contrast, a modern, reddish statement lamp hangs low, but it's subtle enough to avoid competing with the candle burning at the center of the table.

Evie arrives a few minutes later. She smiles at the person helping her find me, and the sight brings up a new feeling to me. Something like... warmth. Caring. It feathers down my chest and pulls from me, until I'm on my feet and itching to hold her and kiss her hello.

Restrain vexes me, but I keep things to a simple kiss on the cheek as soon as we're alone. It's an innocent hello, in light of being in public. Torn between what I'm doing and what I want to do, I grasp for anything I can say that sounds like banter, but there's nothing at the tip of my tongue.

I've never lost my words like this before.

Except her eyes are sad, and everything quiets down without a second thought. We sit and I grab her hand over the table.

I lean forward. "What happened?"

She shakes her head as if that would be enough to deter me. "You are the one who still owes me a question."

"Ask away. For my turn, I'll ask what happened today."

The server comes and lists the specials. We both choose her recommendation, so we don't need to bother with the menu. She leaves us alone once more, and I'm happy to see Evie jump right back into the conversation.

"Do you think I'll get the promotion?" she asks.

"Selena would be making a mistake if she doesn't give it to you."

"You mean that?"

"Of course. You achieved everything Selena asked of you— even made it look easy. She's not the kind to suggest you'll get something and then deny it from you."

She sighs. "I hope you're right."

Water glasses and wine come to our table, alongside a crudo on crackers that melts in my mouth.

I eat another bite before asking more. "But Selena won't make a decision until after the dust is settled for the season. Why are you thinking about that?"

"I thought we were here to put a smile on your face. Get you to laugh."

"We can talk about what's making you feel like this, too."

She hesitates. Even if my heart is trying to move me forward, in this we could be taking a step back.

I push my feelings into a box and close it for the time being. Evie is sad, and that takes precedence.

"Come on," I say. "I'm tackled every day. I can take your heavy days."

The server returns with a busser. They take our starter plates and serve us a meal of risotto with wild mushrooms and herbs. We haven't let go of each other's hand. She holds mine tighter, and my heart demands to be included in the conversation.

It finds a way in. I don't stop it, because it's Evie.

She tastes her food. "I took some time off this morning to go to the bank with my parents. The bank refuses to renegotiate."

"Fuck. Where does it leave you?"

"It leaves me thinking I might need to get a sofa bed to sleep on, so my parents can move in and take my bed."

Her voice is low. It bores down on my breastbone, until I have to use my free hand to rub on the spot. To know Evie is sad, worried about finances and losing the house and taking care of her parents. That she carries this weight on her shoulders...

My chest turns concave. I can't witness this and do nothing.

"We can reach out to my financial advisor," I say. "See what she might suggest."

The words aren't fully out of my mouth when the pain in my chest intensifies. This offer is nowhere near enough.

I frown. "And if it comes to it... you can stay with me until we figure it out. Don't sleep on a sofa bed, when you can stay with me instead."

"That's... a big offer." She sips from her wine. The liquid in the glass ripples slightly, enough for me to notice that her hand is shaking.

Sadness remains on her face. The need to fix it solidifies. It has me tightening my jaw, and my half-eaten food is left forgotten on the table.

My eyes are on her.

She gazes down to her food, and moves some of it around with her fork. "You're way too generous, Logan. Who would have known?"

"You know. So say yes."

"We're not at that point yet with the bank, but thank you."

"So you have a plan?"

We go back to eating. The meal is buttery, with the tang of white wine bursting with freshness on my tongue. The mood is still heavy with the conversation, but there's something familiar about it, too. Like we do this every night.

She sips from her drink. "If I can manage to stall the foreclosure, and I present documentation with my raise and offer to pay a higher interest rate... maybe they'll give me a couple extra years. That may be just enough."

And that would make all of her issues last longer, rather than resolve them.

No, I can't let it happen

I watch her carefully. "What would it take for you to let me help you?"

The line of her lips turns tense. Her eyes lock with mine, but it's a hard stare.

"Logan. No. My parents are already asking about you and whether we're dating and it would be too... too..."

"Let me help. Let me show you I care."

"The fact you want to prove you're going to be a good friend— that's one thing. I know you care! But money? I just..."

"Is this about pride?"

"I'm proud, but that's not it. It's because money and friendship is a risky move. Too... weird, isn't it? And we're having sex!" She hisses the last part to keep it private. "Even if we were a couple— a real couple— if there is a world where our finances are marri— entwined somehow—"

"If we were a real couple, you'd have to come to terms with the fact I'm rich, and you'd never have to worry about money again."

I'd happily share everything with her.

It's scary to realize that. Especially because I know she's still unsure about everything we're doing. I have to be smart about all the things I'm feeling, if I don't want her to run for the hills. If I want her to believe I won't take away what I've offered, I have to make sure not to spook her before she trusts me. If it turns out my feelings are in fact leading me down a path I never expected, I'll have to be brave and play my cards right.

As a pro athlete, I'm used to games defining the course of my life. Figuring out this thing with Evie may be the most important game I ever play.

She sets her cutlery on the plate, like she's done with the dish. "This is all hypothetical. We are... quenching a thirst. That does not a couple make."

"Hypothetically, then. For my own edification. What would it take for you to accept help with this?"

"What's the point of me imagining? Of hoping? I spent years handling things on my own. I kept the only two people I ever gave the title to in my phone and in my pocket, because I couldn't cope with the idea of getting near someone who would ask from me and not give back. Now that I'm accepting some of that closeness? I'm still worried, Logan. Because if I take it in and believe in it only to find I was mistaken? I've told you that would be even worse."

"How can I prove this to you? I know words are not enough, so help me out."

"But what if you change your mind? What if you regret helping me or resent me for it?"

"This is going to make me sound like an asshole—"

We're interrupted again by people who take away our plates and offer dessert. Evie declines, but I ask for cheesecake with two spoons just in case.

I wait until we're alone again to continue.

"Evie, I'm getting a big, fat bonus now that we're going to the playoffs. I'm going to have an extra hundred thousand dollars in my bank account soon. That's on top of the millions I make, and the money from endorsements. I promise I wouldn't resent making your life easier."

"Logan, I..." She presses her lips for a second. "I don't trust myself finding the right limits, don't you see? After years of blurry lines with my parents, when I was too grown up for a child. Or now as an adult, taking more responsibility than my share. Why do you think I kept that fortress around me for so long? Because I don't know how to exist in the gray. I don't know how to make sure I'm giving enough but not too much. And what if I mess up? What if now that I'm finally learning to receive, I take so much that I make someone else feel the way I do and I—"

Her eyes fill with tears. I take her other hand in mine as well. I bring both up to my mouth, where I kiss her fingers reverently.

"I'm an expert at strict boundaries," I say. "I've needed them, picky as I am over who I let close. I promise you, I would let you know if I felt this was too much. It isn't."

In many ways, it isn't *enough* for me anymore.

She sighs. "Okay. I'll think about it."

"Really think about it. Come to the playoff games, be there with everyone in our guest box, and celebrate with me. See if we break the football world by winning our first ring the first year I'm with the Strike. Take my bonus money. It's going to be okay."

When we go out of the restaurant, fans gather and people take our pictures. I put an arm around Evie and hold her close.

Someone asks if she's my girlfriend and, for the first time, I hear a clear yes in my head.

Chapter 33

Evie

The second half of the Divisional game is halfway done, and the Strike has just gotten the ball back. Our team is a few points up, but the score is too close to call. The energy in the box is hopeful. If the Strike win this game and the next two, they might have their first ring. It's unlikely to happen, considering the guys will have to play against the Pythons if they make it to the conference game. To use Logan's words, it would break the football world if the Strike won over the season's favorite.

Winning these three games is statistically low, and the biggest challenge the team has had to face. The odds are stacked against us, but dreams push everyone forward. Now everyone is at the edge of their seat, crossing their fingers. Including me, overlooking the field through the large box windows, with Nat next to me.

She wears Damián's jersey. I wear Logan's. We watch the offensive team take position in silence. My heart beats fast, because every time the quarterback gets the ball, it's a chance to set the win for the team.

The ball snaps. Logan holds it in position as he reads the field, and everyone fights to reach their best placement. In less than three seconds, Saint breaks free and Logan throws the ball at him. The wide receiver catches it, turns, and sprints forward, always aiming for a touchdown— he gains several yards, but is tackled halfway to the end zone.

It's an incredible play. The whole thing takes less than ten seconds and a hundred beats of my heart. The team celebrates on the field. Nat and I hug in excitement. Bear dances and points at Logan, who takes his own couple of simple dancing steps in celebration.

I laugh. The moves are minimal, perfunctory rather than full of joy like when the rest of the guys do it, but it's *adorable*.

My heart melts. It aches with lov— longing. With the sweet dream of us being together, like so many people assume we are.

It's his fault for being so damn cute sometimes.

"What's that?" Nat asks, laughing as well. "Logan's dancing?"

"I think they talked about betting on it? During Christmas dinner?"

The big screen flashes big, bold letters that read, HEAR THE THUNDER in shimmering silver over blue. The crowd goes wild, the roar loud up here and filling up the box. The team gets in their formation again. If they can do the same kind of play again, they'll get a touchdown.

"He lost that bet," Nat says. "I see. But he's winning the jersey one, huh?"

I bite the inside of my cheek. "Yep. I should go check the Hypersquared board one of these days and see who's on top."

Without revealing that I'm wearing his jersey out of a collusion agreement with Logan, I'm sure she takes it as evidence we're together. I should care about that more than I do, especially with everything going on of late.

Like his offer, or the fact that someone filmed us in the restaurant earlier in the week. Social media is evenly split between thinking it was a loving moment between us, or him breaking up with me.

So I posted a heavily edited video of him and what I asked him to do on the venue's terrace after the gala. It went wildly viral. It's also how I discovered our whole conversation on that terrace got recorded. It will never see the light of day outside of my phone, but I may have listened to it a few times.

I'm here shaking with the need to kiss you, fisting my hands so I don't grab you and say, 'fuck it. I need you'.

Gaaaah. I may never recover.

And with the way we still enjoy our time together, and how neither of us seems close to wanting this to end. And how we care for each other, and the friendship between us remains strong... This is all feeling very *hypothetical.*

Roaring reaches us again as the ball snaps. Logan gets tackled but he throws the ball right and Dom catches it. The tight end is open and he *runs*— he crosses into the end zone and it's a touchdown.

Nat and I jump and laugh and celebrate, as Dom and Saint mirror each other with happy, cocky dancing moves. Logan is on his feet again, roaring and making a power pose move. Bear knocks his helmet against the quarterback's and pats his shoulder. Logan holds him by the shoulders right back. I grin and applaud, joy bright and pulsing in my chest.

Until Logan pushes Bear back, makes a heart with his gloved hands, and points it in the box's direction. On the screen, big bold letters read, THE NEW KING OF FOOTBALL.

A somersault springs through my chest. I get lightheaded. My grin softens, because I'm caught processing what all this means, when this gesture might be for me.

"Look at that," Nat says. "That was a bet, too, if I remember correctly?"

Her words are teasing. Her eyes shine bright.

All I do is nod, though I keep my eyes on the field. Happiness still flickers inside, but it's matched by the sharp edges of risk. Logan King is getting everything he wants, and things he hasn't asked for. Like my heart. He's burrowing into protected, tender places in me, and this time it's not because he's pushing to carve a space for himself in my life.

Nat and I watch Damián score the point after. The Strike has a ten point advantage over the other team now, and winning feels closer than ever.

Falling for Logan feels closer than ever, too.

"Look at you." Logan enters the box right behind Dom, and the quarterback comes to me first. He takes my hand and makes me spin in place. "I knew you'd look stunning in my jersey."

We hug. He squeezes me tight but we keep it short. Too many people are around us, and all of them would love to question us. His eyes drop to my mouth, but he doesn't kiss me.

For effect, I hug Dom, Saint, and Bear as well. Damián is cozy in Nat's arms, but he grins right back at me.

"The Strike is on a roll," I say, "but who's winning the Hypersquared so far?"

"Saint," Dom replies. "But it's tight this year. A few bets are ongoing, and Logan has been racking up the points of late. Look at you in his jersey!"

"Wait until I beat Damián in pinball." Logan's voice is serious. "That crown will be mine."

He punctuates the statement by putting a hand on my lower back, and its warmth seeps through the cotton to my skin. My heart flutters. We're closer to acting like a couple than I had realized.

"Worth it," Saint says, "for the sight of you making a heart in Evie's direction."

I gaze at Logan, waiting for him to correct or complain somehow. Just in case I was wrong. He doesn't. I was right.

My heart flutters.

"That reminds me." Nat takes her phone out of her pocket. "I've been meaning to check if the fans are going wild about that heart."

"It's going to help your guys' work project, I bet," Damián says. "Now everyone will be wondering who that's for."

"They won't be wondering," Bear jokes. "Not if what I hear is right."

"What have you heard?" I ask.

"Pen tells me that you two have a chokehold on the quarterback's fans." Leon's smile is bright through his thick beard, and his scar stark. "Word on the streets is that you're the Queen to his King."

"Queen of PR, at the very least." Nat scrolls on her phone. "My feed is full of the touchdowns, all the dancing, and that heart sign. The Strike's thunder is loud everywhere, from what I can see."

"That's biased, Nat," I say. "Your algo knows you want to see that."

She smirks my way. "Me and another hundred thousand people want to see these videos, from the number of likes. This is great fun for all of us."

Damián's eyes are on Nat's screen. "Look at that one. You're there, too."

Nat stops scrolling, her eyes on her device as well. "Someone on the seats right there uploaded this one. It shows Evie and I at the window celebrating the touchdown."

Damián chuckles. "It has an arrow pointing at you, Evie. It says 'Logan King's Queen'."

My stomach twists. Logan holds me closer.

"Send it to the group chat." Saint stares at us, dimples at full force. "For evidence."

"Evidence for what?" Logan asks in a grouchy tone.

"That you two are pros, of course." Saint's grin grows. "That getting you to make that heart worked, and the fans are sweet on the Strike's new quarterback— even more than before."

Logan's eyes narrow.

"So you can make him do it again, then?" I ask.

"You know me more than I thought," Saint laughs.

Later that night, Logan and I relax in his hot tub on the backyard deck. He wants to melt the tension in his muscles more than anything else, and convinces me to get in there— naked.

He leans deep into the water, his head on the edge of the tub and everything else hidden by the bubbles. Jets hit his shoulders and I've never seen his frown so smooth. I keep an eye on him, in case he falls asleep, while I check social media.

Nat was right. Fans are making edits to celebrate the team, all players included. Those that only feature Logan often include the heart he made, and an image of me in the box.

I'm a professional, and only repost those that come from official channels. Yet I rub my lips and take deep breaths, to try to control what my head whispers each time I see Logan on the screen.

You're falling for him.

This isn't just indulging in fun sex until we're done anymore. My heart is getting involved, and it knocks on the walls I've built around the idea of long term love. The kind that gives and takes. It's what I think Logan and I are building together. But should I stop it, or go for it?

I bite my lip. I think I want to go for it.

Terrifying...

A notification for a text comes through and at first I'm grateful for the distraction. Until I see it's from my friend Ren, to the group chat I keep with her and Pri.

> Ren: He made that heart in your direction for work, too? Lol. Evie, I can't wait to hear the whole story one day.

> Evie: The heart wasn't for work. That was a bet, actually.

> Ren: A bet between you and Logan King?

> Evie: Between him and the other players. It's a thing with them

> Pri: I notice you're conveniently choosing not to deny it was directed at you.

> Evie: … yes

I startle when Logan's wet hand touches my face.

"Everything okay?" he asks.

His eyes are heavy with sleep, but I've learned he doesn't need to be wide awake to read me like a book.

"Yeah." I put my phone away. "Are you feeling ready to get out? Are you relaxed enough for bed?"

"Mmh. No." He pulls me from the arm, and I slide close to him in the water. "Five more minutes."

He leads me to snuggle next to him. I set my head in the crook of his shoulder, my hand on his chest, and a leg around his thick thigh. His arm holds me close, his long fingers anchored on the roll of my hips.

"This," he whispers. "This is what will get me ready for bed."

"I could get used to evenings like this."

"Could you?" He gazes at me, his stormcloud eyes serious.

"Hopping in the hot tub on a Sunday evening, to soothe the blues of another weekend come and gone, before going back to the grind on Monday? Hell yeah, I could get used to it."

"Would you still want to work, if you were rich?"

I sigh. "I'm not sure. I think I would, to some degree, but... I guess it depends on what it would feel like to work without the pressures of my parents' debt. Would I like my current job more? I already do, but what would change if I were free to use my salary to live a good life?"

He looks so cute and relaxed, I allow myself the tender gesture of passing a finger down his frown. Like he needs soothing, and I'm the one that gets to give it each time.

His attention doesn't waver on me, but a small smile curls his lips.

I sigh. "If I finally went on that vacation I dream of, and got to spend time in a sunny place by the beach. If I got to actually do nothing for a few weeks a year, and I could indulge in all the dresses and lingerie I want, and go out to see my friends in their small town or to the club when you and the guys invite me..."

"A lot of the wives in the league take care of their family, or have their own businesses or non-profits." His words are thoughtful, like we're discussing hypotheticals again. "Would you have your own PR consulting company, rather than still work for the Strike?"

I ignore the way my heart flutters and run my hand over his chest. His body serves as an anchor to all the feelings wanting to bubble up inside.

"I haven't had the chance to think about that," I whisper back.

So why on earth is he thinking about it? Is this idle conversation after an exhausting game day, or is he... thinking about a future when...

No, he can't be. Can he?

Terrifying...

"Mhh. Well, you have time." He kisses me.

We stumble into bed afterwards. I melt into the mattress, his arm around me, and I let my unconscious deal with how fast Logan is taking over my heart.

Chapter 34

Logan

Evie texts me to let me know we have to talk about a work thing. As soon as I can, I make my way to her office. It doesn't take much to convince me to trek from the field to the admin side of the building. The way my chest feels, I'm eager to see her. Even though I saw her this morning, after waking up together in my bed.

An extra chance to see her. Yes, thank you.

Now I rush through the halls of the Thunderdome, feeling like I'm strolling on clouds. I can barely recognize the sensations, they're so new. I've never felt like this. I may not know exactly what this feeling is, but I know it means I'm down bad.

Fuck. It's a first.

Her door is ajar, and I push it with a finger to open it and check inside. Evie leans on her desk, an elbow on the wood and her head in her hand. Her lovely hair falls down like a waterfall, and she holds her desk phone's headset to her ear.

"Mhh. Yeah. Yes," she says.

I go into her office and close the door softly behind me. The click brings her eyes to me, and they soften as she gazes my way. She straightens on her chair, smiles, and calls me in with a hand.

She opens a notebook she keeps nearby and writes on it.

Sorry, I have to stay on this call.

I kiss her on the temple because why not, before writing my response.

Come home with me tonight?

Yes, she writes back. *Dinner would be lovely.*

Stay over. You might as well bring a few things and keep them at my place, too.

Writing it down means I had time to change my mind, and not put such a thing with blue ink on white paper.

My script looks blocky next to her quick scrawl and, to my infatuated heart, it looks like a great aesthetic combination.

Not tired of what we're doing yet?, she writes.

She gazes at me with curious eyes. The brown of her irises has a soft shine to it, like butterfly wings in the sunlight.

My heart takes on the speed it usually reserves for high-stress situations on the field.

Damn. This feeling inside, it gets stronger by the minute.

I gulp, and I focus on not letting my script look shaky.

Not at all. I would show you, I add, *but it might distract you.*

She smirks before taking the pen back. *You can try. I can control myself around you.*

I smirk. I recognize a challenge when I hear one and, hell. I need the distraction, too.

The beat of my heart stays up, but for different reasons now. I kneel next to her and turn her swivel chair so she faces me. She keeps the phone at her ear, but her eyes follow each one of my movements. The little smile on her face is a dare, and it pushes on every competitive button in my brain.

Sweet, sweet distraction. This isn't a bet, but I'll win it too. And I'll enjoy every second of it.

Lavender reaches my nose first. I kiss her neck. She drops her head to the side to give me access, and I make a long pass of my tongue on the column under my mouth. My hands come up to her chest. I fondle her breasts through the fabric, and note the texture of her bra underneath the blouse. I pop one button open, then the next. I expect her to stop me but she doesn't. Once I've run down her front, I push the soft fabric aside, to find a piece of lingerie I got for her.

I have to bite my bottom lip hard not to groan and make noise. This is why she dared me, too. She wants me to see.

She's still staring at me with a challenge in her eyes. I shake my head. She has no idea what this all makes me want to do.

Our eyes locked, I work her nipples through the lace of her underwear. When she doesn't stop me, I push her loose skirt up to her waist, pull her legs open and kneel between them. With hands firm on her hips, I bring her forward until her ass is at the edge of the chair. Her mouth opens in a silent gasp, and her hand holds on to the headset for dear life.

She clears her throat. "Yep. Absolutely."

I run a thumb over her lip. Her eyes are heated, and I'm hard like a rock. I give her a few seconds to tell me somehow that I should stop... but she doesn't.

I lift a defying eyebrow and drop to her neck again. Her earlobe is soft as I nibble on it. I rub my erection on her like we're teenagers dry humping on the living room sofa, praying no one will pop by unannounced and discover us like this.

She's barely managing her breathing. It's quiet and controlled, but it hitches with a softness that is driving me wild. The creaking of plastic is the loudest sound, because as well as she's keeping quiet, she's gripping the phone hard enough to make it whine.

Her free hand comes to my hair. She pulls from it like she usually does and the pain makes me see stars. I slide two fingers under the silk of her panties.

"Yep. Good idea. Yes," she says to the phone in an almost professional tone.

I hide a chuckle, push my fingers into her wetness, then rub her clit. Her body jerks in a small jolt, but she can't hide that very well. I suck on her neck and rub myself on her thigh, while my fingers work on her.

She undulates on the chair, pulls harder at my hair, and I have to move my hips away to stop myself from making a mess in my practice joggers.

"If you kiss me while you're coming," I whisper so low into her free ear that only she can hear me, "the sounds you make will be mine too."

Her mouth is parted in lust, just like mine. I nibble on her bottom lip and pull. I push two fingers into her and pump, and her eyes turn glassy with pleasure.

"That's correct." There's a tiny hiccup to the last word, but she hides it well. "A-ha."

I add my thumb to her clit, and the trembling starts in her limbs.

"Sorry— just a sec—" she scrambles and pushes a few buttons on the phone. "Don't stop."

She kisses me, hard. I keep fucking her with my hand, and her orgasm squeezes my thick fingers tight. She moans and the trembling breaks into shaking.

"You're perfect," I say. "I can't get enough of you."

Her eyes lock with mine. Her orgasm finally subsides and I pull my fingers out. I suck them clean and moan.

"Wow," she whispers.

"How long can you make them wait?" I ask.

"I shouldn't have paused that call."

I nod. "We'll talk at dinner?"

"Sure. Thank you, I guess?"

I chuckle. "You're welcome."

She kisses me once more, presses the same button, and goes back to her call. "Yes, thank you, sorry for the interruption. I'm here again."

I take the pen and write a final note.

Good job pretending you can resist me.

She smirks and I leave her office with a smile.

Maybe if I keep her happy and well fucked, she'll decide I might as well have her heart.

I think she already has mine.

Chapter 35

Evie

Flashes of what Logan and I did in my office today still pop into my mind randomly, when I pack a few of my things and head to his house that night. I include a couple of outfits to keep at his place, for when I don't want to make the trip back to my apartment.

It was his idea, and it feels like an important clue.

An hour later, we sit at his dinner table. We're spending more time here than back where I live. My neighbors have been paying attention to my comings and goings, and have asked me about Logan a few times. It's simpler for us to be here, and now that I'm bringing some of my things to keep in his room...

I sigh.

"How did the rest of your day go?" he asks.

It's such a comfortable, long-term-relationship question, that my heart decides to skip a couple of beats. It's logical, really. I'm sure it is, if I think about it hard.

"I was in a very good mood for some reason, so that was great." I lift my eyebrows high, and let him connect the dots on his own.

He chuckles. "I count that as one of my good deeds today."

The hanging light is off above us. Only the kitchen pot lights are on, giving us a diffuse, soft glow to eat in.

"Good," I say. "Keep that vibe in the room, because you're not going to like the next conversation."

He frowns and waits for me to come out with it.

"The Sports Media Network producer called. Melanie says they're still happy with your interviews these days, and the ratings are great."

His eyes narrow. He knows I'm stalling and trying to butter him up.

I sigh and go for it. "They want to push on asking about your dad."

His brow knots harder. His jaw clenches. The line of his mouth presses into a hard line.

I give him an apologetic look. "I knew that would bring the return of the killer frown."

"It's still a no, Evie."

I open my mouth to explain but pull back right away. His reply doesn't surprise me and, even though talking about his dad in this context makes my PR instincts tingle, the choice was made hours ago.

His solemn eyes focus on me. "I've told you things about my dad I haven't told anyone else. If you push on this..."

I shake my head and take his hand on the table. "I won't. Of course I'll respect your answer! I already did. I told Melanie the contract is enforceable and we're not open to renegotiating."

His brow relaxes somewhat. "Thank you. Regardless of what happens this season— if I can't get a ring, I at least need to redeem myself by getting us close. I need to know that by the time I walk away from my last game in my first year with the Strike, I'll be out of my father's shadow."

"I understand. I'll help, okay? But part of my job is to tell you what happened... and I should warn you as well, that they will probably find ways to ask about Kenneth King, if they really want to."

He eats a few forkfuls of the big, colorful salad Ames' team sent him. "What can I expect?"

"They could find an indirect way to ask you. Quote one of the few comments he's made on his show, quote social media posts, who knows."

"Mhhh."

"I'll stick around for the interviews, just in case, but you'll handle it. You're a pro at this now."

"Far from it. I still need my training wheels."

He interlocks our fingers, and it clears all tension from the room. Like now that he knows where I stand, we're a unit again.

"Am I your training wheels?" I smile.

He smirks. "I promise only to poke you for advice sometimes."

"You can poke as much as you need. It's my job!"

"I'll do that at work. Here? I'd much rather poke at other things."

His eyes are steady on me, and I keep my smile. We eat some more, with him and his salad and me and my pasta.

It's the kind of evening I want to have every night.

That ache in my heart I felt last week at the stadium returns to my chest. This fantasy is feeling better and better by the second.

"Yeah," I say. "I've learned how much you like to poke at me."

He said he can't get enough of me. Maybe that will turn to more for him, too. Even if he doesn't date, maybe he'll change his mind like I think I have.

"And push," he adds. "Toss around a little."

"That part should definitely be a just-at-home thing."

"I'm sure we can bend the rules sometimes," he says, like we're discussing what we'll have for dinner tomorrow. "You liked it when I poked at work today."

I laugh. "Not too often. Can you imagine getting caught?"

"We'll be careful." He shrugs.

Like it's not a big deal. Like he's looking at the years ahead of us, and that's the least of his concerns.

He stares at me with dark gray eyes. His gaze hides a challenge—

What are you going to do, my Evie?

I can hear it clearly. Maybe I've learned how to read his mind, too.

His fierce eyes study me closely. It's easy to get lost in them, and try with all my might to figure out what color they really are.

I take a deep breath. "I do have a marketing question for you."

He raises an eyebrow.

"I need to settle something for social media," I add.

He cocks his head. "What are you up to?"

"It's one of the most common fan questions I see in the comments."

"I thought they're convinced you're my girlfriend."

I blink a few times at that, but recover fast. The title sounds too good, but I can't entertain it for long. Not when I'm on a mission.

"It's not that." I shake my head. "It's an even more important question."

"Let it out, will you?"

One day soon, I'll have to make up my mind about what all of these feelings mean, and what I'll do about them. But for now, I need the shield of playfulness.

I call him closer with a finger, like I want to tell him a secret. We're alone, but he humors me. The corner of his lips pull up.

"All your fans want to know." I peer into him, and ask the question I want answered for myself most of all. "Logan— what color are your eyes?"

His eyebrows twitch. It takes him a second, but answers in a beat.

"A37," he says.

I startle.

"What?" I'm breathless. "Are you serious? What does that mean?"

"I have no fucking idea, Evie." And he laughs.

My eyes open wide. My lips part. Several emotions move through me at once— confusion, awe, humor, and the realization that he's messing with me.

But that laugh... oh, it's glorious, and it fills me up until I could fly.

A smile takes over my face, but it's soft with the warmth spreading through my chest. Regardless of what happens with us, this is a moment I will never forget.

"Did you make that up?" I ask. "To tease me?"

He nods. I take my hand away in mock offense, as extra playfulness to distract us. He chases it and grabs it again.

His grin is wide and free. "I have no idea what color my eyes are. They are somewhere between blue and gray, but they take on the color of what surrounds me so it's hard to discern."

"I've seen them look purple, for hell's sake."

"Mhh. Was this question really for the fans?" He kisses my hand. "Or just my number one fan?"

"Are you calling me your number one fan?"

He laughs again.

"Worst of all is," I say, "I can't deny it. Not after seeing you laugh like that."

"Was it everything you thought?"

Effervescent mirth lights him up. To my poor heart, he shines like those old church paintings.

I give him a serious nod. "Unfortunately. Yes."

Grin still on, he pushes our plates away. "Am I everything you thought?"

Pulling from my hand, he maneuvers me out of my chair, and onto the table.

"No," I whisper.

"And you still like me."

It's not a question.

I smile. "I still like you, Logan."

"Good."

He kisses my neck and has me for dessert, right there on the dinner table.

Later, he holds me close in bed.

"Just be here with me," he says. "Just breathe with me."

Chapter 36

Logan

It's the Conference game, football's semi-finals. As focused as I am on the game, Evie's presence in the box is a balm to my spirit. It grounds me. Alongside every technique I've ever learned in sports psych, it manages to keep my pulse in check and my mind sharp.

I'll need every ounce of determination and focus I possess— and more— to make the right plays. We're losing 28-21 and, with only two and a half minutes left, every second, every move, and every breath counts.

I purse my lips, get into position, and chant the familiar countdown to the snap.

The ball is in my hands. My mind goes blank. Big guys run at me and even bigger guys try to stop them. My receivers sprint to their positions, but two defenders get free and aim for me. I run out of the pocket, my eyes still on the field. Everything turns into slow motion. From the corner of my eye, I see new threatening figures coming at me from the other side. I dodge a tackle, run sideways, and brush off another attempt to make me eat turf.

My position is off, and their defense blocks Dom. I'm taking too long, and giving the other team too much of a chance to block our plays and I see it— Saint gets open.

I'm in the middle of adjusting for my throw when I'm pushed from the back. My hips absorb the hit, and my back bone itself re-arranges to keep the angle of my arm.

I whip-throw the ball as I fall. The last thing I see is the ball flying in Saint's direction, before I crash on the grass.

It's not a bad fall, and I'm back on my feet within a couple of seconds, right in time to see Gael Santiago, the incredible player that he is, running for the end zone.

I don't breathe. I don't feel. I only watch him, completely useless now, and pray he gets there. From my position it's not clear, but he keeps running. Without my volition, my arms raise slowly as if they knew what I'm about to see. Like they've responded to something my brain understands but hasn't told my awareness yet and I—

Saint crosses the final line with an acrobatic jump, and every fan and Strike player roars. The thunderous sound reverberates in my chest. Bear is screaming at me, a big smile on his face. We grab each other's shoulders, helmet to helmet, and shake each other as if we're trying to make the other see sense.

Do you get what that means? We're tying the game!

"Make that heart, King!" Leon screams. "Fucking make that heart for Evie again!"

In the heat of the moment, I don't hesitate. I make a heart with my hands and point it in the direction of the box. I imagine Evie laughing and shaking her head at me.

No one doubts Damián will score the extra point and, when he does, the Strike has a fighting chance at defeating the season's favorite and going for the big trophy.

The Pythons have the ball now, and I sit on the bench with a blanket around my shoulders. It's branded with a large silver lightning against blue. People around me comment on my play, but I don't register much. They're excited, praising what I did, but it's not until my QB coach sits down next to me that I understand it's big.

He shows me the replay on his tablet. "That will go onto every highlight reel for this season, King. They'll talk about that play for years."

Everyone pays attention to the field, where our defense struggles to halt their drive. Thirty seconds left. An eternity in football and, if they get close enough for a field goal...

My eyes go back to the tablet. I see myself sidestepping defenders, avoiding tackles, and throwing as I fall.

It's the kind of play I would have studied for hours.

My chest does something strange. A click somewhere between my lungs. Cogs aligning after years of disrupted fit. The invisible stone that kept things slightly off is gone, and the whole system is finding a new way to run. After years waiting for an opportunity to redeem myself, there's a film to prove what I'm capable of.

I got the team that fighting chance. Maybe that's plenty. Not *everything* but perhaps... enough.

My chest rises and falls as I process what this may mean.

My coach squeezes my shoulder. "They'll try for a field goal. It's what I would do. But even if they win the game, Logan— no one can take away that play from you."

The Pythons got the field goal and the game. The Strike is eliminated, and the mood in the locker room is somber.

Yet there's a thread of optimism in the air.

Coach Clark is at the center of the space, and all the other players and I surround him. He's been naming every single person who put on cleats and stepped on the field today, and reminding them of the amazing things they did for the team.

I listen to all the wonderful, encouraging words he has for everyone. I believe them all. This is the team I waited for my whole life, and together we will do incredible things.

"Finally, Logan King."

I frown. My arms are crossed.

Coach Clark is a man in his late forties, with white skin wrinkled by spending his days outside. Dark brown hair and brown, piercing eyes. He always looks like he's planning something and, as head coach of the Strike, he probably is.

He directs those sharp eyes my way. "People are calling you the new king of football, but they don't know what that really means. Half of them use it because of your last name, and the other half do it to compare you with your father. They haven't seen what I have seen at the Thunderdome, or know the way you think about the game— but today everyone got a taste of it."

He nods. I mirror him.

"Ever since I saw you playing for your college team," he continues, "I knew you were destined to be one of the best. Regardless of anything else, plays like yours today are a sign of greatness. What you bring into the game is something many of us seek our whole coaching careers and never find. Everyone in the team is ecstatic to have you, and be a part of what makes you a king in the game."

My heart beats fast. Words like the ones still echoing in the locker room are exactly what I've wanted for years.

No one else has responded to Coach Clark, so I don't either. The things I want to say get trapped at a dam in my throat— thank yous and promises for an even better year next time.

Clark talks to the rest of the room again. "Be disappointed that we lost today but don't let it fool you. No one thought we'd make it to the playoffs yet here you are. You turned every prediction on its head and, with what I saw today out there? No one will stop us now."

A few people applaud. I study the crowd. They're disappointed, all right, but no one is crushed.

We may not have won the ultimate prize, but we achieved every other goal we had.

"Be sorry for yourselves for a few hours," Clark adds. "Go to your person and let them make it better. But when we come back to prep for the next season, know we will do it all over again— but we'll end up with a ring next time."

"Hell yeah!" A few people yell.

"This was the year of the warning for everyone else." Clark's face is serious. He means this. "Now all eyes are on us— the underdog who was supposed to be out of the playoff run months ago, but made it to the semi-finals! We'll show them we have what it takes."

More people exclaim their agreement. A shift in my chest tells me this moment is getting engraved there.

"Hear the thunder, the Strike is here!" Clark yells, and we all join him.

The group breaks into hugs and strong pats on each other's shoulders. We promise we'll get the ring next time. I tell them all that I want at least three.

I find the guys I've gotten close to. I'm about to hug Bear when someone grabs me and pulls me into her arms. I know it's Evie before I feel her soft body against mine, and I pull her tight.

"You're amazing, Logan," she says to my ear. "You're incredible. That was electric. How did you do that?"

I take a deep breath, finding lavender among the myriad smells of a locker room after a game.

Her scent is like alchemy to my mind. Every cog and wheel that make up my inner mechanisms run with smooth precision. All friction is gone. The past hour has had highs and lows, but Evie's warmth next to me is the balm to oil the machinery inside. To remind me that I may not have gotten everything I want out of my career yet, but my first year with the Strike has given me more than I imagined I'd ever have.

Her arms are a vise around my neck. "I will never forget seeing that live from the box. You should have heard the screaming!"

I squeeze her tighter. "Did you scream?"

She leans back to give me a radiant look. "The loudest."

I take a deep breath again. Evie is my person, reminding me I'll get everything I want. With her, I have what I didn't know I need.

I'm considering kissing her right there in front of everyone, when she lets go of me like nothing happened.

"On professional terms," she says, her voice suddenly even, "the TV crew is waiting outside for an interview. I'll wait for you with them."

She turns, gives everyone a big hug, and leaves, her ponytail swinging from side to side. On the way out, my last name stands out on her back. The four blocky letters make my heart stutter.

The guys and I form a circle. They all watch me with varied degrees of suspicion and playfulness.

My brow furrows low. "Thank you for everything. Getting to be a team with people like you all is what I've wanted for years. I promise I won't disappoint you next season."

Bear's eyes narrow. "That started strong, but what is that about disappointing us?"

Damián smirks. "I don't think you understand what you've done for us— with us— this year. This *game*. We've wanted a quarterback like you for years."

Saint's dimples make an appearance. "And a friend with the kind of seriousness to ground us will only make us stronger."

I raise an eyebrow. "All I'm saying is I'll do better."

"Do more of the same," Bear says. "The rest is the magic of what happens in the field."

My team's— my *friends'* words of encouragement lighten my chest further. Warmth spreads through me, that I have them to share this moment with and uplift each other like this.

"We'll make magic," I agree.

"No one doubts it." Dom cocks his head. "Especially after today. I hope you're not doubting it either."

I shake my head. "I don't doubt it. I'll make sure to prove it."

"Turn that frown upside down, Logan," Damián insists. "Just the one time."

"Besides," Saint adds, "you got the girl! Isn't that the real prize?"

That steals my attention from the game and football and everything else.

I squint at the pass catcher with the boyish smile. "Explain."

They laugh. All I do is frown harder. If they know something I don't, then I want it. I *need* anything that might help me figure out this thing with Evie, so I may play my cards right.

Bear crosses his big, tattooed arms. "You think we don't know about you and Evie?"

I open my mouth but don't get to say anything.

"Don't bother denying it," Damián says. "Even if we don't know exactly what you two have gotten up to behind the scenes, what we've seen is enough. There's something there."

"She's wearing your jersey to games, for fuck's sake," Saint adds.

"She hugs you and looks at you like she doesn't look at anyone else." Dom's eyes are serious. "I had someone like that— someone I would look at the way you look at Evie, someone to hug like that. I let her go. Don't make the same mistake with Evie."

I shift from foot to foot, arms crossed. It feels wrong to deny what I feel for Evie, or to lie to my friends. And still...

"If you guys were correct—" I try. "What do you propose I do? She's... unsure. She doesn't let people in easily."

Bear puts a large hand on my shoulder. "And yet she let you in. I'd say you keep doing what you've been doing, yes?"

"Tell me." Saint puts his hand on my other shoulder. "Are you two together?"

I push my lips to the side. "Something like that."

"It's not about labels," Saint insists. "Are you, or are you not together?"

I grind my teeth. "I am with her. I don't know if she's with me. If that makes sense."

"It doesn't," Damián says. "All it means is you haven't had the right conversation."

"Are you in love with Evie?" Dom asks.

They stare at me. The answer bubbles up from my chest, a feeling of knowing that's new and yet so familiar...

I may not have ever been in love before, and this grew too slowly to recognize it as it happened, but the past few months have changed the script of what I wanted out of life.

Every part of it includes Evie now.

"Don't tell us first what you feel." Bear squeezes my trap muscle, hard.

I wince. It's a gesture of friendship and a threat.

Bear smiles. "That's something you should reserve for her, right?"

The scar on his lip turns white.

"Mmmh," I growl. "You really have to stop springing interventions on me."

I fail to intimidate them and they laugh. A small smile tilts my lips because, as much as I complain, I'm thankful that I have them all.

These are the bonds I dreamed of, when I first stepped onto a football field.

With them, I finally got what I sought.

Chapter 37

Evie

I'm in trouble. Major trouble.

I'm falling for Logan. Fast and hard.

Almost-run-onto-the-field-because-he-was-tackled fast.

I-have-eyes-for-no-one-else hard.

The TV crew and I wait outside the locker room, in the press side hall. Interviews often occur in this section, and now we hang out as we wait for Logan to appear.

Despite the tense emails we've exchanged— 'as per my last' was used more than once on my end, insisting they cannot bring Logan's dad up into the conversation— I smile at them in an effort to smooth things over. They're polite enough to reciprocate, but we don't chat. It's fine for now. I entertain myself by getting on my phone, even if I'm just opening and closing apps at random. Logan might still take a while.

An old part of me still wants to run and hide from my feelings for him. A bigger, newer part of me knows Logan would find me and make me talk to him. It's one of the reasons I'm so into him, and one of the reasons why I won't run, and I'll stay. Most of all, I persevere because the idea of leaving him behind and not having him close is worse than anything else.

But that means I have to take the risk and stick around. Get used to having a few of my things in his place, and hope we find our way through the jungle of what ifs plaguing my mind. It would likely require me to accept the money he offered for my parents, as a show of trust in us and what he's promised.

If I want to make sure I discover good boundaries with people, the kind that breathe and shift as days go by and life happens, then I have to believe him. He's given me no reason to doubt him.

In fact, he's built a case for himself without me knowing. This morning I received a few emails from the gala organization crew and a few foundations, to thank me for the generous donations I made during the party. Among all the questions I carry with me these days, who is responsible for those donations isn't one of them.

I sigh. Logan hasn't appeared yet. I take the time to tackle the issue of the quarterback with my two long-distance friends.

> Evie: Hypothetically, if one were to admit that maybe there's a slight chance I could perhaps be considering the notion that I might be falling for Logan King... how might one make that reveal to her friends, then ask for help in the same text thread? Consider one might usually struggle opening up and asking for help.

I don't get an immediate response. The app where I post my videos of Logan is an automatic time killer, and I open it to check notifications and get a sense of what people are posting about him. A theme becomes immediately apparent—people are in awe of his play. I scroll past a few amateur commentators, and clips from professional analysts breaking down the play. My heart goes into a gallop. Joy for him and a big chunk of pride over his skill beat alongside the blood-pumping organ.

His play today, with its potential to make history, is the cherry on top to an incredible season. Anyone who knows anything about the sport will recognize Logan's talent. A plan starts taking shape in my mind. I'll edit a highlight reel, force Logan into a media room at TD, and force him to watch how people admire him. I will make him see how people see his greatness...

My smitten thoughts fade when a clip featuring Kenneth King crosses my feed.

The man's hair has gone salt and pepper, in that way that makes a person look distinguished. Wrinkles have taken shape at the corners of his eyes, but it only adds to the air of sophistication. Logan isn't a younger mirror image of his father, but I can see hints of my boyf— I can see clear signs they're related.

"Of course I'm proud of my son," Kenneth King says. "Listen— maybe it's time I break my rules and talk about Logan. You know why I never say much? Because I can't be objective. If someone is going to break my records and leave every quarterback behind, I'm glad it's my son. But if I were him, I'd hate every second someone compares me to my dad. I'd want people to be objective about my skills, and no one has been truly objective when they see what he can do— you see him through the eyes of who I was as a quarterback and that's honestly— I will not participate in that. And neither should you. Especially after a game like today. You all know what he did. That's not how I played. So maybe discover what Logan's career will be, regardless of how proud I am of him."

I blink away the mist in my eyes and save this video to show Logan. It will mean a lot to him. It may even steal another smile from his stern lips.

A text notification finally appears and I immediately click into it.

> Ren: In consideration of how hard it may be for this anonymous person to ask for help or admit they have been fooling themselves re: said football player, I would suggest they start with an executive summary of the state of the union

> Pri: Her friends might be willing to promise to keep the teasing to a minimum, if that would help.

> Evie: It would help. Voice note incoming.

I step away and hide around a corner, and whisper my secrets into my phone. I tell them of our one-night-stand and ending up working with him. How his grumpy ways soften around me, and how he knows when and how to push to make sure I give him a chance. How we agreed to sex that would end in friendship, but now I don't want either to end.

I talk softly into the mic. "So I've been thinking and maybe— maybe that means I'm falling for him? The fact that I enjoy him, and I miss him when he's away for games, and I want every night with him and every dinner. That I want to wear his jersey and I want those heart hands to be for me."

I shake my head and steal a glance at the crew. Logan isn't here yet.

I continue my voice note. "I've depended on such rigid boundaries for so long— no friendship except for you two and— I'm so sorry— I know I've kept you at a distance. There are things you don't know about me. But I thought I needed a steel fortress around my heart, or I'd have no limits at all. It was all or nothing, and I couldn't handle more."

I shuffle the tip of my vintage heel on the carpet under my feet.

I sigh. "I thought I had to choose between friendship and sex, because sex would blur the lines too much. That I wouldn't find them at all, afterwards. But we've had no issues! It's going so well. And now I'm wondering... maybe I can discover what friendship can be with you both, and the guys on the team I'm closer to."

I steal another glance toward the crew. Logan is there, hair wet and fresh from the shower, wearing clothes that although casual— trousers, a shirt, and a fashionable jacket in shades of blue— I'm sure cost more than my car. His frown is in place, but right now it only adds to his sex appeal.

Full-on bird-sized butterflies take over my stomach. I want to run to him, hug him again, praise him, and never let him go.

I keep my eyes on him as I share my final thoughts. "But Logan... maybe I get to discover something else with him. I never thought I'd end up in a universe where I wanted something like this with my first one-night-stand, but here I am. Wanting to see if there's a way to have the friendship we were building and sex and something unique. An intimacy that's only between us."

I sigh and lean on the wall. This message is already long, and I need to go monitor the interview, but I allow myself two extra l lines.

"It's hard for me to share all of this," I say. "But I hope it's another way in which I'm opening up. This time with two friends I really care about. So listen and send me your thoughts, okay? I'd love to hear what my friends have to say, as I discover what Logan and I might have."

I tap on the buttons that send them the voice note. Gathering up my strength and resolution, I wrap myself in joy and hope, and I go back to the interviewing group.

The lights of the camera shine on Logan, making his eyes look light blue. His frown is severe, just like the line of his lips.

He shakes his head. "In moments like those, I'm not thinking how it will look to people watching. All my focus is on making the play work."

"When did you realize what you had done?" The producer asks from behind the cameras.

"I'm not sure I have fully figured it out yet."

"Can you add more?"

"My QB coach showed me the video afterwards. I'll have to study it to fully get it in my head... and do it again next season."

"It must be disappointing to lose so close to the big game."

"It is, but it doesn't erase what the team did this year."

"Some commentators are calling the Strike a one-hit wonder."

"They're mistaken. We'll do this again, and go even further."

"Other commentators have complained that you deserve objectivity you have not received."

Logan frown deepens. One of my own appears on my brow. I watch the scene, getting ready to intervene.

The producer continues. "One show host in particular has a lot to say about it. They said there should be topics no one discusses around you. Do you think people have been objective when they talk about you?"

Dammit. They are ignoring the limits I set and asking about Logan's dad.

I step into the frame before I know what I'm doing. "Uhm... no. I'm sorry. We cannot accept that."

I blink a few times, trying to adjust to the bright light. Logan's eyes set on me, but I'm too busy throwing my most serious gesture in the producer's direction.

My presence in front of the cameras will ruin the shot, but it's better this way. They may not have mentioned Kenneth King, but it's a trap regardless.

"It's not a fair question," I say. "Logan doesn't know you're talking about his father and it could put him in a bad PR situation."

"The question wasn't about his father," the producer says. "We're asking about whether Logan feels he's been treated unfairly."

"But it's an oblique way to get him to comment on Kenneth King's words. So no. Please rephrase or skip altogether."

Logan places a hand low on my back. I turn to him automatically.

He speaks to my ear. "My dad said something? Did you watch it?"

I cover my mouth so no one can read my lips.

I respond to his ear as well. "Yes. It was nice. He was the one to say you deserved the objectivity and that's why he doesn't comment."

He pulls back and searches my eyes. I see my words clicking into place, as he shifts through what it means to him.

I squeeze his arm. He leans in again.

"Thank you." He kisses my temple. "I got this."

I nod and step away. I stand behind the crew this time, to watch from afar.

He faces the cameras again. His serious eyes glint for the crowd he can't see. He looks taller than ever, and grounded like his foundations reach deep into the earth. Confidence exudes from him, to the point I'm certain everyone will believe every word he says.

He purses his lips. "Everyone deserves objectivity. All players and all teams. New and old. When I'm on the field, I want to be seen for what I'm doing there. I want everyone to see how the team and I work in tandem like we've been doing this for years, and how we can only get better from here on out. This is my redemption— that now that I had a chance, I've proven what an amazing team like the Strike and I can do. That in those three seconds I have the ball in my hands, I can promise you'll hold your breath, because you won't want to miss what comes next."

Logan has never given an answer this long or this passionate on screen before. The crew and I watch in awe. I don't know if anyone else's heart drums deep and long in their chest, but mine does. He's talking to us but, above all, he's talking to every single fan at home.

Logan stares straight into the camera. "If anyone has been unfair, this is their chance to do better. Watch us play, and hear the thunder. Everything else is just for show."

We all remain quiet for a second longer. Logan takes it as an end to the interview— or an opening for an escape.

"Thank you," he says. "See you all next year."

He walks right through the crew, with firm steps in my direction. His eyes are intense, but I have attuned to his microexpressions.

This frown is different. It's a decision.

I'm prepared. My smile spreads slowly with each step he takes.

He reaches me, surrounds me with his arms, and pulls me close. I hook my arms around his neck. We kiss in front of everyone else, witnesses be damned.

Chapter 38

Logan

"There's a party at the club tonight," I whisper into her ear. "Come with me?"

She's letting me hold her close, in the middle of the social access hall, where fans, journalists, and Strike employees can see.

I squeeze her tighter and take a deep breath. I fill my lungs with lavender and sigh. I hope she never gets perfume again. This scent is my new favorite.

"I'm not dressed for the club," she says.

"The only thing that looks better on you than my jersey is when you wear nothing." I rock her from side to side. "They'll let you in because you're with me."

"I'm wearing the lingerie you bought me." She smiles. "I thought you liked me in that, too?"

"I do, but I don't want anyone else seeing you in it. It's for my eyes only."

"Possessive, huh?"

"Selfish, really." I kiss her. "Greedy, too. I'd like you next to me tonight. To pull you close with the guys around."

"Would that make you happy?"

I nod. "So happy."

I kiss her again, and I don't have to say much else. We end up in a car on the way to the club. I put the privacy window up.

I bring her to my lap. "Kiss me again."

She does. Her hands go under my jacket, traveling close to my skin.

"Can't get enough of you," I confess again.

Her eyes, so beautifully dark in the back of the car, lock with mine.

"I've stopped expecting I ever will," I add. "We may have lost today, but I'm on top of the world, just because you're here. I've redeemed myself. People are seeing me as my own man— in part thanks to my dad, funnily enough. And I have a team and a group of friends I fit with. People I want to keep around."

A small smile appears on her mouth.

"I want you around, Evie. You're at the core of me. This new version of me— it's in part because of what I feel for you."

She opens her mouth to speak, but I put a gentle finger on her lips.

"I know hearing this can be a lot," I say. "And you know I can be pushy. You've called me stubborn and persistent and yeah, I am those things. But perhaps in this you'll find that it's really loyalty— a belief in what I think we can have together. I'll wait until you can see it too. If you'll keep giving me the time to show you that you can believe in me, this way too."

I expect to see signs of worry or suspicion on her face, but there's none on that.

The line of her lips curls into a teasing smirk. She takes my hand and puts it above her heart. It beats fast, but her eyes remain open.

The drum in my chest is an echo to hers.

She runs a thumb over my bottom lip. "What if I told you my stomach isn't in knots? It's filled with butterflies instead. Even if my heart is racing, you know what? I can breathe easily."

She caresses my face. I pull her closer with the arm around her lower back. My other hand remains on her chest, counting heartbeats.

She grins. "All it took was you grinning at me. Laughing with me. And now I'm here, realizing it's not quite friendship that I want with you."

"No? What do you want instead?"

"I'm going to be a better friend to the ones living in my pocket. I'll go visit them and include them in my life even if they live somewhere else. And I'm going to accept the friendship the guys have been offering for a long time. That's where I'll discover what friendship can be like."

"And with me?"

"With you I want friendship mixed with something else. Intimacy. A life we might share. To think of each other as we go through our days, planning dinner and a vacation together after you're done the season. A set of toothbrushes in each other's home. A conversation with HR to let them know we're together. I want to face all the people teasing us, and for us to ignore the comments on social media together. I want to discover where a journey like that might lead us."

I close my eyes for a second, and let her words become one with my marrow.

I got the girl.

"I see." I open my eyes. "You're in love with me."

"Logan!"

I laugh.

She scrunches up her face. "It's not fair when you laugh. Now I forgot what I was going to say."

"You were going to tell me you're in love with me."

"Right." She lifts an eyebrow, a soft curl to her lips. "Well, I see cocky Logan has made a return. I'm on my way there, sure, but that's very different from the brave, bold statement you made. You know the kind of balls it takes to say something like that?"

"I know. You're familiar enough with my balls to know I have nothing to fear in that regard."

"It's not the part of your anatomy that I'm the most interested in, to be honest, so I may have misjudged."

I adjust her on my lap. The weight of her brings deep satisfaction to my insides. I grab handfuls of her flesh, and suddenly I'm a cat making fucking biscuits.

I grin. "You probably didn't think to check, impressed as you are with my cock. But I got balls big enough to put into words what you're not saying."

She holds back her laugh. "Oh my god. You're *that* certain that I'm in love with you, aren't you? Shameless, I tell you. I said I could potentially see getting there one day. Maybe. Perhaps. We'll see."

"That's plenty of ground covered, in my opinion. How many yards, would you say? Might as well say you're approaching the end zone."

She breaks and laughs. "'I might as well' none of it. I can't believe you're changing my words like this. And you haven't even told me where in the field you are!"

I take her face in my hands. "Where do you think I am, when the first thing I said was you've made me a new man?"

"Is that what you said?"

"And that I don't want to imagine my future without you."

"I feel like I haven't quite heard that before."

"Weren't you listening? I said that it's time we reframe the past six months and admit we've been dating from the start."

"You're saying this club party isn't our first date?"

"I'm saying I started falling for you years ago, and that every second we spent together— regardless of what we called it— I got closer to the goal line. Now I'm staring at the last yard, standing in place and looking at you, waiting until you catch up."

"We'll get there together?" She grabs my wrists with gentle hands.

"I'll carry you through, my Evie," I say, and I kiss her.

The VIP section of the club is packed with players and friends. Saint, Dom, Evie, and I stand in our own tiny group. Bear sits with Pen, Nat, and Damián nearby.

I have an arm around Evie's shoulders. She made a knot on her jersey, pulling the fabric to the side and highlighting her shape. It's distracting, with the way it accentuates the curve of her generous hips, wrapped by a pencil skirt. All I want to do is grab and hold on for dear life.

"Okay, but what is this exactly?" Saint makes small circles in front of Evie and I. "Where do we stand as a group with all of this?"

"Saint, please," Evie laughs.

The receiver with a diamond earring points a finger toward my face. "Logan's classic frown is in place, which isn't surprising. Grumpy vibes? Check. But his arm is around you so I feel like we need an update."

"We don't need to provide an update," I say.

"What kind of update?" Evie asks. "As in, you have information that is outdated?"

Music is loud in the background, but focused on the first floor so we don't have to yell to talk.

"We have staged a few interventions with our quarterback." Saint scratches his chin in a thoughtful manner. "Hasn't he mentioned it to you? Shocking, to be honest."

"What's this?" Evie asks, her eyes on me. "You haven't said anything about interventions?

"Mmh." The sound out of my throat is grouchy.

Dom laughs.

"You may appreciate this." Saint seems unconcerned about my response. "Many months ago, when we were just coming together as a new team, we told him no one plays with Evie Moreno. So of course, we had to make sure he wasn't playing with you."

"You think he's been playing with me?" Evie smiles at them, also completely unconcerned.

"We quickly realized he's obsessed with you, so not that." Dom laughs. "Lately, the interventions are about making sure he won't let you go, not to mess it up, et cetera."

Saint's dimples deepen in his pretty face. "We're just trying to figure out what direction to take the interventions next."

Evie laughs. We don't get to respond, as Ames joins us alongside a put-together type of masculine individual. His dark, curly hair is perfectly combed for a modern look, and his eyes would probably look dark blue in the daylight. They compliment his dark blue suit, and contrast with his white skin.

"Hey guys!" Ames links arms with this person. "Thanks so much for inviting us to the party, Saint. Aidan and I are excited to be here with you. Everyone, this is Aidan, my partner."

"It's a shame about the game. The Strike deserved the win." Aidan's Irish accent is a soft burr as he shakes Saint's hand. "Not that I'm an expert, of course."

Saint nods. His usual spark evaporates, and he forgets all about the teasing he's been casting my way.

I smirk. Saint definitely has feelings for Ames. Considering she just introduced Aidan as her partner, she's the one person in the city he won't get to date. I'd tease him about it as retribution for all the interventions he's put me through, but I'm not an asshole. I wouldn't kick a man when he's down.

Dom pushes a hand forward and introduces himself to Aidan. I do it next.

"Logan King," I say. "This is Evie Moreno, a PR exec for the team, and my girlfriend."

That gets a reaction from Saint, whose dimples appear again. Dom laughs.

"All right, then." Saint smiles in our direction. "Happy for you guys. Now that that's settled, I'm going to go. There's a lucky someone out there I don't know, waiting for me to sweep her off her feet."

He gets a cocky playboy look on his face, bows to us, and leaves.

Ames looks confused for a second, but soon we're chatting casually again. We learn Aidan works on TV, and they met when Ames' team catered for one of his shows. Soon the whole group is sitting near Leon and the rest.

I only last twenty minutes before I pull Evie to the side. We find a spot further away from the group, in an empty cushion at the edge of the sofa. I bring her close, and we create a bubble just for us in the middle of the club.

I caress her face. "What are the chances I can convince you to hide in the bathroom for a little while? It's fancy in there. I can show you."

"Very low," she scoffs. "You'll have to wait until we go to your place. Right now, I want to be here with everyone and *bond*."

I let out a dramatic sigh. "I suppose that's a good thing, considering."

"I have different plans for later in the car, though."

"Oh? Tell me."

"I... will... make you watch your dad's comments tonight."

"That's not as fun as what I had in mind."

"It will be wonderful. I'm on a mission to make sure you are inundated with messages of how amazing you are. I want to make sure you have zero doubts after tonight."

I lift my eyebrows. "What if I already know, and all I want is to celebrate with you?"

"We are celebrating!"

"Okay, fine. I am happy to let everyone see you looking at me adoringly like this."

"I'm looking adoringly at you?"

I nod. "It makes me want to puff up my chest with pride."

She laughs. "Then I'll show you the texts my friends sent after I told them about us. They will put a smile on your face."

"Mhh. Will you tell your parents, too?"

"I have to talk to them for sure. They need to know I have a boyfriend I adore, to start, but also... that we may have found a way to save the house. If your offer still stands?"

I raise an eyebrow. "The offer to help with the money you need?"

She rubs her lips and nods.

"I'd never offer and take it back, Evie." I put a hand on her face. "So why do you look unsure?"

"I didn't want to seem like I'm assuming, and it's still such a big deal, a life-changing kind of deal—"

I smirk and kiss her softly. "I like that I get to be the person doing this for you. So please let me do it."

She seems to struggle for a second longer, but the tension leaves her in a deep sigh.

Her face softens. "Thank you. A few plans are starting to take shape in my mind and finally— finally I feel like there's a light at the end of the tunnel. A real end in sight."

"I hope to be involved in these plans."

She takes my face in her hands. "You're involved in every single one of them."

I kiss her. "I'm glad you're finally seeing sense."

"Logan!"

I laugh. A few faces turn our way in shock. I ignore them.

I gaze at Evie. "My pleasure, Mystery Girl."

Chapter 39

Evie

As hard as it was to wake up early this morning, after celebrating until late with the team in the club, I wouldn't change anything about Sunday. Even if my Monday looks like any other Monday for me, with emails piling in my inbox and PR calls on my schedule, my mood is impeccable.

For one, I got to wake up with Logan by my side. As soon as my alarm went off, he brought me closer and mumbled in my ear, asking me to stay for another five minutes. I did, because I couldn't help myself. Then I rushed and got through work with a smile on my face.

Not even my new debt repayment spreadsheet ruined my mood. After talking to Logan last night and inputting all numbers in the document, we came up with a plan that lets me breathe a little easier. I keep opening it and closing it during my morning tasks, just to stare at the numbers again to make sure this is really possible, and really happening.

I have just sent a text to my parents, letting them know I'll be there before they go to work during my lunch break, when Selena herself knocks on my open door.

I smile. "Selena! Hey! Can I help you? You didn't have to come to my office, I would have been happy to go to you."

She waves my words away, dismissing my protest.

She sits on the chair in front of me. "Do you have a minute? I wanted to chat with you."

"Of course."

"I'll keep it short. This season has been everything I wanted. I'm here because I know you have a part in that."

"I'm glad to hear you're pleased."

"I am, very much. That's why I'm excited to give you the promotion I promised."

I barely hold back the gasp, or the joyful scream building in my throat. Excitement and relief entwine inside, and my hands go to my chest, like I need them to contain my heart in there."

My smile grows wider. "Thank you, Selena. You have no idea how much this means to me."

I got the promotion. My work as a PR exec is valued, and I earned this recognition. It doesn't matter that the raise may not convince the bank, when I have a much better plan now. Because it means that I don't need the promotion as much as I want it, and I got it.

"You deserve this promotion ten times over, Evie. I'm here because I wanted to make sure you know I see what you've done this year. Not only did you help me with the vision I had for Logan, but you remained on top of your role with everyone else. I'm happy to show you this way how much we appreciate you."

She gets up and I do too.

Selena shakes my hand with a bright smile on her face. "Someone from HR will pop by shortly with the offer letter. I'm glad to have you supporting the team for this new era of the Strike."

I sit back once she leaves, my chest light. My grin is a million watts in potency, and I dance on my chair. Without much thought, I grab my phone, take a selfie, and text it to Logan.

> Evie: say hi to the new Senior PR Executive for the Strike.

I can still feel tingles all over when I make it to my parents' house.

We face each other much like we did months before, when they first told me about their plans to expand the business. They sit in front of me on the couch, and we all have coffee by our sides. The difference is that, unlike that time, I feel weightless. Not because there are no challenges, but because there's a plan. And I won't have to face any of it alone.

"I have good news," I start. "I got the promotion I've been counting on."

"Felicitaciones!" They grin with joy for me, though I can see nerves in their eyes, too.

I smile. "Thank you. I'm very happy. The owner was so nice to me. Very encouraging for what I've been doing this year."

"We're so proud," Dad says.

"Thank you both." I nod, but my smile falters. "It's a great step in my career, though... well... we all know that with the latest letter, it won't be enough to save the house."

I've known this for a while, and it still manages to dim the shine on my day to say the words out loud. I lick my bottom lip and watch my parents' reaction.

My dad slumps. My mom's face crumbles. They share a long, sad look.

"Maybe it's a good thing," Mom says. "To finally have this over with."

"You have carried this with us too long, hija," Dad adds. "You did everything you could."

Regret fills his face. A weight pulls my chest down, begging me to make it better. And I will, but I'm learning not to rush to their rescue.

I take a deep breath to soften the feeling weighing me down. "The thing is, I have a new plan. I think we can save the house."

The change in my parents is immediate. They perk up and stare at me with confusion and hope.

"¿Qué?" Dad asks.

"I just need to know..." I gaze from one of them to the other. "Is the business secure?"

"Dile, Ismael," Mom says. "Let her know what we're doing."

They exchange another look, before my dad faces me with serious eyes.

"We did an entrepreneurship course," he says. "Through that, we got connected to a not-for-profit that helps people with businesses like ours. We got a grant. A really good grant."

"We had to reorganize our business plan." Mom gives me a small smile. "We will be able to buy the food truck. We will get to minimize liabilities and give ourselves the raise we have been needing. If we manage to pay the debt principal, hija... Mamá and I can take over the penalty payment."

"What?" I breathe.

Dad nods. "We were waiting to hear from the grant people to tell you. We didn't want to give you false hopes, in case we didn't get it. Or if we had to make a whole new budget, if we lost the house."

I stare at them, trying to process their words. My brain is silent, like it's waiting for the punchline, or the other shoe to drop. Until the first thought clicks, then the next.

This means the business is secure. Their retirement is planned for. The house is safe. And I'm free from carrying debt too big for me, that I never accrued.

My parents will be okay, and so will I.

"We are..." I say.

My mom smiles and finishes for me. "We are going to be okay."

We hug. A few tears fall, but smiles fill the room. Eventually, we all sit on the same couch.

"So what's going on with the house?" Mom asks. "How are we handling the debt principal?"

"You see..." I suck on my lip. "I have a boyfriend now... and he's amazing."

"Logan King!" my dad guesses.

"¿Él es tu novio?"

I nod. "And he's going to help me with the money we need."

They are almost as excited about that as they are about saving the house.

We make plans for how we're going to handle the next few months. They have to go to work soon, but we're too happy to let go yet, and Logan is on his way. He's picking me up on the way to the Thunderdome. We asked for individual meetings with HR to announce our relationship, according to policies.

The doorbell rings. I open the door and jump into Logan's arms. The kiss I give him is fueled with the relief and freedom I feel. He reacts seamlessly, wrapping me tight and keeping me close to him.

"Hello, there," he says before giving me another kiss. "We should always say hello like this."

"Deal, Your Highness."

As soon as we come apart, my parents throw a hundred questions at him. They thank him for helping me and us in one big sweep, and they get us to promise dinner with them soon. I have to remind everyone we're all going to be late for work, before the three of them agree to say goodbye for the day.

Logan is chuckling by the time we're walking to his SUV. "You know what was the best part of all of that? Your barely contained panic."

"They flooded you with comments! And I don't know if you have the fortitude. Do you even know what alfajores *are*? They'll forgive you for not knowing Cerati, though. Eventually."

"Excuse me?" He gets on the driver's side.

I close the door behind me on the passenger side. "Do you know when the last time was I introduced them to anyone? Eighteen months before I met you at the bar, when I told them I was dating the one and only boyfriend I've ever had."

"I knew I was a rebound," he said.

"You were not. You were my first one-night-stand. I was very over my ex by the time I found you."

"In any case, I have the fortitude, thank you very much. I'm not scared of your parents."

"Maybe you should be. I'm scared of yours."

He tsks and turns on the engine. "Don't be. I'm the frowniest of the bunch."

"I think that helps. Maybe."

"It's fine. We have all the time in the world to figure it out. For now, let's go to work and announce our relationship to everyone. What do you say? If everything goes according to plan, I will come home tonight with a crown, too."

Logan goes to his HR meeting first, and I catch up with work in my office until it's time for mine. The players will have time off now that they're out of the playoffs for the season, but I don't. Still, I check my accumulated vacation time and dream. For the first time ever, I let myself fantasize of all the things I couldn't afford, when my time and my money were carefully planned to help my parents.

It's easy to plan for great things to come our way when we're happy, and I'm the happiest. Logan and I are together. He got his redemption with a spectacular first year with the team, too. People have continued to praise him, and no one is talking about his dad.

On my end, by late next week, I'll be able to close all pending matters with the bank. My money will be mine to spend and save. It's time to start planning for a couple of weeks lounging on sand, surrounded by sun and sea. I can't wait to talk to Logan about it.

My time has come, and I'll get to share it with someone I'm head over heels for.

I'm still in a far distant land, full of sun and sea, when it's time for my HR meeting. The employee relations manager goes down a list of questions, quickly taking notes for their documentation.

"Did you enter into the relationship with Mr. King willingly?" Justin asks.

"I did."

"Did you ever feel pressured by Mr. King?"

I did, but I liked it.

I rub my lips to keep that in.

"Uhm, no," I say instead.

They lift purple eyes my way. These are contacts, rather than the magical reaction of Logan's irises to the light.

It works for Justin. They wear bold clothing, and their nails are painted black. I'm a little intimidated, but I don't show it.

They repeat the question. "Did you feel pressured at any point by Mister King?"

I smile. "Nope. He's persistent, you know? But it's one of the many things that make him incredible at what he does."

"Okay." Their eyes go back to the list in front of them on the desk. "Do you foresee any issues between the two of you that could make you unable to work, or cause issues to the organization?"

"No. We're good."

And so we go on. I shake Justin's hand on the way out and, with a smile on my face, I make my way to the locker room.

"Please cover the goods!" I yell as I approach. "There's only one of you I'm interested in seeing naked. I don't want to see anyone else's privates by accident!"

I hover around the corner, waiting for the green light from the group. They're not training today, but I don't want to take the risk.

People are laughing and I hear a few jabs directed at Logan that I can't make out. He appears around the corner, rolling his eyes at everyone and ignoring them.

Saint trails behind him. "I'm here as a witness, to make sure he doesn't cheat. You'll see."

Confusion gets worse when Logan ignores him too, and gives me a quick kiss.

He speaks loudly enough for everyone to hear. "If you see my privates, it's never going to be an accident."

People laugh in the locker room. Saint smirks.

I chuckle. "Yeah, I think we'll pretty much always do it on purpose. What's going on?"

Saint shrugs. "Can't tell you yet."

Logan lowers his voice now. "Did everything go well with the meeting?"

"Yes. We're good to go."

He kisses my temple and leads me to the locker room.

The usual suspects hang out in the space, plus several other players. They all wear casual clothes.

"What's going on?" I ask.

"Logan has to ask you a couple of questions," Saint says. "Please answer truthfully."

I gaze from the group, to Saint, to Logan. My insides go still, and I wait for the big reveal.

"Evie," Logan says. "Is it true that you and I are together, and you entered this arrangement willingly?"

I would have laughed, but the question is strange.

"I already talked to HR." Suspicion laces my words. "What's with you guys?"

"Just answer, please," Logan half-growls.

"Yes." I roll my eyes. "I entered it willingly."

"At this point in our lives," Logan continues, "you're forsaking all others for my grumpy face."

He seems irritated and so out of character I'm starting to get worried. The energy in the locker room is mischievous, though, so I play along.

"This is so weird," I say. "Yes. I am 'forsaking all others for your grumpy face.'"

A few people make frustrated sounds. Saint's eyes narrow.

"What's going on?" I ask again.

"Two more questions." Logan holds me by the shoulders. "Will you do me the honors of letting me whisk you away to a surprise vacation, as soon as you get some time off? My treat."

I gasp. "Are you being serious right now? A vacation?"

"Will you do me the honors, Evie?"

"Fuck yes!" I try to hug him, but he makes a gesture to stop me.

"Now the speech!" Someone says.

People are getting excited. My heart still beats fast, too eager for this surprise vacation and this time off coming sooner than expected. All I can do is gaze around, trying to collect clues.

"Make it good, King!" Someone else adds.

"Evelyn Moreno." He steps close to me. "Hear this declaration."

"Oh my god." I snort and cover my mouth.

I finally put the pieces together. This is a bet.

"Ever since I met you, I've known we have chemistry," Logan says. "But as I've gotten to know you, I can't call it any less than alchemy." He takes one step closer, and places both hands around my face. "I planned to go through my life happy with everything I got, content with football and friends. Then you came into my life, and showed me how much more I really wanted. I wasn't looking for gold, yet I found it in you. But I did better than any scientist from olden times, because I got you."

If I was ever tense, his words make it all disappear. I thaw, ice pooling into water at my feet, that he shares his feelings freely for me in front of his team.

Everyone stares at him. I give him a happy, soft smile.

He smirks, like my reaction is all he wanted, and all he needs.

"Fuck, that's a speech," Damián says. "Did you even have to destroy me at pinball, if you were keeping that under your sleeve?"

"Make the heart for an extra hundred points!" Someone screams.

Logan makes a heart with his hands and points it my way. I laugh.

"Aaaand he gets the crown!" Dom exclaims.

Saint groans.

Bear brings the crown the players fight for during the season. He gives it to Logan, who places it on my head.

"Oh, I see who won, then," I laugh some more.

"Thank you," Logan says, before smacking a kiss on me and bending me backwards. I can barely react fast enough to keep the crown on my head.

People laugh and applaud around us. I'm laughing as Logan straightens me. He grins and keeps me close. The sight of his grin still has the same effect— I could melt in his arms.

"He beat Damián in pinball by a landslide, but that only got him to a close second place," Saint explains in my direction. "A few last minute bets were allowed, considering how many people doubted you were actually dating him."

"The Beauty and the Beast Bet for the Best of the Best Betting Board Team Builder." Leon laughs. "Now say that three times fast."

"Now the king has a queen and a crown," Damián says. "Unbelievable first year with the Strike!"

"I couldn't ask for more," Logan says, and he kisses me once more.

I couldn't ask for more myself.

Epilogue

Logan

Fifteen months later

Last year, the first trip we took was to Laguna Island to visit Ren and Pri. A few weeks afterwards, we left for a warm place by the ocean. We enjoyed it so much, we returned a year later.

This vacation spot is incredible. Evie mentioned wanting to go somewhere that made her feel like she was in a movie, and Saint said he knew the exact place. He was right. This private beach house is surrounded by exuberant plants, sand, and ocean. The water is the perfect temperature, and the days go by slowly.

Like last time, we don't do much. We swim, eat, nap, and engage in the best recreational cardio of my life. I have to keep my condition in the off season, after all. Not to say anything of how neither of us can seem to get enough of each other, all these months later.

I don't expect it to ever be enough. Even now, with Evie in my arms, I want this to last forever.

The property isn't fully isolated, so we wear bathing suits. We're in the water, her slick body plastered to me as I keep us in place. My feet anchor us in the sand, while peaceful waves bathe us and keep us cool under the sun. The light around us has started to turn orange, with the star's journey toward the horizon. It reflects on the water and on her skin, and a deep, satisfied sound hums out of my throat.

Her eyes are closed, and a placid smile rests on her lips.

I kiss her jaw, then her mouth. "Evie. I have a question for you."

"Mh?" She doesn't open her eyes.

Her arms spread like wings, treading water and letting me hold her close.

"How long have we been living together?"

"Officially? Like a year. Unofficially a bit longer." The words come out dreamy, like the memory pleases her. "There was a lot of 'I don't like it when you're not there. Too much house, too little you' from you during that time, if I remember correctly."

"Mh, I remember the same. Though I'd like it on record that it's not like I had to fight you too hard for it."

A wave slightly taller than the rest raises the water level to her shoulders, and she shivers. We don't react much to it otherwise.

She gazes at me and shrugs. "Not denying it. I was just hoping to hear you tell me again how much you love me and why you can't live without me."

"Mhhh. Have I been slacking in that regard or...?"

"Not at all, I just like to hear it as often as possible."

"I say 'I love you' every day."

"You do, but I've spent too much time with you and now I'm greedy too. It's that speech you gave me when you won the Hypercubed crown last year. It spoiled me. You can understand that I want more, right?"

"Right. Yeah, I understand."

She surrounds my hips with her legs, and my shoulders with her arms. Cold drops of water run down my back, and it's me who shivers this time.

She raises an eyebrow. "I'm ready. You can start whenever."

I smirk, but I relent. "Ah, Mystery Girl. My Evie. I love you."

"Good start."

"I wasn't looking for love until you came into my life. I thought romance was a pretense, but now all the songs make sense. You're the best puzzle I ever solved. The game we played was the most important one in my life, and I never knew."

She sighs. "Yep. It's working."

"When you're in my arms, I know peace." I kiss her. "I'm selfish. Wanting to make sure you're within reach every night I'm at home. And cocky, sure, because I know you can't get enough of me either."

"I can't even deny it. We both know that, given enough time, you always get your way with me."

"On that note, we should start thinking of our dream home. We should build something."

Her mouth opens like she's confused. "Wait. What?"

"The house we live in— we didn't pick it or decorate it. I want a home we created together. I want to see your wildest dreams come true."

The humor in her eyes continues to sparkle bright, but her soft smile is the kind to have my heart skipping a few beats. It's the kind that tells me she's happy with me. It never fails to muster awe, shining bright into every shadowed corner still living inside of me.

She kisses me. "You make me believe you want my happiness. You make me feel cared for. You are steady and generous and..." she sighs. "Little by little, you know how to bring me to my knees."

"Then say yes. Send me a hundred pictures of your vision. We'll argue about a color here or there, or a tile design. But bar a few exceptions, I think I'll let you win most of it this time."

"Most?"

I nod. "I have a few requirements."

"Such as?"

"A hot tub. Privacy. Strong windows overlooking the water."

"Strong... windows?"

"They need to be able to take some repetitive force on them. I need to be able to say, 'hands on the glass' and not worry about accidents of any kind."

"Logan—"

"It will keep me going when the contractors are late, or when the tile we picked after an argument is discontinued. I'll say, 'it's okay. I'll still get to fuck Evie against the windows first thing once this is over' and it will all be better."

She laughs. "First thing? As in, 'we got the keys. Let's go!'"

My nod is serious. "First thing, Evie."

"Got it," she laughs. "Thanks for the warning."

She gives me a long, languid kiss.

"Can't wait," she adds.

"Now let's go chill on the couch and watch the sun set. What do you say?"

Evie and I lounge on a large, circular outdoor sofa. Thirty cushions of many colors lay about, providing support for anything we can think of. Let's say, we've been getting creative. Some risks have been taken outside.

Right now, we're content to watch the sun set. Light has turned golden everywhere, hinting to the bronze hiding in all things. She sits against me, between my legs, her head resting on my chest. We breathe in sync, our eyes on the horizon.

The evening is turning out to be everything I wanted.

I smile. "What's on your mind?"

"Just thinking how good my life is. We're together, we're moving forward, we're going to build a house together... I think I'm getting used to having a lot of things to look forward to."

"You're just getting used to it now? We've been together for a year and a half."

She chuckles. "Yeah, you've been slacking after all."

I snort. "Unbelievable."

"I need someone to feed me cold grapes, I think. That would really help."

"Unbelievable," I repeat, but I diligently make my way into the house.

I come back with a bowl of grapes and a couple other things. We sit side by side, with her snuggling against me and my arm around her. I cross my legs at the ankles and set the bowl on my lap. Green, shiny grapes fill the dish to the brim, and I take one to her lips.

Playfulness shines in her eyes as she chews. "Thank you. You are the best."

"Remember this moment moving forward."

I take one grape for myself, then give her another. Sweetness explodes on my tongue.

"Even when I pretended not to remember," she says, "I couldn't help it. Every moment we share takes hold inside of me."

"That's what I was hoping to hear."

"You know one of the ones that repeat in my mind?"

"Mhh?"

I feed us again.

"When you guys won the championship a few months ago. When we all ran from the box to the field— I was so focused on finding you I didn't even notice Ames and Saint."

"I didn't either."

"All I cared about was finding you. My heart was in my throat, and everything was so loud, and confetti made it hard to see—"

"But you found me."

"And we forgot about the world, and kissed and kissed."

Her eyes glitter. A small smile appears on my mouth. It was one of the highest highs I've ever had.

Yes, this moment is perfect.

"Even though reporters wanted to talk to me," I say. "I just kept you close and kissed you some more."

"Even though some of those reporters took pictures, and released the ones where your hands are on my butt and pulling me closer."

"Can't say I'm upset about it. It was a good photo."

I liked it so much, I made it my phone's screensaver. Evie, on the other hand, printed it and keeps it in her office.

"This is it, isn't it?" Evie asks. "We made it. We have everything we want."

I cock my head. "Almost."

A small wrinkle appears between her brows. "What? What is missing? Are you happy, Logan?"

"Very happy, but things are unbalanced." I put the bowl away on the side table.

I shift until I can see her better and caress her face.

She still looks a bit worried. "Unbalanced, how?"

I drop a soft kiss on her lips. "I have a ring and you don't."

I breathe slowly, patiently waiting for her first response. My thumb makes a pass over her cheek. It takes her a second to understand my meaning, but she eventually gasps.

I frown. "I can't stop thinking about it, since I got my first ring."

"We've never talked about marriage." She places a hand on top of mine.

The sun is halfway gone, and light is turning softer around us, the sky painted in shades of violet. Her warm brown eyes look deep black, and it brings a sense of being seen, being known, being loved that I craved for a long time.

I smirk. "Is this you letting me know you'll have to think about it?"

"No— I mean— I just—"

"I love you, Evie. I didn't fall for you because I was lonely, or because I was missing anything. But we fit in a way I didn't know was possible. I don't want to imagine a life without you. We're building a home. We have each other. But I'm greedy, and I want more. I want the whole package now. The party, the promises. I know you'll cry reading your vows and I'll frown and dry the tears away, because I can't help myself."

"Logan—"

"If you need me to convince you, I'm prepared to wait and work on it. I also got a ring for you. I thought I might show you. See if that helps."

"You got... a ring?"

I lick my bottom lip, and take a breath to calm the nerves I didn't expect, but that appear nevertheless.

I search in my pocket.

"You're just carrying it around casually?!"

I chuckle at her response. "I didn't just bring grapes back from inside."

The right ring waited for me at the third jewelry place I visited, only a month after winning the big game. I've had it since, thinking about this proposal, hoping it would be as simple and genuine as every moment we've ever spent together.

I sit and she mirrors me. I open the blue velvet box in front of her. The ring I picked is engraved in my mind, so I gaze at her instead.

I lower my voice. "I thought it was time for me to have a proposition for you."

Her lips part. Tears come to her eyes.

Yeah, I got this one right.

My Evie likes to indulge now. At one point in her life, that was just about keeping a few pieces of lingerie. These days, I get to be the one showering her with things she loves, and this ring can't be any less. She picks it up from the box, and admires the three-stone set up. All diamonds, the center one big and bold in an emerald cut, flanked by tear-shaped stones to soften the design. The points draw the eye to the shank, made of shiny platinum.

"Three stones for every ring I'll have," I say. "If I have more, I'll add a pendant. Maybe some earrings. We need to keep it balanced."

"Logan..." She lifts her eyes at me. A tear falls, and I gently dry it with a pass of my thumb.

"Do you think you'll say yes?" I whisper.

She nods.

"Will I have to work too hard?" I ask.

She shakes her head.

I smirk. "Can you talk at all, my Evie?"

She shakes her head again, hiccups-laughs, and kisses me hard.

I kiss her back, but soon I'm chuckling.

I hold her in my arms, the sun almost gone. Outdoor lights turn on around us, as the skies turn a deep blue. She still holds the ring in her hand.

"Evie. Will you marry me?"

"Yes. Yes! I'll marry you, Logan."

With a smile that echoes hers, I kiss her again. I put the ring on her finger, then we kiss some more.

I'm pretty sure neither of us will ever get enough.

Do you want to see if **Logan really tests the windows** of their new home like he promised? Then subscribe to my newsletter by visiting leonorsoliz.com/game-ep and you'll get to see what happens when they get the keys!

Thank you

It's been a bit over two years since I began this authoring journey, and I'm now starting my third series. It's incredible to look back and see everything that has happened since I decided to publish my writing. I've learned so much!

I wouldn't be here without the support of my community, for whom I'm eternally appreciative and endlessly grateful.

First, as always, thank you to my two loves. Your continuous support in time, labor, and understanding; plus all dev editing ideas and emotional crisis intervention skills mean the world to me. I left everything I knew behind for the two of you, and I have been fortunate enough to get to celebrate that decision every day.

Thank you to Sookh Kaur for understanding like no one else can, and providing feedback with a sharp eye and the kind of enthusiasm that gives me life. I also want to thank my Beta readers, whose feedback helped make this story what it is. I'm grateful to you, Katie, Cassie, Lynell, & Beth. Every thoughtful comment you've made has made me a stronger writer, and has helped create a stronger story. When I can't be objective about my words anymore, your mind and generosity make all the difference.

Next, to Janelle, the best book-consultant-slash-genius I could have, who was the first to challenge the original idea for this book. Thank you for being the amazing friend you are, and making time to see me despite your busy schedule and preference for neighborhood living. I can't wait to see how you react to these words, now immortalized forever. Your turn now ;)

Last but not least, to you, my reader. I'm honored you chose to read my book, and you're making time to read this final note. Especially for those of you who have been here from the beginning, and shout about my stories to anyone who will listen. You're essential to this dream I'm pursuing. I hope my books make you feel good things in a world that can be rough.

Other Books by the Author

THE COZY LATINE BILLIONAIRES SERIES

Yours, For Now

Book 1 – Gabe and Lina have to fake a relationship if they want to reach their business goals.

Yours, Forever

Book 2 – Max and Eva get married in Vegas and promptly forget about it...

Yours, Finally

Book 3 – Jake and Violeta finally find their Happily Ever After.

Yours, For Good

Book 4 (final) – Javier and Nora. Modern Daddy Long Legs retelling.

To check all my series and plans, visit

leonorsoliz.com/upcoming

About the Author

Leonor wrote her first Meet Cute at eight years old and never really stopped. After many years of practicing and dreaming, she took the plunge and wrote a full-length romance novel. Then she wrote some more.

Her books are cozy and fun: low conflict, slow burn books that will make you swoon... and will reward you with great spice. With a healthy dose of humor, these stories guarantee a happily ever after to her plus size and latine characters.

Leonor is a Latina living in Canada, working as a therapist during the day and fitting as much writing to her life as she can. She's also a multi-crafter, trying her hand at watercolor, jewelry, and anything else that strikes her fancy. She illustrates and designs her own covers!

You can connect with me on:

www.leonorsoliz.com

hello@leonorsoliz.com

Instagram: https://www.instagram.com/leonor.soliz/

TikTok: https://www.tiktok.com/@leonor.soliz.author

Facebook: https://www.facebook.com/leonorsolizz